VANISHING POINT

Maurice Crillon is a brilliant French artist and art forger with a silver tongue and a silken touch with women. When his mother dies he learns that his father was an English baronet. His curiosity gets the better of him and he decides to meet his parent. But then he becomes entangled in an adventure in which he unwittingly becomes the quarry of the security services of two nations. Agents for the Mafia are also extremely interested in Crillon — and all of them are bent on recovering certain incriminating documents which have now fallen into his possession . . .

Books by Victor Canning
Published by The House of Ulverscroft:

BIRDS OF A FEATHER
THE BOY ON PLATFORM ONE
FALL FROM GRACE

The Arthurian Trilogy:
THE CRIMSON CHALICE
THE CIRCLE OF THE GODS
THE IMMORTAL WOUND

SPECIAL MESSAGE TO READERS

This book is published under the auspices of

THE ULVERSCROFT FOUNDATION

(registered charity No. 264873 UK)

res   s.

R

Gre   n,

You   n
by   y
c

T

T
c/o   d

94-98 Chalmers Street, Surry Hills,
N.S.W. 2010, Australia

With over thirty novels to his credit, Victor Canning had also written many short stories and serials which were published in the principal newspapers and magazines of England and America. Born in Plymouth in 1911, he was a features writer for the *Daily Mail* before World War II, during which he was commissioned in the Royal Artillery. He had worked as a scriptwriter in Hollywood and lived in Devon.

VICTOR CANNING

VANISHING
POINT

Complete and Unabridged

ULVERSCROFT
Leicester

First published in Great Britain in 1982

This Large Print Edition
published 2012

The moral right of the author has been asserted

British Library CIP Data

Canning, Victor.
   Vanishing point.
   1. Suspense fiction.
   2. Large type books.
   I. Title
   823.9'12–dc23

   ISBN 978–1–4448–1280–0

Published by
F. A. Thorpe (Publishing)
Anstey, Leicestershire

Set by Words & Graphics Ltd.
Anstey, Leicestershire
Printed and bound in Great Britain by
T. J. International Ltd., Padstow, Cornwall

This book is printed on acid-free paper

Secret de deux, secret de Dieu
Secret de trois, secret de Tous
French proverb

Prologue

At midnight on Monday, June the Tenth, Nine-teen Hundred and Forty, Italy declared war on France, and on the following Thursday Italian SM81 three-engined bombers attacked Toulon. Turning away from their attack one of the bombers developed engine trouble and rapidly losing height crashed on the rising ground just north of the coastal road between the resorts of Aiguebelle and Cavalière.

The bomber ploughed into the façade of the Villa Colombier and within three minutes the whole place was ablaze, burning like a great pyre. The heavy pall of smoke drifted on a light southerly breeze out over the purple darkness of the sea while the leaping flames from the burning building cast erratic, twist-ing shadows from the gnarled olive trees that covered the slopes around it.

Within half an hour, and long before any effective help arrived, walls and roof had collapsed, as supporting timbers and the rafters were burned away. Oleanders and other shrubs in the garden and nearby olive trees flared up to encircle the holocaust and to set the dry grasses and heather clumps of the hillside alight to form a barrier which barred any close approach to the villa. At daybreak the smoke rose in an unwavering column into the calm morning air while small tongues and sporadic runs of fire still lived and leapt from heath clump to bush and tree on the tinder dry hillside. The villa was the property of an Englishman, Andrew Starr, the only son of Sir Albert Starr, Bt, of Avoncourt Abbey in the county of Wiltshire.

On that morning the Germans were poised to capture Verdun and their 7th Army about to cross the Rhine opposite Colmar while the French Army General Headquarters was moving south from Briare on the Loire to Vichy. Far away in North-West France Captain Andrew Starr was helping in Operation Cycle, which was designed to evacuate over thirty thousand British troops from Cherbourg. He himself never left for he had received secret orders to remain behind. On Monday, June 17th, while Rommel was racing towards Cherbourg, covering two hundred and forty kilometres a day, he went to a small hotel in Cherbourg, said one word to the proprietor, was shown without comment to a top floor bedroom, and shortly after emerged from the hotel in French workman's clothes. Mounting a bicycle which leaned against the hotel wall — a bicycle which had not been there when he entered — he rode off.

In the South of France at that moment, his wife, Christine, dumb to all feeling, stood some distance from the blackened pile of fallen masonry and charred wood and metal which had once been the Villa Colombier and the Italian SM81 bomber. Stiff-faced, her eyes wide and black shadowed, her grief was still so great that her beaten spirit was to be denied the balm of any tears for days to come. Pray she could but weep she could not for the grief she held had numbed all within her. Somewhere under the great pyre — burnt beyond any hope of recognition or formal burial — were the ashes and dust of her near-month-old child Angus Starr and his French wet nurse. The two had been alone in the house while she had been away in St-Tropez arranging for a fishing boat to take her and her son and nurse to Spain.

She crossed herself and turned away. Far out on the line of meeting sea and sky Port-Cros and its islands lay like a still cloud of pale smoke. On the path down the hill a bearded goat, forefeet raised against the trunk of a gnarled olive, turned from its browsing and watched her. A bee-eater flashed across her path but she saw nothing of its brilliance. Her eyes were veiled with a grief which had yet to be muted by time and tears.

1

Through the leaded lights of the small bedroom window Monsieur Louis Bonivard, the curé of the scattered Dordogne living of Cragnac, could see the narrow stretch of garden freshly planted with young lettuces and onions and the green growths of hazel-staked peas and runner beans. Madame Crillon loved her garden. There were few times when he passed on his pastoral duties that, despite her age, she could not be seen there, heavy-booted, skirts tucked up and, in the summer, wearing a wide-brimmed straw hat, tending to her crops, watering and hoeing and, although old, seeming indestructible . . . until, as now, the day had come when the good Lord smiled and gave the call for the end of all her labour and all the frets and cares of her earthly life.

Almost automatically he wrote slowly and in a neat, precise hand as she spoke, her voice clear mostly, but sometimes wavering into silence while she caught her breath and found fresh vigour. Sometimes he held up a hand and stopped her speaking while he re-shaped her words into ordered sequence and form, so that her statement should be coherent and without ambiguity. And sometimes when she was silent, regaining her strength, he looked out of the window at the garden until she was ready to go on.

At the end of the garden beneath a row of poplars was a small seat of roughly trimmed birch lengths where many, many times he had walked down to greet her and to sit with her and watch the waters of the Vézère idling past in summer drought, sometimes in autumn flood. Once she had said to him, 'Monsieur, I know all the voices of the river. Sometimes they speak angrily . . . scolding. And another they sing gently . . . giving peace and a little time of forgetfulness for our sins.'

Out of the corner of his eye he caught the movement of a pair of siskins moving in the top branches of a laburnum tree looking for a nesting site. He wrote on to her dictation and there was no surprise in him at the words which came from her. There had been a time when confessions stirred him to extreme compassion and, sometimes, to unworthy anger. Now . . . he accepted all calmly, knowing that behind each human act and thought God worked and there was no questioning His ways.

When she had finished, he said, 'There is much here maybe to cause unhappiness to others. You must think on that, my child. Your son for instance. Sometimes it is better to bury one's past for the sake of others' futures.'

'No, monsieur. It must be this way. God does not want any truth hidden. I have been too long in accepting that. With this done I can go with more of peace in my heart than I have known for years. God has spoken to me. It is His will. And I wish you to do as I have said. This you will promise me and then give me your blessing. Now, give me my glasses so that I can read it and then I will sign it.'

She smiled suddenly and through the crabbed, wrinkled face he saw briefly the phantom of the young woman who had once been tempted and now at the last moment would put herself right with her God and he knew that there was to be no turning her, nor perhaps could there be for behind her stood the years which God had ordained for her and who could make quarrel with that?

He went to her, gave her her glasses, and helped her up to read and sign the statement she had made and was surprised momentarily at the firmness with which she wrote her name until he realized that it came from a new strength and peace within her since she had now unburdened herself of a sin which had haunted her for so long.

This done, he gave her the last rites and was mildly amused that even in his ritual she turned her head and through the window watched her garden and the bright flow of water between the riverside bushes, knowing that her garden had been her place of peace and her work in it a happy penance which she made for Him, not in hope of forgiveness, but as an act of service and charity since most of what she grew she gave away to the surrounding villagers.

When he returned that afternoon she was dead. Two days later she was buried and the villagers, who all loved her, filled his church in a way that seldom happened for any other of his services. Her son, to whom he had written in Switzerland, was not present, nor was there any communication from him. Angry a little at the son's absence, but with charity enough to know that the man might well have been away from home, he stopped at the *Postes et Télégraphes* and sent a telegram to the same address advising the son of his mother's death. Until he could meet or speak with him he knew that there was nothing further he could do.

On his way back to his own place he stopped at Madame Crillon's cottage to make sure all was locked and secure. An old man was in the garden, hoeing slowly down between the rows. He went down to him, knowing him, knowing, too, that he was an atheist who would loudly proclaim so after a few drinks too many.

He said gently, 'Gaston, you were not at the service . . . not even for her?'

Gaston eased himself on his hoe and said, 'No, father. Why should I have been? She was not there. I told her that when she went I would still take care of her garden. If she is anywhere, she is here. Was her son Maurice there?'

'No. He obviously cannot have got my letter telling of her illness.'

Gaston spat. 'You waste your charity, father.'

Monsieur Bonivard smiled. 'I hope I have more than enough to miss it.'

Gaston shrugged his shoulders and turned back to his hoeing.

* * *

The ringing of his telephone brought Maurice Crillon slowly from sleep. Naked he rolled out of bed, squatted on its edge, and yawning rubbed his hands through his hair and then slowly massaged his still sleep-filled eyes. A glance at the wall clock told him that it was seven-thirty. He went through into his studio and picked up the telephone receiver from the ledge of the great north-facing window which looked out over the Lungarno Soderini and the River Arno. Florence was well awake with the movement of cars and pedestrians, and the river — mud coloured — had risen during the night from rains up in the mountains. The whole city was grey and gold and scarred with black shadows in the streets where the sun had yet to reach.

A woman's voice over the telephone said, 'Telegram for Signor Crillon.'

'That's me. One moment.' He reached out and took a pencil from a jar filled with pencils and brushes. 'All right. Go ahead.' He spoke Italian well, but the girl at the other end knew at once that it was not his native tongue.

He wrote the brief message on the plaster of the wall at the side of the window and as he did so was touched with deep grief but knew no surprise. His mother had long been ailing — and now her days were over. As the girl finished, he said, '*Grazie* — there's no need to confirm it.'

He stood by the window and blacked out the few words he had written down. As he did so he acknowledged the gesture with a wry twist of self-recognition. In this life it was safer to give nothing of importance away or to leave traces of one's private life, no matter how trivial they might seem. The instinct of self-preservation had long become habit. What you give to other people may be turned against you. Don't let people pry even marginally into your private life — particularly (he smiled to himself) since there were too many parts of his that would not bear examination. Even in love, a man should watch his words.

He turned away from the window and paused for a moment or two at a canvas that lay free of its old frame on his work table. It was a mid-eighteenth-century country scene by Giuseppe Zais — a *paesaggio* with villagers dancing on a green bluff, a rushing, mountain torrent in the background and distantly a river bridge below a hill-town golden in the afternoon light. It was a variation of a much better known example of the artist's works at the Accademia in Venice. On an easel alongside the table was a copy he was making. His eyes went from one to the other. He smiled to himself. The world was full of vain, undiscriminating, gullible fools.

He went back into the bedroom, picked up a towel from a chair and was moving towards the bathroom when the woman in the bed sat up, yawned with the backs of her hands across her mouth and smiled over them at him.

'I heard the telephone, Maurice. What was it?'

'Nothing, Carla *mia*.'

'Not my brother?'

'No.'

She grinned. 'Or someone telling you the end of the world was coming? Surely you would tell me if it were that?'

'That, yes.'

Her hands came away from her mouth and she yawned and spread her arms wide so that her naked breasts momentarily flattened against her chest and her dark hair fell backwards, freeing to sight the long upthrust of her neck. Momentarily he felt the itch to have in his hands red crayon and dark paper to catch the beauty of her body.

'Between us,' she said casually, 'it would be nice to have nothing but truth.'

He smiled. 'There is that already, Carla. Stupid little facts are not truth. You and I are truth.'

'Poof! You escape in words. I shall come and shower with you and you shall soap me. When you do that I feel that I am a baby again. And after that, you shall towel me dry. And after that I shall make coffee and — '

'And then you will go back to your brother, Aldo. I have to go to France.'

'France? Why?'

Pausing before replying he was tempted to tell her the truth, but resisted it. She would be all over him with the tenderness of concern and consolation — and this he did not want.

He said, 'It is a matter of business. I will be back as soon as I can. I will finish the Giuseppe Zais then.'

Standing under the shower as the water began to run she put her arms around him and said, 'You know I would leave him. Come with you now were it not for the money. I cannot touch it until I am thirty-five without his consent.'

He grinned. 'You could forget the money and come with me now.'

'You would accept that?'

'Of course.'

She shook her head. 'It would be stupid ... all for the sake of a few years. *Caro*, money is money — and with you it goes through your fingers like sand. You need me and you need my money. Then I will look after both.'

She bit the side of his chin gently and went on, 'You should not treat money as though it lay there like fallen leaves for the gathering.'

'You think so? It is spring now — not all the money in the world could buy you a basket full of autumn leaves at this moment.

But money is always there, somewhere, for the gathering.' He ran his hands over her body and went on, teasing, 'Now you are like Correggio's Danaë. But one day — '

Before he could say more she raised her head to the shower fall, filled her mouth with water and blew it into his face.

He laughed and went on, 'But one day you will be beautifully fat and I shall love you the more.'

'You swear?'

He grinned. 'I swear.'

An hour later when he had packed and driven off she stayed on in the studio apartment to tidy and clean it. At the window by the telephone she searched the wall which was where he usually scribbled notes during a telephone conversation if it were of importance. They were all, as usual, blacked out with thick pencil. Three years she had known him and through all that time she had learned little of him. What knowledge and memories she had of him had all been created in those years and the knowledge was scanty; an old mother somewhere in the Dordogne whom he partly supported, some years in Paris and Zürich . . . art schools, an obligatory period in the French Army . . . other women, too, she guessed but never mentioned . . . a man almost twice her age, a man with magic in his

14

fingers when he caressed her, but with more magic when he picked up palette and brush. *Mamma mia* ... that was all her brother cared about. But for that he would never have allowed their relationship — he still adamantly refused to release her money from their mother, hoping one day she would never be able to hold him here in Florence, that one day the ties between them would break and she would marry a man of his choosing ... *Porca miseria!*

She went over to the table where the Giuseppe Zais lay free of its frame, still only partly cleaned and restored, the dirt of years gone mostly from it, bright and luminous as the day probably when Zais' elderly idol, Marco Ricci, with a few years to live, might have seen it. One day her brother, Aldo, would take the family picture back to its owner, some obscure Italian aristocrat or jumped-up Milan millionaire and — according to her brother's whim, for sometimes when his bank balance pleased him he had bouts of conscience — it might be the original or it might not. But in the studio would be resting the original or the copy to be shipped and sold through her brother's friends abroad, or to buyers elsewhere who asked no questions and kept their own collections private. Maurice often said that vanity of possession clouded most eyes, but more importantly that most people went through life not using their eyes properly because they had never bothered to look long and hard for the signs of truth. At this thought she smiled to herself for in so many other ways Maurice was a greater stranger to truth than most men. There was no moment when one could be sure of his word . . . not even when he swore he loved her and would love her still when she grew fat. It could be true . . . and in love, if one did not believe, then there was no true ecstasy of spirit or body. So when they married, and if she grew fat and he wandered now and then, what would it matter? She had love enough for two. In no relationship was there ever true perfection. Nowhere in the world at any time, he had once said, had any man or machine drawn a perfect circle and had added, which had surprised her, 'It is against God's will.'

At that moment the telephone rang. She picked it up and said, 'Studio Crillon.'

'Carla.'

'Yes.'

'Put Maurice on.'

'He's not here.'

'Why not? He's always there in the morning.'

'He's gone. And before you begin the

questions let me go on. He had a telephone call this morning. Early. Then he came and woke me and said he had to go back to France for a few weeks — on a business matter — and that he would be back as soon as he could. That's all I know.'

'Didn't you ask him?'

'I never ask things like that. You know Maurice.'

'Has he finished the Giuseppe Zais?'

'No.'

'The man drives me mad.'

'And makes money for you.'

'And treats my sister like a whore.'

'That's right. And she enjoys it. Give me my money, you bandit, and we could marry and I'd be respectable and give you little nephews and nieces to fuss over. You'd like that. You're such a great family man.'

'He's got a mother in France, hasn't he?'

'Yes.'

'Perhaps he's gone there. Where does she live?'

'Somewhere in the Dordogne.'

'The address, idiot. He might have gone there.'

'So he might, pig. But he didn't say and I don't know the address.'

'You need a damned good beating to make you civil.'

'I expect Maurice will get around to that one day. *Ciao*, Aldo.'

She put back the receiver and went to the window and looked out over the river. Some way up the river she could see the Ponte Santa Trinitá and she smiled to herself as she remembered her first meeting with Maurice. She had been walking over the bridge on her way to the boutique in which she worked — Aldo did not let any of the family of which he was head idle at home if they were old enough to go out to work, though he was rich enough to keep two mistresses — when Maurice had come towards her. She had paid little attention to him until he was about to pass her. It was then that he turned back abruptly and began to walk a little abreast of her. Without looking at her he had said, 'It was on this bridge that Dante first saw his Beatrice. Would that be your name, too?'

She had made no reply but he walked with her without another word until she entered her place of work. For two days he met her each morning and was waiting for her each evening as she walked home to the family apartment in the Piazza Santo Spirito, speaking no more than to give a greeting on meeting and a goodbye on leaving. On the third evening as she walked home and was about to enter the apartment building he handed her a large brown manilla envelope. In the apartment she had opened the envelope. On a grey sheet of cardboard was a red chalk drawing of her head and shoulders. On the back was written — *Quite apart from having fallen in love with you, I would like to paint you. Tomorrow morning on the bridge if you hand this back to me without a word I shall probably commit suicide if I can find the courage to do so. Maurice Crillon.*

Aldo, whom she had already told of her encounters with Crillon, was in the room and without a word she had handed the drawing to him, saying, 'Do you think when I walk past him without a word he really will jump into the river?'

Aldo had said nothing for a while, intent on studying the drawing. Though he had no aptitude for art himself he had an eye which could instantly sort the gold from dross, and in his coarse, avaricious soul there lurked an aching, passionate love of beauty and craftsmanship. He was a pig of a man, full of coarse appetites, a bully and a ruthless man — but deep within was a man who would have walked from Florence to Rome and back barefoot over thorns to have been born with a tenth of the talent and genius he recognized in the portrait.

He said quietly, 'You walk past him without

19

a word tomorrow and when you get home I'll put you over my knee and beat your bare arse so that you won't be able to sit for a week.'

And so it had begun; her love for Maurice, and Maurice's work for Aldo.

★ ★ ★

Two days later — he had driven via Thun in Switzerland — Maurice Crillon arrived at his mother's cottage. Getting out of his car he saw Gaston down at the bottom of the garden working the handle of the pump which drew water from the river to fill the garden's two water tanks. He walked down to him, remembering the days when, as a boy, he had worked here with his mother — not enjoying it much but fully aware of her passion for the things she grew. Although as a mother she had not been outwardly affectionate, he had loved her. She had put nothing in the way he wanted his life to go when he had left school. She had given him money when he wanted it . . . sometimes squandered it . . . and when life had often beaten him over the head he had always been able to return here to lick his wounds, knowing, too, that she would ask no questions about his life that would embarrass him. At times he had felt that she served and comforted him, had given him money without question — did things for him, in fact, that in an odd way made him feel that she owed him something. Perhaps because of his father who had been taken prisoner by the Germans at the Fall of France and had never been seen again. Perhaps she had felt that no boy should be without a father, and that she should have married again ... Himself, he had no such feelings. What you've never known you could never miss. And anyway, with a father he would never have known the freedom he enjoyed with her.

He stopped, pulled a young spring onion from a row, washed it in one of the filling water tanks and ate it. Above, a pair of buzzards swung idly on the rising air currents. If he shut his eyes he knew that the sight of them and their movements would stay etched somewhere in his memory, ready to be recalled whenever he chose. So it was with Gaston. The old man's face lay in his memory, like so many others, always available. In the Uffizi Gallery at Florence there was a Domenico Veneziano painting of the Madonna and Child with Saints and one of the saints was John the Baptist, and the face was the face of old Gaston — who was far from conventional holiness, but undeniably had his own form of holiness.

The old man stopped his work on the

pump, spat, then pursed his thick lips before saying with little friendliness, 'You've arrived too late.'

'I came as soon as I knew. The curé's letter was delayed in the post.' It was not strictly true but it would serve, he thought. But the delay had been a genuine one. Had he received it he would have come at once.

Gaston fished in the pocket of his pale blue working blouse and handed him the cottage key, saying, 'Monsieur Bonivard wanted to know when you arrived. I'll tell him on my way home. I'll keep things going here, too — until you decide what you're going to do. But — I do it for her, not for you.'

Maurice took his case from the car and let himself into the cottage. The main room was as he had always known it. Everything had its place and had stayed in it. The room was swept and cleaned and free of dust. Gaston would have done that. There had been times, he knew, when his mother had been ill that Gaston had come in daily and looked after things for her. In Cragnac there had been a period when all had thought that Gaston would eventually marry his mother. He made a wry face at the thought of Gaston as a stepfather. However, despite the old man's censure of him, he liked him and was grateful for the companionship he had given his mother over the years.

Going upstairs he found his mother's room tidy and aired and there was a small vase of wild daffodils and violets placed in the wall niche which held a blue-robed figurine of the Virgin Mary. Looking at it he closed his eyes and crossed himself and said the first genuine prayer in years. The flowers, he knew, must have come from Gaston — and that small act of Christian observance, against the grain of all the old man's beliefs, could never have been made for any other woman.

His own room with the low bed under the window looking over the garden was also unchanged and the small watercolour which he had made as a boy of the house and garden, crude, but with, he saw now, the touch of waking passion in it for line and colour which was to grow and obsess him over the years. Later, to amuse his mother when he came home on holiday from Paris, he would draw caricatures of the villagers that would make her laugh. Her laughter still hung in his memory, and now disturbed him for he knew that he had far from served her well except in material comforts. On the wall above a wash-hand stand was a faded photograph of the father he had never known, a tall, slim figure in a dark suit, holding a fedora in one hand to his breast and a walking stick in the other, his legs crossed as he leant against a studio pillar, his side-buttoned boots highly polished and a cat-that-had-had-the-cream smirk on his face. Early in his thirties he had come home once and without her knowledge had studied the face and then drawn it, putting back its life and true nature, and given it to his mother. She had wept for the first time he had ever known, and there had been nothing to tell him whether it was from joy or sadness.

Disturbed by the memory, touched briefly with a nameless remorse and dissatisfaction with himself, he said aloud, 'God makes us, and His will shapes us.'

Recognizing the rare mood and knowing from experience that it might last if not challenged, he went down to the large living room and opened the walnut-wood hanging corner cupboard. His mother drank nothing but a little wine and water, but in the cupboard against any chance coming of his was a bottle of whisky. He poured himself a drink.

He sat by the window watching the setting sun low over the hills beyond the river. It was higher up the river in one of these hills that he had, at the age of sixteen, found a small cave and had made his first forgeries. With red and black ochre he had drawn imitations of Palaeolithic art and made engravings on the rock face of outlined hands, black-spotted horses, a charging bison with a spear through its neck and also the figure of a naked, heavily breasted woman. He never attempted to profit from them, and never told anyone about them. But at times when his oncoming adolescence troubled him he would go and sit up in the cave's mouth and smoke forbidden cigarettes. A year after he had done the drawings heavy winter rains had collapsed the hillside above the cave, blocking it off. Someday, he thought now, in a hundred or a thousand years they might come to light . . . so what?

At that moment he heard a car stop outside the cottage and knew that it would be Monsieur Bonivard, the curé. He got up and went to the wall cupboard and brought out another glass and a bottle of Monbazillac which his mother always kept for the priest's visits.

2

Monsieur Bonivard, glass in hand, the golden wine taking the last of the day's light through the window, their preliminary greetings and his condolences over, said, 'She would have wished you here, of course. It is a sadness that you could not be reached in time, my son.'

'I was away from Switzerland, father. On business. But I thank you for all the trouble you have had and taken on my behalf. I shall not forget it.'

'I do God's work. And the way He works is sometimes strange to us. This we can only but accept. And I speak now not of your being unable to come here, but of your mother — for there are things you must know about her which when you know them will leave you with decisions to make. Before she died she gave me something for you . . . a letter, which is also a form of confession. I wrote it at her request and she signed it and I witnessed it. I have it with me and I wish you to tell me whether you would like me to go away and let you read it alone, or whether you would wish me to stay?'

Frowning a little, Maurice Crillon said, 'Is it so disturbing, father?'

'I think so. There was a point after she had dictated a little to me when I stopped her and asked her to consider whether what she was doing was wise. Whether, in fact, God was with her. She said she could not speak for God, but only from her conscience and from her love for you because she knew that you could then make your own decision and she was sure that God would direct you.'

'I can't believe that there was any true sin on my mother's conscience, father. If she wanted me to read the letter then she must have had good reason. She was in her true mind when she got you to take down the letter?'

'Absolutely.'

'Then because she wished it I must read it.'

'And you wish me to stay?'

Maurice smiled. 'Your glass is empty.' He reached over and filled the priest's glass.

As he did so the curé took an envelope from the pocket of his soutane and handed it to him, saying, 'I will leave you alone for a little while and take my wine into the garden to catch the last of the sun. If when I return you hand me the letter and tell me to burn it I shall understand.' Monsieur Bonivard stood up and went out through the garden door.

When he was gone Maurice opened the letter and switched on the electric table lamp. He spread the sheets of paper on the table before him and even as he did so found himself admiring the priest's handwriting which was in a meticulously formed Italianate script. The man was old but his hand was that of a young man. The letter read:

To my dearly beloved Maurice,

I have tried to get in touch with you so that you could be here and have all this from my own lips and then give me your forgiveness. Now you can only read my words and then pray to God to give you a true direction.

You know that I was born and lived all my early life at Lalinde, not far from Bergerac, and it was here that I met my husband to be, Paul Crillon, a journeyman carpenter from Sarlat. We were married in June 1939 and went to live just outside Toulon because, through a friend, your father had got a job on a big building contract nearby. We lived in two rented rooms. But at the beginning of September that year when war was declared on Germany your father was called up under the general mobilisation orders. I stayed on doing domestic work and sometimes helping in a neighbouring shop. I never heard any more of him. Nor much later could the authorities help me. It was thought that probably he had died in a German Prisoner of War camp.

In October I knew that I was going to have a child. I worked as long as I could, and was helped out by your Uncle Maurice who when he died left me this cottage and a small legacy. My baby, a boy, was born on 30th April, 1940. He lived, poor soul, for only one week. If you were here I could speak of that time, but since you are not I can only leave you to imagine my feelings. What matters now is the truth which I owe to you.

Through the midwife who had attended me I got a position as a wet nurse to the boy child of an English lady, who lived at the Villa Colombier near Aiguebelle, where naturally I lived in. The child had been born on May 15th, 1940, but the mother had no milk to feed it. And at this time she was trying to find a way to leave France and I was frequently left alone with the child and one housekeeper who came in daily from Aiguebelle.

Late at night on Thursday June 13th an Italian bombing plane which had been attacking Toulon crashed on the villa and the place was completely destroyed. Earlier that night the baby boy had been feverish and I had taken him from the villa, hoping the cool night air would soothe him. I walked some way along the hillside with him and from a safe distance saw the air crash and the burning of the villa.

Then I committed a sin for which daily I have asked God's forgiveness. I walked away with the child in my arms along the road to Toulon, and then partly by train and partly by getting lifts I found my way back to Cragnac and your Uncle. I never told him the truth, or anyone else until this day. But to you, my dear son, for I can think of you no other way, the truth is owed. What you will do I know not. Monsieur the curé knows all the facts of your true parents and will give them to you if you wish to ask. I have sinned against you greatly, but I have always loved and cherished you dearly as my own.

May God grant you the wisdom to act charitably and with compassion. God bless you my dearest child.

The letter was signed by his mother and, under his authentication, by the curé. Maurice put it down on the table and without clear feeling or thought picked up his glass and finished his whisky. A long shadow fell across the evening sunlight coming through the door. The curé stood there, his face in the shadow, his tall bulk like some hunch-backed stork. He said nothing, but moved into the room, sat down at the table across from Maurice and poured into his glass the last of the Monbazillac. He touched his lips with the wine and then putting down the glass said gently, 'You know what I wish to hear from you, my son, before anything?'

Maurice nodded. 'Yes, I know, father. I loved her. There were times when I was not a good son to her. I am glad, too, that she died with the burden taken from her. And with the whole of my soul, father, I forgive her.' Then he grinned and added, 'But you must agree that for a Frenchman to discover that he is an Englishman is no pleasant surprise?'

The curé smiled. 'It could be worse . . . *un sale Boche*. But please do not quote me on that. So what do you propose to do? You know the counsel I would give.'

'I know. But somewhere still living there are my true parents. Or are they dead?'

'They live.'

'And if I ask you will tell me where?'

'Yes, I promised that.'

'I must sleep on it.'

'Then when you say your prayers you must

ask God to give you true direction. If you look and listen He will make it known to you, my son.' The curé rose and came to him. Briefly he held his face between his hands and bent and kissed his forehead.

The curé gone, Maurice walked out into the garden and down to the river in the growing dusk and sat on the seat overlooking the now darkening face of the waters. One part of him was all compassion for his mother — he could think of her in no other way. But part of him now, like an itch that suddenly rises and with scratching grows stronger, was the inevitable curiosity about this other mother, his true mother. In his heart he knew what he wished. That his mother had said nothing. How could a man dismiss such knowledge? How could a man not fail to find himself wondering about his true parents, wanting to know where and how they lived? English or not, it made no matter. Wanting to know was an itch the mind relished. It was like having a blank canvas in front of you and with nothing in your imagination to put to it. He gave an angry grunt. He had lost one mother. And now he was being asked to bury another. Surely God would not have wanted it that way? Suddenly the surface of the water was foamed grey with froth as some unseen pike harried a shoal of small fish.

For a while his mind was incapable of absorbing let alone analysing the central situation of his present state. Only one thing was clear. He was not the man he had always thought he was. Instead of the blood lines of honest, almost peasant stock, French to the backbone, he had to acknowledge that his real character and every gene in his body came from, at the moment, unknown stock. That at least solved, even if it did not soothe, some of the contradictions in his character. His talents — he knew himself to be so endowed — came not from any worthy Gallic source but from those still unknown English parents who had passed on to him a racial culture and possibly an insular stance which, now he saw, could account for many of the ways he thought and acted. Perhaps even for — he grinned briefly and wryly — that rogue element which ran parallel with his talents. Through those unknown parents God had endowed him with the hands and the eyes of an artist, and also — it seemed — with the heart of a rogue and the rashness of a buccaneer. What kind of parents were they? There was an itch to rest uneasily in his mind.

Wet nurse to an English lady with a villa in the South of France . . . His imagination could easily encompass the situation of his mother (and mother she would always be in his mind and heart) and the tragic, terrible moments of temptation. *Pauvre chère Maman.* He could understand it all, and there was no smallest part of anger or censure in him. The Devil knew how to tempt in moments of grief, and how to twist the forces of all forms of love to make men and women step aside to take the wrong path and, taking it, to find that after a few paces there was no turning back. He had done it himself while a student in Paris with his first little forgery of a Dufy which he had sold to an American tourist . . . and from there he had moved slowly into the more sophisticated and shadowy world of dishonest dealers . . . The world was full of wealthy ignorants who saw themselves as experts, so full of a pride in their own judgments that when they came to know they were cheated they refused to acknowledge it openly. They still bedded their false mistress, and cherished her, knowing how to be deaf, dumb and blind to save themselves the pain of truth and the ache of their own warped judgments. But not he. He knew the world he lived in, knew the rarity of virtue and truth and, like a chameleon, shaded his modes and manner of living in the complicated and enchanting exercise of survival. The one great maxim was to give little of yourself away to anyone else, even to be ambiguous where no need existed, but might in the future. And now the world had played a trick on him. Right from the first moments of walking, talking, and finding himself a person — the world had been cheating him while the gods above chuckled as they watched the growth of the cuckoo in the nest.

He could acknowledge now with a new complacency some aspects of his character which had always puzzled him. His talent, genius if others wished to call it that, though he knew better, came from a still unknown source. And so did so many other qualities of his personality. And that source lay in England; and to have owned a villa in France spoke of no journeyman carpenter like his never seen, long dead, supposed father. What kind of people were they? That was an itch in the mind which would have to be eased. He knew himself too well not to acknowledge that. Even if only to view from a distance the true mother and father who still lived had to be made fact. Just to look and see might be enough. At least it had to be done because he knew that he could not wipe from his mind his mother's confession. He knew himself too well to think that he could go to the curé and say *There is nothing to be done except to forget.*

★ ★ ★

He drove into Cragnac the next morning, taking with him flowers from the cottage garden to put on his mother's grave. The freshly turned, red slaty soil was slicked to a darker colour by a faint drizzle which fell. He said a prayer for her and was surprised to find his cheek muscles jerk with an emotion that suddenly engulfed him as vividly, all those years now past, he saw her with a babe in her arms walking, almost running, perhaps stumbling, away from the villa. How much more vividly, he realized now, had she carried that moment in her mind, and in all his days with her there had never been any sign of the agony of the truth she harboured within herself.

Monsieur Bonivard appeared out of the church and, seeing him, came over, the skirts of his soutane taking the wetness of the grass and dragging a little at his legs. He gave him a greeting and then said, 'What would you like done about the grave, my son?'

Crillon said, 'Gaston will grass it and keep it tidy. And then, sometime, I will cut and inscribe a stone for her.'

'You will?'

'Yes, I will. I worked for a stonemason and monumental sculptor for a while in Switzerland. What the hands can shape on paper they

36

can also find in stone.' He smiled. 'She shall have her garden flowers and — unless you object — some of her fennel and lettuces.'

Monsieur Bonivard smiled. 'Why not? And will you be staying here long now?'

'No. I have a life to live. But I shall keep the cottage. Gaston will look after it. This is my home. I shall always keep it.'

They turned away from the grave and walked down the path to the road where Crillon's car stood. Not until he stood with his hand on the car door handle did the curé speak.

'And the other thing, my son?'

Crillon nodded. 'Yes, that. I have thought about it, father.'

'And?'

'I have too curious a nature to live the rest of my life not knowing. It would always be there . . . '

'Yes. I understand. It would be too much to ask. But when you know, you may find other compulsions. When this happens I ask you, my son, to consider carefully what you do. They are both alive, your father and your mother. Through no fault of their own, life has wrought this strange circumstance for them, just as it has for you. I ask you to think hard and pray for true guidance before you commit yourself one way or the other. Only that I say. Think not alone of yourself. You know now the truth about yourself and you are young and strong enough to come to terms with it one way or another, but your parents are elderly. You must place them first in your thoughts. I say no more on that issue.'

He raised a hand, made the sign of the cross and gave Crillon a blessing. Then he reached into the deep pocket of his soutane and pulled out an envelope and handed it to him. Without another word he walked away through the light drizzle that was falling.

Maurice Crillon put the envelope in his pocket, got into his car, and drove back to the cottage. Once inside he put the envelope on the living-room table and poured himself a glass of wine. Outside the rain, thickened and driven by a rising wind, hammered against the glass panes of the garden door. He drank a little of the wine and then opened the envelope. Inside on a lined sheet torn from an old exercise book and written in black ink in his mother's shaky handwriting was the following:

My dear Maurice,

The English lady I worked for as wet nurse at Aiguebelle is the wife of Andrew Starr, the only surviving son, so I now understand, of Sir Albert Starr who I learned some years ago is now dead, which means that your father is now Sir Andrew Starr. He is a Baronet which is something I don't clearly understand. Their family house, which my mistress often talked about, is called Avoncourt Abbey, near Salisbury in Wiltshire, England. They also have a place in this country somewhere near Thier, I think.

My dear son, if you ever read this I shall understand and from the love I bear can only pray you will act wisely and from the heart.

God bless you my dearest one.

Enclosed were two documents, a Birth Certificate for Maurice Crillon registered at Toulon on 30th April, 1940 and a Certificate of the same registration place for the death of Maurice Crillon on Tuesday, 7th May, 1940.

He sat back in his chair, suddenly overcome with emotion, wishing that his mother had never made her confession. What was in the past and unknown was better left that way. But that was not her way and she must have suffered for it every day of the years left to her after she had fled from the Aiguebelle villa. There were some confessions that should only be made to God. Now whether he liked it or not there was a new element in his already complicated life — and it was not one he could ignore. He acknowledged that now. This was not something he could leave alone. His nature made that impossible. What he made of it lay in the future and he held back any desire to speculate.

Once, when he was eighteen, he had gone to England during the summer vacation for two months, to improve his already fair English and had enjoyed himself, lodging in Brighton and missing most of his classes but taking more of the English language from his contacts with the holiday girls and youths so that he could speak it more than adequately. Languages came easily to him. Too much, perhaps, he thought, came easily to him. Salisbury he knew was a Cathedral city and he had a feeling that he had made an excursion there at some time. So his true father was now a baronet. He was a little hazy about the word's exact meaning. His mind could supply an imaginary background. No matter how inaccurately shaped, there were indubitable elements that had to exist . . . they were no paupers for sure. He raised his head suddenly and sniffed the air as though a familiar and exciting scent had flaired past his nostrils and he recognized from past adventures the beginning of the slow rise of anticipation in him. What he might or might not be able to make of all this was not the most important aspect of this revelation. It was the rising, lancing, excitement in him which he had known so often before. A woman coming across the Ponte Santa Trinitá with the morning breeze of the Arno flattening her dress against thighs and breasts, a girl sculling a boat on a Swiss lake, sun-brown, more naked than naked in her bikini . . . a Juno who had made his hands itch to possess her, first in the flesh and then in stone or on canvas.

He got up, suddenly determined, and went to the telephone he had made his mother have and always paid for. He sent two telegrams. One to Switzerland and the other to Florence. He then went up to his bedroom and packed himself two suitcases — one for his clothes and the other for his basic working materials.

Gaston arrived in the garden as he came down. The light rain had thinned and died. He went out to him and asked him to go on looking after the place and making him take money for the service. He finished, 'If anyone wants me — there is always the Swiss address which will find me.'

Gaston said, 'It's a stupid fox that only has one earth. But one day, Monsieur Maurice, you will be caught out in the open. I can

41

speak frankly now that your mother has gone.'

Maurice laughed. 'You read character from what? The eyes, the whole face?'

'No, Monsieur Maurice. I read it from what the eyes and the face never show naturally. You smile for people but the smile does not start in your heart, and you give them your face, but it is an actor's face, something you put on each morning. But you must know all this?'

'And my true face?'

'It is a long time since you have seen it. And now you never will for it only comes back when you sleep. You agree?'

'Yes, I do.' He shrugged his shoulders. 'But now I have long learned to live with the stranger who has taken me over.'

Gaston smiled and said, 'For your mother's sake I will look after things.'

★   ★   ★

Fräulein Trudi Keller stood by the stone balustrade at the top of the steps which ran down to a small half-moon of beach on the shores of Lake Thun. The top of the steps was guarded by a pair of wrought iron gates which were always kept locked during school hours to stop the young children from reaching the lakeside. Across the lake, still a little mist-hazed under the morning sun, she could see the distant town of Spiez and, high above it, clear in the cloudless air the crest of the Niesen. Three swans foraged the weed growths away to her right and far out on the lake a steamer was making its way up to Interlaken. Behind her a group of a dozen small children romped on the grass, shouting and running and playing games, enjoying their mid-morning break. In the small beds on the garden side of the terrace the canna lilies were stiff, green, glossy, almost heraldic growths with a few buds already broken to release the first display of flaring red and yellow blooms.

Footsteps clattered on the pathway behind her and she turned as the kindergarten housekeeper came down to her, wearing the heavy clogs which meant that she had been mopping and cleaning the kitchen floors. She was in her fifties, as broad as she was tall, her face creased with lines, her eys bright blue like the morning waters of the lake.

'Fräulein,' she said, holding out a buff coloured envelope to Trudi, ' — this has just come for you. I signed for it. I will now take the children in for their milk and biscuits.'

'Thank you, Frau Horst.'

As the housekeeper turned away and began

to call the children, Trudi Keller opened the envelope. She knew it was from him for no one else sent her telegrams. It would be nice one day, she thought, to get a proper letter. But no — it was always a telegram or a telephone call, and these only when he wanted something. Sometimes, but so rarely, he came himself as a little while ago and they met without her parents ever knowing for since the day years ago when he had ceased working for her father they had forbidden her to mention his name. But nobody could forbid or prevent her feeling for him.

The message was simple. *Please telegraph the Florence number and say — Business matters complicated. Cannot say when I shall be back. Maurice.*

She put the telegram into the pocket of her dirndl skirt and shrugged her shoulders. She was so used to it now that she had long ceased to be surprised or even to question what went on in his mind. Her own common-sense had long told her that she should right from the beginning have refused to be used by him, used and always without the faintest idea why he wrapped himself in mystery and needed her as a go-between for what seemed the simplest and most innocuous of reasons . . . coming and going without warning, suddenly, as she wheeled her bicycle out of the school drive, seeing him waiting for her and then finding herself lost again, going to an hotel with him for the night. But once with him, once in bed, nothing mattered. No other man existed or ever would in the way he existed for her. Years ago he had wakened a hunger and then fed it, taken advantage of it and made her his creature, used her and abused her — but had never given her anything of his true self. The day in Zürich he had come to work for her father had been a bad day for her because, against all her attempts to free herself, she had found herself his slave, but not one entirely lost to common-sense. That there was another woman in Florence, and other women God-knew-where, made no difference for some deep instinct told her that the other women were probably tied to him exactly as she was.

In the lunch break she sent the telegram to Florence for him, not using the school telephone but walking the short distance to Gunten down the lake towards Thun.

★　★　★

The following evening Carla, coming back from her work at the boutique — she had ceased working full-time some little while

45

after she had met Maurice Crillon, but still did two or three days a week — called in at the flat and found Maurice's telegram waiting in his post box.

She smiled at the phrase — *business matters complicated*. Knowing him well now she knew that could mean anything. There probably were no business matters at all, and instead of the phrase *Cannot say when I shall be back* she felt that the words *Will not say when I shall be back* would have been nearer the truth. She was used to his ways now and was more or less convinced that his obliquities had long become more a matter of habit than necessity — though there was no doubt that he and her brother were often engaged in very risky business. Her brother was astute enough, and anyway if trouble should reach him he had many friends to lie on oath for him, and others whose influence reached into high places. But she knew, too, that if it were needed he would sacrifice Maurice without a moment's hesitation to save his own skin. She could hear him say, all red-faced and outraged indignation, 'That one . . . out of the goodness of my heart I pick him starving from the gutter and give him cleaning and restoration work and all the time he makes copies of the paintings which go back to their owners and — Santa Madre

— he keeps the originals to sell to his crook friends in Paris or God knows where.'

When she got back to the house Aldo was eating by himself in the dining room. His two children never ate with him except on high days and family occasions or when they all went out on some celebration to a restaurant. He was crouched, as though afraid someone might snatch it from him, over a dish of thrush pie. Before she could make any greeting he said sourly, 'Whoever sold these thrushes to Luisa cheated her. I should know. Anyone who hunts should know. These are fieldfares. The world is full of liars.'

'Then you're in good company, dear brother.'

To her surprise he looked up at her and grinned — and she saw for a moment the brother who had once badly knifed an older boy who had tried to interfere with her, a brother who had said, 'Anyone touch any part of the Pandolfi family!' He had spat and flicked the edge of his right hand across his throat.

'So,' he said to her now, ' — you are in a good mood. So what is it so bad that makes you so happy at the thought of telling me? You are pregnant, maybe? Then I kick you out of the house. Or you have lost your job? Then I kick your arse and go to them and arrange it. If they say *No* — then I buy their shop. So what is it, little sister?'

She put the telegram in front of him and went to the door and called to her sister-in-law, Luisa, that she was at home and then came back and helped herself to a glass of marsala from the sideboard. Sitting down at the end of the dining table she raised the glass to her brother and said teasingly, 'What? No explosion?'

Sourly, he said, 'Too long ago I run out of explosions over Maurice. He is a genius, and what they say about them is true. They are difficult to live with. That you will learn if you ever marry him. Every day I pray against that — because you will never be happy, never, never . . . '

'So what? I am happy now. Does one have to look at a man who takes one's fancy and say *Will he make me happy?* No, there is no saying of words.' She tapped her bosom gently. 'In here . . . no matter any words there is born the beginning, like no other beginning before — and you must trust and accept it.'

Aldo picked a bone fastidiously from his mouth and laid it on the side of his plate. He shrugged his shoulders, and said, '*Cara sorella mia* — you are like all women, a fool. But more so than most. And as for Maurice, one day he will find that he cannot treat the world like a coloured ball with which to make games. You think I am a pig that never looks beyond its trough. But I am a clever pig — not just to make money, but to make it so that no one ever points the finger at me without finding that before he can speak the finger is chopped off — like that!'

He chopped the edge of his right hand down on the table and made the crockery dance. Carla smiled to herself as she noted that his free hand had held his wine glass firmly on the table so that it should not fall over. She said quietly, 'Oh, Aldo — you do not deceive me. I know the truth. You love Maurice like a younger brother loves his elder. More than that. You would have liked to be as he is — with that in your eyes and hands and heart which he has before an easel. I have seen your face sometimes at the galleries . . . once I most remember at the Uffizi before Tiziano's *La Flora*. Two things you showed without knowing it . . . Adoration and longing. Why do you try to make the world believe that you are an unfeeling pig? Pig, you are — but not unfeeling.'

Aldo was silent, face expressionless, for a while and then he said gently and smiling, 'My little sister, perhaps it is a good thing for men that few women have eyes like yours.

But now I have had enough of your witchcraft. But first answer me a question truly. What has Maurice got in Switzerland?'

Carla shrugged her shoulders. 'Does it matter? He worked there for a long while. You know that. Maybe a woman.'

'You don't mind that?'

'Why should I? Maurice needs women as you need food — unthinkingly. When the meal is finished, he is already looking forward to the next.'

Aldo rolled his eyes. 'And you would marry a man like that — you with all your money to come?'

'What has the money to do with it? You live for making money and for your food and drink — but Luisa married you because she loved you. When I marry Maurice he can have as many women as he likes so long as he loves me and sleeps more or less regularly at home.'

'Holy Mother — you make marriage sound like the Common Market!'

Carla laughed. 'Marriage means little. Love is all.'

Aldo snorted. 'Now you goad me for your pleasure. But enough of this nonsense. One day I shall send Maurice away.'

'When you do then I go. But the truth is that one day Maurice will leave you. Maybe he already has.'

'Why do you say that?'

'Because he has curious habits. He has a bible by his bed which I have never seen him read — but written inside is a birthday greeting from his mother when he was ten years old and he once told me that it went everywhere with him when he changed jobs. Now it has gone.'

'But how could he know he wasn't coming back?'

'I don't think he did. But something made him take it.'

'Then happily that's the end of him for you.'

'Oh, no. When he wants me he will send for me — and I shall go.'

'But what about the Giuseppe Zais?'

'Somebody else can finish the cleaning. But the copy will never be finished. All you will get is the money for restoring the original — unless you can find another Maurice.'

She smiled gently at the almost apoplectic Aldo. On the spur of the moment she had made up the story of the bible. Now, since she could not do it openly, she mentally crossed herself and prayed that the lie never became a reality. But her uneasiness was soothed by the behaviour of Aldo — he lay back in his chair like a stricken man. She said gently, 'Perhaps if you agreed to release my

51

money now and give a blessing to our marriage he would come back.'

'You think so?'

'I know he would.'

'How can you tell?'

She put her hand over her heart, enjoying herself. 'In here.'

Slowly Aldo said in his head of family voice, 'I shall think about it. But it would not just be for finishing the Zais.' He grinned suddenly. 'For such a rich prize he would have to do a few more first.' Then suddenly bursting out laughing, he almost shouted, 'You are a liar . . . a liar. I can see it in your eyes. Like the first time you told me you had never slept with him . . . like the time you said the priest was familiar with you . . . oh, and a dozen others.' He stopped suddenly, finished his glass of chianti, and then went on quite seriously, 'But hear this now — and I swear to the Holy Mother that I mean it — you get Maurice back here to finish the Zais, and maybe do two or three others and you shall have my blessing and your money. And don't tell me you have no ways and means. You know more about Maurice than you tell or he guesses. No woman can sleep with a man for more than six months and not know things he never guesses. Find him, get him back here, and you have my word.'

'And my job?'

'That stinking little boutique or whatever it is can sink in the Arno as far as I am concerned. I will give you the money for whatever you need.'

Carla stood up and said, 'I will think about it.'

'*Grazie*, my dear sister. After all, we are one family. We help one another.'

3

He had spent three nights in Salisbury, staying at the Red Lion Hotel, and during that time he had visited Avoncourt Abbey twice as an ordinary tourist to walk its gardens and to go round those limited parts of the house which, largely unused by the family, were open to the public in the afternoon on Tuesdays, Wednesdays and Thursdays. On all other days, although the house was closed to the public, the gardens which ran down the gentle valley slope to the Upper Avon were open. The guide book told him that part of the building was Elizabethan, built on the site of an even older house which had been destroyed by fire, and the rest early Georgian. Standing a little apart from the house was a late, fourteenth century chapel dedicated to St John the Evangelist, the patron saint of travellers, and which was also a chapel of the Commandery of the Knights Hospitaller of Saint John. On the wall of the nave was a tablet commemorating the Commanders of Avoncourt and the earliest inscribed name was that of a Sir William Starr for the years 1326 to 1338. Other Starr names followed up until 1540 when came the dissolution of the monasteries. The tablet finished with the lines —

The Knights are dust,
Their swords are rust,
Their souls are with the Saints we trust.

The whole business, now that he was here, had originally overwhelmed him. There had been times when his instinct was to turn away and forget the uncomfortable truths which had come to him through his mother's confession. The only time when he had felt completely at ease so that his natural opportunism was revived was when he had gone round the two large galleries of the more modern part of the Abbey which housed the collection of paintings the family had acquired over the centuries. Here he had found peace, excitingly laced with envy, and had experienced a *frisson* of rare humility before the works of so many masters. All this, he told himself, could one day belong to him. They were there, waiting for him to claim a right to them when one day his true father should die. His father he had now seen more than once, walking a Jack Russell terrier and a springer spaniel through the grounds and down the lower meadow slopes to the river

— a tall man in his late sixties wearing khaki drill trousers, an old Harris tweed jacket with leather elbow patches, and serving a gammy right leg with the help of a long thumb stick. He sported an old fishing cap, adorned with trout flies, and smoked a pipe with a burnt-down bowl and the stem wound about with adhesive tape. The possibly eccentric English gentleman par excellence — and his father. His father. The first time he had seen him and a gardener nearby weeding a flower bed had identified him for him, he had had only one reaction — *Mais, c'est ridicule!*

After his second visit to the Abbey he returned to his hotel and before dinner walked into the nearby Cathedral close, the great spire thrusting high into the late May evening sky. As he sat down on a bench to consider his course of action he automatically took a small sketch pad and pencil from his pocket and, occupied by his thoughts, began to draw the Cathedral. It was a thing he often did when he had some problem to work out and now, as he considered his plan of approach to Sir Andrew Starr, his hand moved automatically.

His real problem lay in the embarrassment of making a direct approach. He was — and so often to his own advantage — instinctively aware of other people's feelings. It was the first step to taking advantage of them. And there was absurdity here at the thought of writing a letter to Sir Andrew enclosing his mother's confession and the supporting documents and politely asking for an appointment to see him. The situation was bizarre enough, and at the beginning would remain so, to call for an unusual — for him — considering of his father's feelings. Since the situation was delicate and capable of many developments — he had even considered an offer to sell the evidence for a large sum and a promise of forgetting all about his birthright — he felt that whatever his first approach should be, there must be nothing done to prejudice his own position and freedom of choice. He could, of course, take no action at all. He had come and seen. He could just drive away without doing anything. He could, but he knew he would not. That was not in his nature. The problem was to find the right approach which would leave him scope and room to make his own decision or compact later. Oddly enough, too, he now discovered that there was a leaven of charity in him for the Starrs. They were owed the truth about that night at Aiguebelle. Once that was in the open both he and they would be free to arrange an agreed solution. Reaching this point he saw at once how he must act. Knowing what he had to do, he finished his sketch and was about to put the pad in his pocket when a voice at his side said, 'I hope you will forgive me, but I wonder . . . well, I think your little drawing is marvellous, I would like to have it. Buy it, I mean. Oh God, am I sounding awful and pushing?'

He turned and before he saw her properly he was smiling. He took his time before replying, but in that interval, his eyes went over her and he knew that any time he wanted her to return to memory in the future she would be there at recall. He knew other things, too. Things that were a matter of instinct and experience. Women's voices and women's eyes, the shape of their faces and the lines of their bodies, clothed or unclothed, crowded his memory ready to come forward at his call. And beyond these outward things he could always sense the emotional drive which in unguarded moments made them act sometimes a little out of character and sometimes quite contrary to their nature. Here was one, he thought, who in a few moments would be overwhelmed by her forwardness. To save her from that, and with an eye to the possible future, he said, 'Do you live in Salisbury?'

'Yes, I do. Oh, dear — you're not annoyed with me?'

'On the contrary. All artists live on praise.'

He pulled a blank leaf from his pad and handed it to her with his pencil. 'Write down your name and address. This is only a rough sketch which I want to work up properly. You shall have it when it's done. Go on — write and I'll bring it to you.'

Her face hidden from him as she wrote, her fair hair falling forward a little, he saw that her hand wore no wedding ring. As she handed the paper back to him, she said, 'You're not English, are you?'

He laughed. 'Well, in a way no. But then in a way yes. Does that confuse you?'

'Well, yes, I suppose it does.'

'It does me too.' He put the paper into his pocket without looking at it, and went on, 'When is the best time to bring it to you?'

After a moment or two of hesitation she said, 'In the evening. After I get back from work.'

'I will come soon, and you shall have your cathedral.'

'Oh, dear. I do feel awful.'

He shook his head. 'No, not awful. Not that. I know what you feel. I have suffered from it all my life. *Le coeur a ses raisons que la raison ne connait point.*'

★　★　★

Sir Andrew Starr knew that the man was waiting for him. There had been too many times in his life when he had known that men were waiting for him — men seen perhaps only once or twice, but no matter how briefly some instinct signalled that their presence went beyond coincidence. There was always this bond between the hunter and the hunted. Not that now — as in the old days — the presence of the other carried menace. Life was full of pleasanter encounters. At a hundred yards he could now pick out an Abbey visitor who stood waiting, debating between propriety and natural diffidence to establish the impulse to step forward and ask for an autograph. But this man wanted no autograph. He had seen him before. Today he had followed him down through the grounds to the river and then sat on the fishing path stile to let him take his walk up the river, and now was here still, his back turned to him but — he knew — perfectly aware of his coming.

He moved downstream unhurriedly, the two dogs behind him. May was on its way out, the river ran with a smooth, green-glass gentleness. There had been a hatch of mayfly further upstream and the water surface was pocked with the greedy rise of trout and grayling. A cuckoo called up on the valley slope. The wild garlic was in flower and bees were working over the blossoms of rest harrow and bugle. Once in France . . . how many lost years ago? . . . he had walked down a river somewhat like this to find a man waiting for him and had known there was no turning, only a going on to kill or be killed, to defeat betrayal or be killed by it. He lived still but his gammy left leg was a souvenir of the encounter which carried no gain for him except that it was a reliable barometer of changing weather. That other, long ago, had kept his hands in his pockets until the last moment. This one's hands were free from the pockets of the suede jacket he wore and there was no bulge in either of the pockets of the neatly pressed, cream coloured jean-type trousers. Continental. Clothes make a man — and if he were foolish could unmake him.

As he came up to the stile the man stepped down and stood aside a little to give him passage, but not immediately because one hand was moving inside his jacket to an inner pocket. The movement wakened a remote but no longer important *frisson* of expectancy in him. Those days were long gone. Only when he went back to France did the smell of them sometimes catch him . . . Gauloise smoke, sour wine odour from the sabot roughened floor, the aroma of *potage* and *fritures* moving from the kitchen into the bar.

61

The man said, 'Monsieur, may I have a small moment or two of your time?'

The voice told him enough to place him, and the hand coming free of the inner pocket, holding a long manilla envelope, removed the tired *frisson* of memory.

Sir Andrew said, 'My days are full of it. So I have plenty to spare.' He spoke in French.

The man smiled and tapping his chin with the edge of the envelope said, 'Is it so obvious?' He spoke now in French.

'Few people can truly escape from their mother tongue into another. God likes us to keep our place in the world.'

The other laughed. 'Can the leopard change his spots?'

'No. But they are hard to see against the right background. What is it that you want from me?'

'I would like you to have this and read it when you get back to the Abbey. My name is Crillon. Maurice Crillon. And I am staying at the Red Lion Hotel in Salisbury. I shall be there when you want me.'

He took the offered envelope and put it in the pocket of his Harris tweed jacket. 'Very well.'

'Thank you, monsieur.' Crillon stood aside to let Sir Andrew cross the stile.

Sir Andrew climbed over, the dogs slipped

through underneath. Without looking back Sir Andrew followed the path up through a coppice of young spruce. He followed his routine; a talk with the head gardener, a visit to the stables, and then the morning fifteen minutes he spent in the old chapel — some little time of it spent in his own form of prayer and devotion, but now more in considering a growing feeling in him, the mysterious human condition of sensing change, some slip in the working of time. Something was happening today . . . He had had such days before. Many and more frequent when young as though the Fates — and, God, how often had that happened during the war years? — were bungling some message, some warning that they wanted him to have, but were not using the true code for the day.

He went up to his sitting room in the private part of the Abbey and Hanson, his butler, brought him his mid-morning coffee and biscuits and the first of his three prescribed medicine doses for the day. Before leaving Hanson said, 'Her Ladyship telephoned from London, Sir Andrew, to say that she won't be back until the end of the week.'

'Thank you, Hanson. Did she say why not?'

'Yes, sir. There's some auction she wants to go to on Friday.'

'I see. Thank you.'

When Hanson had gone, Sir Andrew drank his coffee — the unopened envelope he had been given on the table before him. When he had finished, he filled a pipe and, not until it was going well, did he open the envelope and lay its contents on the table before him. There were two letters, a long one and a short one, written in French, and two certificates, one for a birth and one for a death, both registered at Toulon. Neglecting his pipe he read the letters and then examined the certificates. He then read the two letters again. Putting them down he waited for some emotion to take him, but nothing came. Nothing could in these moments. There was some rising spate waiting to break in him, to surge high and fast and flush the old bed of time past and then drop back between its banks where the waters would clear so that a man could see distinctly every rock and river-smoothed pebble of its floor.

He got up and left the room and walked the Tudor panelled passageway to his bedroom. Some ghost of memory had haunted him while he had been speaking to the Frenchman . . . Maurice Crillon. The windows looked out over the garden and hillside fall to the river. Against the morning sunlight the coming and going of nesting house-martins to the eaves above threw flickering shadows about the room.

Over his dressing table was a portrait of himself as a young man by Augustus John. Studying it he saw that it had something of Crillon about it. Or was that imagination? Anyway . . . One was always, he supposed, a stranger to one's own face. One could never see one's self truly through one's own eyes. Still, with a little imagination and good will . . . there was something of Crillon there.

He went back to his sitting room and telephoned his wife at their London house. He was told she was out and left a message for her to ring him. Until she returned there was little he could do or wished to do without consulting her. He went to his desk and wrote a note to Maurice Crillon and then gave instructions for his chauffeur, Lloyd, to drive into Salisbury and deliver it to the Red Lion Hotel.

Later that afternoon Maurice Crillon returned to the hotel to find the note waiting for him. It read —

Dear Monsieur Crillon,

I have read the documents you kindly left with me. I do not have to tell you that they moved me very considerably. At the moment Lady Starr is in London but she

will be back at the weekend and then you must come and see us. So I will be in touch with you. I am sure you will understand that this is not the time for me to go into any description of my emotions. To say that they exist is enough. And please forgive me, if, for the moment, I sign myself —
Yours sincerely,
Andrew Starr

Crillon read it twice. Then with a shrug of his shoulders he put it in his pocket. It was neither more nor less than he had anticipated. The moments in life of intense surprise were the ones that drove most people, not only to hide their confusion to gain pause to think, but into the need for an interval of complete withdrawal to give emotion and shock time to weather a little; to give the body as well as the mind time to test the nature of the change in the coming new climate of their lives. Anyway, he was in no hurry. For some things there was no hardship in waiting. For others, though, there was only foolishness in delay. Opportunity was a flower with a short life, to be plucked promptly.

He had spent a couple of hours that afternoon in the Cathedral close doing a much better pencil drawing than the one the woman had admired. One way or another he could guess that he was going to have time on his hands. Some time he must send Carla a card. He could hear her brother exclaim — *Mamma mia! What does he do in England while the Zais waits here unfinished?* Well, maybe it would be forever unfinished and Aldo would have to complete the cleaning of the original and break his heart taking it back to the owner. For a moment or two he thought about Carla and Trudi, the one with the sweetness of a ripe peach ... ah, what was Trudi if one should eat her? A cheese? A fine Emmenthal? But he was in England and the palate sought a change.

He pulled the piece of paper with her address on it from his pocket. Until now he had not looked at it since being given it. Margery Littleton. The address meant nothing to him — Flat 10, Amesbury Court, London Road. Well, the hotel porter would know.

He went out and bought a bottle of wine and a bunch of white lilacs and drove to the address just after seven. It mattered nothing to him if she had people with her — though he had the impression that she lived much to herself. People with friends and contentment seldom sat on public benches and steeled themselves to make conversation with strangers.

She opened the flat door to him and her surprise was unguarded and his eyes marked the quickening of her breath and the swift agitated movement as she crossed her arms and her hands clung to her elbows, fingers moving with a fine tremble. At once he was sorry for her because he knew she hung between disbelief and joy not untouched with apprehension. Everything was there to be read in her face. How different from Carla on the Ponte Santa Trinitá ... *noli me tangere* ... walking like a well-fed panther. And Trudi ... the gorgeous Amazon who had watched him for days without true recognition as he worked in her father's yard and who, the first time he had come up behind her, put his hands round her waist and kissed the back of her sunburnt neck, had turned and back-handed him so that he had sprawled among the marble chips in the yard. *Eh, bien, chacun à son goût.*

He said, 'When I make a promise I keep it. But if you wish me to go, please accept the flowers and the drawing — I've redone it for you, larger, so that you can frame it. But, if you send me away, I shall take the wine with me.'

She laughed then, a breathless laugh slowly easing, and stood aside to let him enter and said, 'The place is in a muddle and I was just going to cook myself something and — '

He raised a hand, stilling her, and said, 'You have eggs?'

'Yes, why?'

'If you permit — I will make us omelettes in the kitchen while you do the tidying that worries you.' He paused for a moment smiling at her and then said quietly, 'I am a Frenchman bearing gifts — not a Greek. You have no need to beware of me — '

'Oh, I didn't think that for a moment.'

'Good.'

She led him into the sitting room and one glance told him that his drawing of the Cathedral would be among bad company. White horses rose from a stormy sea over the mantelpiece, and there was a semi-Cubist painting of a fishing village, angular boats and sails and white, red and blue cottages clinging to the side of a steep cove and — cut from some magazine he imagined — a colour print of a cat sprawling in a basket while kittens romped over her. But the kitchen to his surprise he liked. It was airy and well ordered, everything in place, spotless and shining, like some well-lit Aladdin's cave. He turned to her and said smiling, 'This is your love?'

She smiled, too, and said, 'Yes — the room out there . . . I rent the place furnished. But this . . . well, I like cooking and I like things to be right. Just as at the office.'

Nothing was hurried. The was no desire in him to force anything. Time was always a man's best ally. She tidied the sitting room and then came and laid the small dining table at the end of the kitchen, and when he felt the occasional rise in her of awkwardness, he smoothed it over by telling her about himself, not the truth of course, but off the cuff inventions. Yes, he was French. From Bordeaux. Did she know it? No — then he felt free to invent an art school and himself one of the masters, and he was over here with some vacation time still on his hands after fixing up a summer position as an art master with an Adult Education school in Brighton. With time on his hands he was free to indulge his own pleasure . . . visiting and drawing English country houses and cathedrals and churches. Had she ever been to Rheims or Chartres? No. Notre Dame, of course. Yes. And she went every summer with an aunt for three weeks to Majorca. And as his correctness gave her confidence, and her second glass of Petit Chablis smoothed the disturbed surface of the emotions he had aroused in her, she loosened and laughed and came to meet him with her own little burden of memories and regrets. She had been born in Devon and worked in a local government office in Taunton until both her parents had died and then she had come to Salisbury to a position as secretary in a solicitor's office. And later . . . later . . . his correctness by now fully gentling her, offering sympathy with the odd catch of humour to lighten it . . . he learned of the young Green Jackets officer, to whom she had been unofficially engaged (in time the rather disapproving Indian Army father and the point-to-point and horse trials mother would have come round to it), who had gone to Northern Ireland on a tour of duty and an IRA land mine had blown him and three of his men to Kingdom Come. The smallest seed pearls of tears had briefly starred the corners of her eyes so that he had felt genuine sympathy and, under its cover, reached out and held her hand in a brief caress which, probably without knowing it, she had returned and so sealed the compact to come between them. And when he came to Brighton in high summer . . . he opened a brief glimpse of a possible friendship to be renewed.

As for now he realized — more than surprising himself — there was no exigent passion in him to spur him on to take *une fille si mal gardée*. He left her at a polite hour, shaking her hand and formally thanking her for her hospitality. There was no need for rush. He would be here for a while, and Avoncourt Abbey waited. He needed no demanding attachments until his position there was clear.

Two evenings later on returning to his hotel he found a letter waiting for him, hand-delivered, from Sir Andrew Starr.

It read —

Dear Monsieur Crillon,

My wife and I will be very happy if you would come and have dinner with us tomorrow evening. My chauffeur will call for you at six-thirty.

Yours sincerely,
Andrew Starr

The chauffeur did. Lloyd was a middle-aged, short, slightly bow-legged man in bottle-green jacket and trousers, wearing a peaked cap with a little green rosette at its front. His face was like something out of a Rembrandt drawing, collapsed flesh about his mouth and a dark apple shine to his cheeks. The car was a Rolls-Royce of fairly recent date. He was driven in silent state to Avoncourt Abbey and for the first time he felt a slight sense of the ridiculous and unreal. All this and the rest to come was a world far, far removed from his mother's cottage, from the untidy studio over the Arno and Carla padding around naked — but a world which he could either accept or reject. He held that thought firmly in his mind. But accept or reject, one way or the other he meant to take from it some profit or pleasure, or perhaps some other gain to which the gods would in time point the way. But for the present he was content to go with the smoothly regulated current of events.

He was taken around the far side of the Abbey to the entrance to the family's private wing. A butler took him along a badly lit corridor, the limed wood framed panels covered with a soft mouse-brown antique leather and hung with pictures that sang briefly for him as he passed, his quick eye noting and identifying many of them. There was no nervousness in him. He was his own man — and nothing could ever change that.

Sir Andrew Starr, dark suited, guessing that he travelled without evening clothes, was waiting in a pleasant, well-lit sitting room. He was alone and greeted him with a slight twist of a smile, pleasant but masking . . . well, what emotions? He did not know and did not choose to guess. He knew himself and his position. On his father's side, he guessed, similar constraints held their place. Whatever changes time might bring in were problematical and still distant.

They shook hands, and Hanson the butler left them, and Sir Andrew went to a table in the window to fetch them drinks. With his back to him, Sir Andrew said gruffly and with a short laugh, 'Well, this is a fair turn up for the old book, isn't it? Leaves us both like a couple of fish stranded out of the water. Where does one begin?'

Crillon laughed. 'The beginning was long ago, Sir Andrew. Perhaps I did wrong by coming to you?'

'Oh, no — not that. We shall weather it one way or another. My wife will join us soon, but I wanted a little time to be alone with you so that we could get some things straightened out. I should warn you that she is a woman of sharply changing moods. You will do me a kindness by making allowances for that . . . and for the shock. One moment she is telling herself that this is all nonsense, and the next she is weeping, playing the part of the mother to whom a long lost child has been restored. Like something out of an old Drury Lane melodrama.'

'Drury Lane?'

'A London theatre.'

'Ah, yes, I see. Well, sir, it is melodrama. And that is the stuff of women's nature.'

Sir Andrew lowered a bushy eyebrow and said, 'Don't know about that. They can be damned deep and as precise as a surgeon's knife when they wish. Are you married?'

'No, sir.'

'May I ask what you do for a living?'

'I am an artist and picture restorer.'

'And you live at Cragnac?'

'No, sir. My mother did. But I go wherever I can find work. Which is not difficult.'

'Know about pictures, eh?'

'I think so.' As he answered he realized that Sir Andrew was probably as emotional and changeable as his wife in his own way, and that all this conversation was deliberately held off the line of the real purpose of this meeting in order to allow him to come to some assessment of his own. Was he dealing with a deceit or a genuine melodramatic truth?

'You've been through the galleries here?'

'Yes, I have.'

'What would you take if I offered you your choice?' Sir Andrew grinned under his bushy eyebrows, his face creased like a too long stored apple.

Crillon considered this, and then said, 'Well, there are many I would like to have, but as I am a travelling man, going where I find my work, I would happily settle for the Eugène Boudin you have — *Dieppe, La Plage*. It would go easily into the bottom of a suitcase.'

Sir Andrew laughed. 'Not bad, not bad. Though, by God, I have very different memories of Dieppe.' He was suddenly silent, lost in thought, and then said quietly, 'Anyway, if all this is as it seems it will be yours one day. And, eventually, a title, and the worries. Aye, worries. I'm lucky as far as money is concerned, but cash don't buy off all worries.' He laughed again suddenly and said, 'My dear boy, my advice to you is to turn now and run. You won't have any money troubles here — but, by God, you'll have others if — as I do — you think out of fairness you should share some of your good fortune with others. They'll rob you of peace. They'll steal your plants, ruin your shrubs by taking cuttings, leave their disgusting crisps and chocolate papers all over the place, write their names on the backsides of any handy statuette, and let their unruly children fall down the long steps in the water garden and bring an action for damages — and that's not all. When they've all gone and you're alone and can call your home your own again you find you can't walk round it at night if sleep escapes you without setting off magic eye alarms and God knows what. Take my advice, lad . . . aye, even my son . . . ask me to settle a handsome sum on you and go. Be free to wander and do the thing you like doing. Eh, how does that seem to you?'

Before Crillon could answer, a high, fluting voice came from the doorway of the room. 'Like the stupid, self-pitying nonsense it is, my dear Andrew. And, my dear boy, my dear long lost one, pay no attention to your father. Life has given him so much happiness that it has turned him sour. My dear boy! I knew it . . . I knew it . . . Come let me embrace you!

Lady Starr advanced on Crillon, a tall, white-haired, still good-looking woman, full-bosomed, long-legged, wearing a red velvet evening gown, the room light sparking the rings on her hands and the emeralds around her neck, and she threw her arms around him and kissed him almost boisterously on one cheek after the other. Then, holding him away from her, went on, 'Yes, yes. Of course. Your father's eyes — but not his crabbed nature I hope? And you hold yourself well, as I do. Stand tall and face the world fearlessly. And what a nice, well cut suit. Just right for the occasion. Dress, you know, tells everything. My dear boy — welcome home.' She kissed him again on the brow and both cheeks and then stepped away leaving with him the ghosts of more than one large brandy.

From behind her and a little to one side Sir Andrew winked at Crillon, and then said, surprising him, 'Tell us, my dear boy, what were your reactions when the good curé landed all this on your plate?' He spoke French now, and that language was held to for the rest of the evening largely, and Crillon soon realized that it was a language in which they both were fluent.

Smiling, he said, 'Well, Sir Andrew, what would you and your dear lady have thought if after years and years of being French you learned that you were in fact English? *Moi, j'étais étourdi.*'

'My dear boy — how natural! The English really, most of them, are impossible. They are the bastard descendants of too many races and take a pride in it because they assume that it is a mixture designed by the gods to elevate and distinguish them from all other races.'

Lady Starr moved forward, patted him gently on the cheek, and then sitting down said to her husband, 'Andrew . . . a brandy, I think. The whole thing is so improbable and delightful, so excessive that one's mind reels and needs calming.'

'Yes, my dear.'

As Sir Andrew moved to get her drink, Lady Starr smiled and gave Crillon a little wink and said, 'It was a tremendous shock, you know. Oh, a happy one. But nevertheless one's whole psyche reels at the happy unexpectedness of it all and needs support. Your father has been marvellous about it and I share his feelings with him. Late come it may be . . . yes, sadly very late come. But we must accept God's will. And your dear mother . . . how she must have been tormented over the years. My heart bleeds for her. Naturally, I don't remember her very well. She was only with me a matter of weeks at Aiguebelle. But I understand the temptation . . . Oh, I do. I do.'

'Darling,' Sir Andrew came back with her brandy, 'I don't think we need to go into all that. In moments of crisis people act spontaneously often without a thought for the consequences. If you're going to blame anyone, blame the bloody Boche and the spaghetti boys. It all happened a long time ago. Monsieur Crillon is the one who really has had the bombshell dropped into his lap.'

'What an extraordinary metaphor, my love. But I see what you mean. The present is the thing and the future to come. Of course, Andrew. Let us drink to that — the future to come.' She drank without waiting for them and afterwards took a tiny lace-embroidered silk handkerchief from her evening bag and wiped a small trace of a spillage from her chin.

Maurice Crillon had a swift memory of his mother, sitting at the red velvet-covered table before dinner with her one glass of wine hardly touched before her, her old face lined with years of weather and worry. This lady's age near enough — and carrying a burden of conscience of which he had never dreamed. He had a sudden impulse to get up and run out into the early summer darkness and never return. His mother had been a person who loved God yet had lived in the quiet, persistent agony of her sin. God would forgive her. And so did he. In the depth of his heart he could wish that she had never made her confession to monsieur the curé. He could have been eating *melone prosciutto* and then *spaghetti bolognese* in some *ristorante* at Fiesole now with Carla, night and bed and love waiting, and the real Giuseppe Zais also waiting to be finished cleaning and the fake copy to be completed and the whole of the world and his life before him to do with as he chose. He had the swift sensation that things were closing in on him and that there was no handy bolt-hole.

They went into dinner and were served by a manservant, and their talk became general. The dinner service was *rose verte*, and the table light came from two six-branched silver candelabra and he smiled to himself at the

80

thought of the two oil lamps they had used in the cottage until he was working and could pay for electricity to be installed. And, oddly, he began to have the impression that for Sir Andrew and Lady Starr — but far, far more particularly for her — all this, his coming, the somersault of part of the past into the present, was a welcome divertissement since their life was full of boredom which no part of their money or position could adequately dissipate. To be honest, he could admit — the piquancy and possibly future profit to himself ignored — he would have preferred to be eating with Margery Littleton. *Le style — c'est l'homme.* This could never be his style — not for long anyway. These people meant nothing to him. Never could. And — after all these years how could he mean anything to them? Time had long watered down all blood ties.

Later — after coffee and brandy for him, and more than one Grand Marnier for Lady Starr before she retired leaving them alone, embracing him a little too closely, tears marring her mascara — Sir Andrew got up, offered him a Scotch, which he refused — heavy drinking gave him no pleasure — and then, standing by the fireplace with his drink in hand, gave him a long stare and suddenly laughed and said, 'Well, Maurice, my boy

— this must have been quite an ordeal for you?'

Crillon shrugged his shoulders. 'I'm not sure about ordeal. No, not that. More a dream, sir.'

'Do you wish it were?'

'I don't know . . . '

'I think you do. When I was little more than half your age I more than once saved my life by being able to read people's faces. Just now you'd like to turn and run and never come back. Or — and I mean no offence — take some cash and let the credit go. A nice settlement on you, a gentleman's agreement — and off you go. And the baronetcy goes to my great-nephew, a decent enough fellow who has the worm of religion in his mind and will probably turn this place over to a bunch of monks, with a handsome endowment, and so make sure that the heavenly gates will swing open for him as he rides up on a cloud top. Not that I'm against religion. Just against most of the people who come poncing and preaching in under its umbrella and to hell with those left out in the rain. Is that what you'd like?'

Crillon smiled. 'Well — not knowing by any means what it involves — I must confess that if you offered me the pick of a few of your pictures, and a car big enough to carry them, I would happily go.'

Sir Andrew laughed. 'Honestly spoken. Tomorrow or sometime we'll walk the galleries and you can tell me which you'd take. I'll make my own list and then we'll compare them. Now that would be fun. Fun, anyway, even if you're not going to run. We'll do it sometime.' He paused for a moment or two and then said with a touch of sadness in his voice, 'I'm not going to say that I am not delighted knowing now I have a son — and the more I see of you the more I see it in your face. Some time I'll show you a painting Augustus John did of me when I was eighteen-odd. My God, he was a man of moods and merriment and as foul-mouthed as a bargee when he wished. But I digress — which is a thing I do often and people must put up with it. Where was I? Oh, yes — your happiness. You're not married, are you? Or have I already asked that?'

'No, I am not, Sir Andrew.'

'Well, that's something. No wife to nag you. Just your own decision. Nobody else knows about this business?'

'Only monsieur le curé.'

'Ah, yes, well — that would be no problem. The Church has a Pandora's box full of human secrets. So, nobody but you, and my wife and myself. And I can tell you that

83

my wife, after a little obligatory weeping, will keep her counsel. So?'

Crillon was silent for a while, during which he lit a cigarette and found himself waywardly thinking of having the pick of a few pictures from the galleries — to sell half and live merrily ever after. And was this man, his father, really suggesting that he should be bought off? This upright, honest, battle-scarred English nobleman? Was that it — or was he genuinely concerned about his home-coming, lately-discovered son's happiness?

He said, 'Which decision would make you the happier?'

Sir Andrew drew away from the fire and patted his hot bottom absently with one hand, and said, 'Aaaah! Ball back in my court. But not difficult to play. I could say — the one which would make me happy. For you to stay. But I don't, because if you're not going to be happy, then how could I be? So, *mon cher* Maurice, your papa has put the ball back into your court. And anyway, I suggest you sleep on it, live with it for a while. It can easily be arranged. You come and live here as a guest — clean and restore a few pictures if it would make you happy. Only myself and Lady Starr know the truth. And it will stay that way. How would that suit you?'

'I think it is a very sensible suggestion. But

I would like to ask one further question before I go back to the hotel.'

'Be free. Speak as son to father. By the way do you shoot or fish or ride?'

'None of them.'

'Well, that makes a change. But if you stay the County won't like it. But to hell with them. Now, what is it you want to know?'

'Well, sir — you've made your position clear. But what about Lady Starr? How would she feel if after a while I went?'

'Ah, a good question. Well, as you must have realized, she is of a very romantic, exuberant cast of temperament. With everything we have you might think she was a well-contented woman. And for the main part she is. But I must be honest — too many years have passed for your arrival to have any real meaning for her. She would deny this because at the moment this is all novelty, fairy-tale stuff. The kind of situation she knows so well from the trashy novels she reads. For once, she finds herself the leading character in a romantic melodrama. Lovely stuff, my boy — when you're just reading about it and when the book is finished you can close the covers and turn to something else. Mind you, she would spin out the reading of this book for your sake, for mine and for hers — but in the end the book would be closed with a sigh of relief. Everything happened so long ago. The grief she felt at Aiguebelle no longer exists. Old age as you will find one day likes to imprison such extraordinary situations as ours between covers. In life . . . well, there comes a time when, if the gods lay down an unexpected hand too late in the game, one doesn't care a damn either way. Let me make it plain. I could grow to like you quite easily, already am fast beginning to, and between us as men there would be no trouble. But with Lady Starr — though she would deny it right now — the time would come when you would just be part of the scenery. We are both too old, frankly, to be bothered with such a major upheaval in our lives — my wife more so, I am sorry to say, than I am.'

'And at the moment this secret rests just between the three of us?'

'Of course. There is no wiser course than delaying to go to a lawyer — or the Standing Council of the Baronetage — until you have to. Make a thing public and you often find it becomes a rod for your own back. You're free, white, and long, long past twenty-one. Come here, enter into your own and — *pouff* — whether you like it or not your whole life must change.' He laughed suddenly. 'You know the romantic novels have got it all wrong. Poor Cinderella . . . I bet her Prince led her a hell of a life, mistresses, squabbles about her table manners, jibes about her family, and always penny-pinching over her dress allowance. When magic finishes — life begins, and good fairies get heartily cursed. So, my boy — the ball is firmly in your court for you to play as you wish. Now — we'll both have a night-cap and then Lloyd will drive you back to your hotel.'

It was only as he was being driven back to Salisbury that Maurice Crillon suddenly realized that there was much in his father's character which he had inherited. The man would have survived anywhere. He took things as they came and made the most of them — in his own interests. All the talk about Lady Starr could be true — but the real truth was that Sir Andrew just did not want his own life turned upside down. Lady Starr's feelings were simple camouflage for his own. It was an attitude that he perfectly understood. All that had to be settled was how he, himself, could make the most of the situation. For one thing was certain — from the little he had already seen — he knew that the last thing in the world he wanted was to become the heir to a baronetcy and have his life inexorably fore-ordained. That would be to kiss freedom good-bye.

Lady Starr always took her breakfast in bed, and always at the same hour, and always — no matter how she felt — the same breakfast of bacon and eggs, and toast which she spread with a liberal covering of peach jam. Marmalade she abominated. And always — precisely timed so that he could help himself to the last cup of coffee from her pot — Sir Andrew came to join her. The ritual was unvarying and its provenance stemming from the first days of their marriage, a ritual broken only when first war, and then the separations of civilian life dictated it. It was a time when truth reigned small or large, and the unshakeable accord between them openly showed its face.

This morning he came in, gave her a kiss and his greeting, stuck one finger into the peach jam jar and stood licking it while he filled his coffee cup. Then he carried his coffee to the half-opened window and looked out at the gardens and the distant river, and noted the track marks of a fox across the heavily dewed lawns and thought — *Vixen probably. Cubs. Scrounging the dustbins round the back of the servants' quarters. Plenty of young life about now to hunt and kill, but why bother when sloppy humans laid their table remains out on offer? Killed a German collaborator once, sitting on the seaward side of the Biarritz golf course. Right through the head while he was eating petit pain and jambon. Hardly dead — rifle with a silencer — before a fox came out of the bamboo growths and proceeded to finish the meal for him. One man's death provides another's breakfast.* A magpie flew across the lily pond at the head of the grand garden stairway and settled on the head of the tallest of the three naked Graces, the one with two fingers broken and a face that reminded him always of a Greek tart in Bordeaux who had been good to him in every way she could a month after Rommel had come racing into Cherbourg. He crossed his fingers to ward off the evil eye and said, without turning:

'What did you think of him?'

'Impossible . . . ' The word died in a long sigh.

'No Aiguebelle stir in the heart?'

'Really, Andrew — that was another world, another time and another me.' Her voice was firm, each syllable given full value.

'If he'd come at the age of twenty, say?'

'It might have worked. But not now.'

'He knows his onions about pictures.'

'He could have Saint Peter's keys in his pocket for all I care. My dear — it's an impossible situation for him and for us. He must see sense.'

'Tricky. Now he's here and he's seen — he might start feeling his oats.'

'Don't tell me you can't handle him?'

'I started to . . . just a little. There's no doubt about his credentials you know.'

'That makes no difference. That damned wet nurse . . . really it's all like a bad Victorian melodrama and I'm too old to just play a walk-on part two minutes from the final curtain. *Mother! . . . My boy! My little one! My goodness — how you've grown since I last saw you in your dainty chintzed crib!* Andrew, you've got to do something. He's Maurice Crillon — not Angus Starr. Oh, I know it was hell at the time. If he'd only turned up earlier, in time for a decent school and all the rest . . . but now! Oh . . . ' She sighed. 'I can just see how tedious all the talk will be. And more because that damned great-nephew of yours will raise his hackles and contest it and get a great badgering of bishops behind him and a retinue of barristers rubbing their brief-blistered hands in glee. The whole thing could go on for years.'

Sir Andrew laughed. 'My dear, you're in great form.'

'And so had you better be. I wash my hands of it — but you know what I want. You know I always thought there was something odd about that wet nurse.'

'You think she signalled to the Italians so that they could crash their plane on the villa?'

'Don't be ridiculous and flippant. Anyway, in a little while I shall go down to Les Hirondelles and stay there until you've got it all fixed up. Why don't you have a word with Warboys? You're seeing him soon, aren't you?'

'Warboys? He's practically retired.' He turned and faced her.

'Andrew, don't be ridiculous. That kind never retire. And don't look at me like that. I know more about Warboys and all that Birdcage Intelligence crew than you think. And don't tell me that they ever let you go. Oh, all very gentlemanly. But, by God, once in you're never free from a call until your dying day . . . Oh, yes, they'd haul you back if it were necessary. All right, love, don't look so po-faced. I won't say any more. But you must do something. I'm too old to start being a mother. And anyway, it was never a state I really aspired to. All that initiates it, yes.' She smiled suddenly and added, 'Do you think me a horrible old woman?'

He moved to her, kissed her on the cheek, and then going to the door said, 'I will see what I can do. But you be nice to our Maurice while he's here. That's all I ask. You do go on a bit, you know, when you've had — '

'Say no more. But you see what's already beginning to happen — I must reform my drinking habits just because our long lost son has turned up. You tell me — what deprivations is he going to have to suffer?' She smiled suddenly. 'I'd quite enjoy it if I were watching it all being played at Drury Lane — preferably as a musical — *but* to have it actually happening! My dear, I think the whole thing is just too tedious, and my heart bleeds for you because you have got to handle it.'

★　★　★

They made a compromise — or rather it emerged little by little from both sides. Crillon kept his room on at the Red Lion — *Good to have your own bolthole, my boy. Things bound to get a bit on top of you here at times* — but he was given a small apartment at the Abbey; his own little suite of rooms, quite self-contained, where he could eat alone if he wished and also entertain. *Feel free my lad. Come and go as you wish. I remember how I was at your age.*

And — to avoid the boredom of idleness or lack of interest while they got to know one another — off one of the smaller picture galleries Crillon found a well-lit work room which was kept free for a craftsman who came three or four times a year to check the paintings and do minor work on them, cleaning and restoring — and here he settled himself to work. He found a Stubbs of an early eighteenth-century Sir Robert Starr mounted, cocked-hat, on a grey mare against a background of the hillslope down to the river. It took him a few days to clean and when Sir Andrew saw it he was full of delight. *My God — marvellous. Just as it must have come off the palette.* After that he had *carte blanche,* and because he liked her — although he sensed that a great deal was being held back — he did a small red chalk drawing from memory of Lady Starr standing by the drawing room window arranging a bowl of flowers. She was delighted and for the first time kissed him on the cheek with genuine emotion. When they were out and he wandered through the two main galleries on a day when viewing was closed to the public he was entranced, though not so far gone that his eyes did not immediately reject some of the rubbish which over-enthusiastic Starrs had collected. There was a so-called Luca Carlevaris painting of the Piazzetta at Venice from the south-west which was so clearly the work of a minor and undistinguished hand that Aldo would have kicked his foot through it. And thinking that — the thought of Carla inhabited his body for a while and for a moment or two he was tempted to get up and walk out of the Abbey for good. Instead he drove back to his hotel wanting to be free of the Abbey for a night for the routine there had quickly palled. Had there been only Sir Andrew things would have been more than endurable, but Lady Starr — his dear mother — how could it be? — was frequently impossible. She drank much less — perhaps out of a feeling for him as a guest (for he was sure that he held only that status with her) — but as a result was often in a bitchy or bad-tempered mood. One night at dinner she took quite unjustifiable and unpardonable offence at something Sir Andrew said, rose from the table and in an icy voice announced, 'My darling, you really are a most stupid and unbearable bugger at times.' And left the room.

After she had gone Sir Andrew smiled at him and said, 'She has a bad migraine today. Always makes her like that. Well, we all have something, don't we? Me — well now, I can't stand it when travelling in a train I have to take one of those seats where the ashtray is on the left-hand side. Popping your right hand over all the time to get rid of ash as though you were crossing yourself continually from the thought of some great sin . . . By the way, we're both going up to town tomorrow for a few days. Some things I've got to attend to. Bloody bore but there it is. When I come back we'll have a real long serious talk and get things finally sorted out. Be obliged if you'd do some thinking on that score while I'm gone.'

Crillon was silent for a while, and then he said, 'You really are quite serious about this?'

'Of course — and chiefly so on your account. I'll make you a once and for all handsome payment and you can pick a few pictures if that appeals to you — and then off you go. Seem blunt, do I? Well, that's the honest way. You're forty-odd and I'm damned near seventy — though I frequently feel far less. We have a gentleman's agreement — and off you go.'

'What would you say if when you came back you found that I had gone?'

'That that was what you wanted — and good luck to you. You've got a bank account in France?'

'In Switzerland.'

Sir Andrew pulled a note book from his pocket, slipped the pencil from its spine and said, 'Give me the details. I'll make a transfer while I'm in London tomorrow.' He grinned.

'Tempting you, you see. But I'm sincere. If you don't chose to go — the money will still be yours. My God, my father used to keep me as skint as a journeyman tinker until I was twenty-one and came into some money of my own. I promise I'll do it in London tomorrow. You can ring the Swiss bank and check. Of course — I keep your mother's statement and the birth and death certificates.'

'To destroy?' Crillon was enjoying himself.

'My God, no! They go into the family archives to be unopened for a hundred years. Like to see whichever baronet's face it is when they're opened.' He laughed, almost brayed, and went on, 'Bit of a shock, eh, for some stuck-up bastard? Another skeleton to be tucked away in the family cupboard. Well, there isn't a family in the country that doesn't have them.'

Sir Andrew, his own glass still full, pushed the port decanter to Crillon. Outside the wind was rising and a scattering of heavy rain assaulted the window briefly. Crillon filled his glass and then raising it drank, and said, 'Maybe, a farewell toast?'

Sir Andrew nodded, drank with him and then said, 'There is no problem in life which can't be settled if there's money on one side and goodwill on the other.'

4

She was typing the firm's final statement of costs for handling the sale of a farm when the telephone rang. She picked it up absently.

'Yes?'

'Miss Littleton, will you take a call from a Mr Crillon?'

She was silent for a while, caught between surprise and pleasure. Then she said, 'Yes, I will.' She hung for a second or two in the almost childlike spell of rising excitement, felt her cheeks flush and was glad that she was alone. She had not heard from him since their last meeting and had assumed that he had either gone back to France or had no wish to continue their so brief acquaintance.

He came on the line and said, 'Margery?'

'Yes . . . yes, Maurice . . . '

'You don't mind me calling at your place of work?'

'No . . . no, of course not. But how on earth did you know where — '

His laugh cut her short. 'Well, it wasn't difficult. The yellow pages of the telephone directory. There are not all that number of solicitors in Salisbury. I got you at the third go. I'm sorry I haven't been in touch with you before, but these last few days have been very busy. I will tell you all about it at lunch. That's why I'm ringing. Since it is your half-day it would give me great pleasure if you would let me take you out. Perhaps to some little place in the country and after we could drive around — ' He broke off for a moment or two, and then in a different tone went on, 'That is, if you have no other engagement?'

'No, no — I haven't. But how did you know it was my half-day?'

'Ah, well, yes. Not difficult. My excellent little tourist's handbook tells all such things about English towns. You will come, won't you?'

'Yes, of course I will. It's a lovely surprise.' For a moment or two she wondered if she had sounded too eager, and then decided that if she had she didn't care. He had been often in her thoughts and she had wondered whether she had done or said something which had turned him from her.

He said, 'You have made me very happy.'

For a moment she felt like saying — and you have made me very happy, too — but settled for, 'I leave here at half-past twelve.'

'I shall be waiting. *A bientôt* . . . '

She put the receiver back in place and sat

staring unseeingly at the bill of costs in her machine, her thoughts scattered, flighting wildly, and then going back to the moment when sitting on the seat she had been surprised by the sudden and undeniable impulse to speak to him, and then . . . how nice he had been when he came to dinner and how soon it had become clear that he had put no wrong interpretation to her forwardness. So correct — but undeniably liking her, and taking that ghastly little sitting room in his stride. There was something about him, some instinct he had for understanding, sensing the truth but declining to abuse any advantage it might have given him . . . not that she would have minded. It had happened twice before, and each time — except for the briefness of high passion — she had been left, over-eager for the man to be gone and never encouraged again because she had felt like a tart. And then . . . Oh, God — if she had known she would have worn something different! But that only for the sake of her natural vanity. For him she sensed it was unimportant. Just for a while, the memory came back to her of annual holidays with her aunt in Majorca . . . the awful men who looked you over as though you were something in a cattle market. And her aunt — the first time to her intense surprise — who loved it all, and was old enough to know better and too old for conquest, but just loved the atmosphere of sexuality as hungry children racing into a kitchen relished the high, enticing aroma of food cooking.

When she left the office, he was waiting for her — not as many another man would have done right outside the doorway, but a few yards away, discreet and ready to defer greeting should she be with some other member of the staff. As she came up to him, he just touched her hand for a moment and then moved her away to walk the little distance to the car park, talking as though they had known one another for years. At once she was soothed of high throat-tightening excitement and became herself. Magic. How could it happen? As though she had known him for years, and, since she was no fool, she didn't care a damn that there must have been plenty of other women before her. No past or future. Just this present moment, and then another and another — smoothly riding the crest of Time.

They lunched at a small inn lower down the Avon valley below Salisbury, eating in the garden beside the flag-bordered river, swallows dipping to ring the water with the brief caress of their breasts, swans riding in state, aristocrats and haughty until the odd bread crust was thrown and then scrambling like unruly beggars over the scraps from the king's high table. And she laughed from pleasure and the wine and his company. Before they left he took the menu and on its back — and not even telling her to sit still, to pose, not even looking at her — he sketched her head and shoulders, the river beyond, and to her the thing was a miracle and — when she said so and how could he do it — he said, 'God gifts everyone at birth with something. But most people are too lazy to find out what it is.'

'Everyone with something?'

'Of course. Something — great or small.'

'And what did he give me?'

'You don't know?'

'No.'

'Then I tell you. Courage. The real kind.'

She laughed. 'Courage! I'm as timid as a mouse!'

He shook his head. 'No mouse is timid. It is the only wild animal which has the courage to live with man and make him its provider . . . whether he likes it or not.'

'But I'm *not* courageous.'

'You are. Sometime soon I will prove it to you. But for now — we shall continue our drive and you can be the guide. I go where you direct — but later we must stop at a place where we can do some shopping for things for dinner.'

She laughed then, enjoying herself, feeling absolutely free with him, warm and relaxed within his magic circle. She said, 'I know what you are going to do.'

'Of course you do — but tell me.'

'You're going to come back with me and cook a meal.'

'Yes — agreed?'

'Of course. Lovely.'

And it was lovely. The loveliest day she had had for years. She took him through the New Forest and then back through Winchester to see the Cathedral and to do his shopping. At her flat he borrowed an apron and cooked. She liked the apron touch. He was neat and precise in everything he did. They started with hors d'oeuvre, black olives and little strips of pimento, and then fillet steak *poivré* with asparagus tips followed by a piece of *brie* which was absolutely *à point*. They drank a bottle of wine with it all and she found herself laughing and chatting without constraint, enjoying herself more than she had for years, and knowing perfectly well what was to follow. And when that came it was as perfect as the whole afternoon and evening had been and there was the slow balm of deep happiness in her as afterwards she lay naked with him in bed. The day had to finish as it had begun and run . . . a wonderful break in the calendar, a trip to paradise and with her no wish to return from it until she had to. And he was as no other man had ever been . . . or was it that she was as she had never been able to be with any other man? Not caring for herself. Abandoning herself so completely to a new tide in her feelings, a tide that bore her on its crest and, finally, left her stranded in the abandonment of a slowly ebbing physical joy that made her feel that she and her body had for the first time become fully acquainted.

They slept and when they awoke they made love again and this time to a different rhythm — like tried lovers, without haste for the wine of their passion had changed, matured miraculously.

As the first sparrows began their chattering and bickering on the guttering outside the partly opened window Maurice said, 'You know, I have to go back to France soon. You know, too, that it is not good, not honest, to say we will find means to meet. Life does not go that way.'

'I don't care — this while it lasts will be enough.'

He laughed quietly. 'For me, too — if it

were anyone else. But I am greedy. You are as no other woman has been. So I want to keep you as long as I can. I have to go back to Bordeaux in ten days' time.'

'Then for nine days I shall be happy.'

'We could be happier. I would so much like to show you France. We could pack my car and go together and then, when the days are done, I will put you on a plane somewhere and you can fly back. It would be dishonest of me to say that I will come back, or that one day I would send for you. Life doesn't allow that. It can be tried, but little by little it begins to die. We are joyful with what we have, but we both know that it can't last. But there is no reason why by coming with me we should not make it last a little longer. There is still a lot of wine in the bottle to be enjoyed, *ma chérie.*'

The truth of his words caused her no upset. She had known from the first moment his hands had taken her naked body that it could not last . . . no matter what she might have wished, had wished. She had too much common-sense to delude herself. But to keep him a little while longer . . . Oh, God, yes that . . . but how?

'Oh, Maurice . . . but I have my work. I can't just walk out.'

'But you have holidays, no?'

'They come in August. I can't change them. The office rota is all made out.'

'Oh, pouf! One can always arrange that.'

She laughed then. 'Oh, Maurice you're impossible. Of course I'd love to come. For a handful of days like that with you I'd do anything. But I don't see what.'

'But it's simple. You have your aunt alive still, yes?'

'Yes. But she's in Scotland.'

'Ah, that's good. A long way away. This morning when you go into the office you say you have had a telegram that she is ill. You have to go to her. *Et voilà* — you will be free!'

She laughed loudly then, delighted at his calm wickedness, delighted at the prospect of more days with him, delighted at the directness with which he had come to a solution of all difficulties. Then suddenly she broke her merriment. 'No, it can't be done. You see sometimes my aunt — particularly if she's feeling bored or not well — telephones me at the office for a chat. She might do that — and then where would I be?'

He traced the tip of his forefinger down her nose and let her take it between her teeth gently. The frown went from his face and he smiled. 'You say your aunt when she goes abroad with you to Majorca is . . . well, you know how she is. So, no matter her age, she is romantic. She is on your side. Tell her the truth. Phone her and ask her to send a telegram from Scotland for you. Tell her why. You know that women always like to get the better of men. She will enjoy it. No?'

'I don't know.'

'When I come to take you out to dinner this evening, you will tell me, Yes or No? Oh, come, *chérie* — paradise is not a fixed place. It is a lot of little spaces in Time through which we pass now and then.'

She sat up suddenly and bent over and kissed him. Then she got out of bed, slipped on her dressing gown and moved towards the kitchen. Over her shoulder she said, 'I will telephone her this morning from here and ask her to do it today.'

'*Bien.* '*L'amour rend inventif.*' No?'

'What does that mean?'

'All that we have been talking about, *ma chérie.*'

★   ★   ★

Later that morning when he was back at his hotel, having shaved and changed his clothes, a telephone call came for him from Switzerland. An official from his bank informed him of the transfer made to his account by Sir Andrew Starr. The amount involved surprised him by its size. It was far more than he had anticipated . . . in fact, far, far more. But not less, he told himself after a moment or two, than was reasonable considering what he was giving up and the peace of mind which would now be with Sir Andrew and his wife.

He drove up to Avoncourt Abbey and finished the cleaning of a small panel by Osias Beert, a still life of flowers and fruit in a marble bowl with a brilliant red admiral butterfly hovering over one of the bowl's white tulips. Then he went up to his apartment and began to pack his suitcase. But before he had finished a sudden thought struck him . . . he was going and renouncing all that Avoncourt Abbey stood for, cutting himself off for ever from his real father and mother. Oh . . . he was being paid well, but no matter all that . . . no matter that this going was what he wanted as much as his parents, there was a small quirk of sentiment in him to which there was no denying house-room. And, anyway, he thought — Sir Andrew could not mind. He had once made — putting the money settlement aside — the offer himself of a gift of some paintings. Surely at least he was entitled to some physical memento . . . something to remind him of these brief Avoncourt days?

He walked down the long, oak-wainscoted passage to Sir Andrew's bedroom and went in and stood in front of Augustus John's small canvas. It was reasonable as a painting, but not of a nature that really appealed to him. It was too facile . . . bread and butter, or maybe wine and caviar . . . no, perhaps beer and skittles. But nevertheless — it was his father to whom he was drawn far more than to Lady Starr. Had his father been a widower, he had a feeling that neither of them would have let the other go. They would both have relished the upheaval in the Starr world.

Then, remembering the alarm system to which all the gallery paintings were wired, he went back to the cleaning and restoring room and threw the main switch off. Returning to the bedroom he was glad he had for as he lifted the painting down he saw the picture hook slide up an inch on its vertical wall bracket and smiled to himself. When Sir Andrew did something he did it with Army thoroughness. He pulled the picture hook down and heard the slight click as it locked back into place.

Ten minutes later, saying no good-byes, he drove off to Salisbury, the painting safely wrapped and in the bottom of his suitcase. He telephoned the solicitor's office and spoke to Margery. Her voice was a little breathless, excitement running high in her. She had telephoned her aunt from her flat before leaving that morning, and her aunt had telephoned the office in mid-morning. Everything was arranged.

He said, 'That's wonderful. Come along to the hotel and have some lunch with me. Then we'll go to your flat and you can pack. We can catch an early evening boat across from Southampton. What did your aunt say?'

'Oh, dear — once she knew, she was all for it and chirping like a canary. I really was surprised.'

He laughed. 'Sounds like the kind of aunt all girls should have.'

★ ★ ★

Over lunch at the Ritz with Warboys, Sir Andrew Starr realized that this was not one of their now traditional meetings . . . old friends keeping in touch . . . same school . . . same so many things — Oxford, the Army, same club and the same war — though Warboys had sat at home around the streets to roam while he had gone to be a soldier and a dozen other things besides. Good chap, though, Warboys — even if you didn't always know what he was up to, except that in some way you were going to be used for the greater glory (or protection) of the three estates. Lanky, like a bean pole with the crop picked and the vines drooping, lank white hair with a touch of silver, jaw like a pike and the pure blue eyes of a child, and hands, frail and long fingered, that had pulled so many strings. Hands now liver-blotched — but still holding the reins though somewhat loosely, death inconceivable except some day for certain an unexpected fanfare of trumpets on high, his ears just picking them up as he collapsed, probably over his fly-tying desk, a part-finished Silver Doctor still in the vice. Getting a little tetchy, too. Never used to fuss so much over his wine, or leave so much to go cold on his plate.

As the waiter left them from serving brandy, Sir Andrew said with a sudden impatience . . . at their age it was a thing quite unremarked, 'Well now, why don't you come to the bloody point, you old warhorse? You've been fiddling and farting around ever since we met, like an old aunt who's suddenly taken a dislike to you and isn't quite certain yet how to get into telling you she's cut you out of her will.'

Warboys smiled then, and said, 'Am I so dithery? Yes, I suppose I am. Well, old Father Time is not so many swathes away, scything at his own pace, Andrew. I like the old aunt

110

bit. Fact is it's rather like that. Well, it's about the handsome conscience money you've been collecting from certain would-have-been unpatriotic gentlemen — save the word — for years. When the thing first started there was a gentleman's agreement between you and the Establishment — us. You collected your tribute yearly from these high-placed bastards — and we just manipulated them now and then for our own purposes in the clandestine interests of the State. But now you are going to be cut out of the will. Time was when I could have given you an apt quotation to soften the blow. Trouble is when I search for one now — mostly all I get are tag ends of music hall songs. There was I waiting at the church . . . '

Sir Andrew laughed. 'Would — *Nullum sine auctoramento malum est* — fit the bill?'

'Clever boy. I knew you would help me. Yes, the compensation has to stop. You've seen it coming?'

'I suppose so. Three of the bastards have died and of the other four, two have decent sons with families.'

'And the other two have daughters — one married to the law, an eminent Q.C. — '

'And the other to a millionaire playboy so that in her own right she could probably pay the dole out of her dress allowance. I've no

111

sympathy for any of the original bastards.'

'Unto the third and fourth generation?'

'No — just the first. Our generation. Because of what these people would have done so many of them are long dust. And think what would have happened if the thing they thought was inevitable and were prepared to support had happened?'

'I won't be so ungracious as to suggest that you are worried on the money side.'

'Then you're wrong, dear Warboys. I needed the money at first, before you knew anything. But I don't now. But hundreds of others do. That's where most of it goes — discreetly.' Sir Andrew laughed harshly. 'Of course, I keep a percentage for handling charges and buying the odd picture now and again. But I don't regard those as mine. They're all being left to the nation. Are you really calling a halt?'

'Not me. I'm just the messenger boy. Oh, I still sit a few days during the week in Birdcage Walk, and go round keeping the boys and girls happy. But the real tiger you have yet to meet . . . will have to, in fact, when you hand the original stuff over.'

'Quint?'

'Oh, no. He retired last year. Got his K. Now lives on the Isle of Purbeck, with plenty of unattached companionship of the kind he always favoured — and collects fossils. I thought of applying to join his collection.' He sighed and looked around the restaurant. 'Sometimes I come in here and before I even get to the *sole tartare* I long for the sight of a white face. *Tempori parendum* — I find that difficult.'

'And the real tiger?'

'A Quint protégé, named Kerslake. Not our background. Humble origin. A moon-faced yokel from the leafy lanes of the West Country. Began life as a police constable in Barnstaple. Steady rise. Occasionally human out of office hours, but never in. A new kind of breed in the dark galleries of the underground complex of Her Majesty's Service.'

'Well, these are changed days. You never know what's coming out of the compost heap. You can't be enjoying this.'

'I'm not.'

'Well, then give yourself the pleasure of telling them that what I've got I keep. You've got photostats — let 'em be content with those.'

'They won't like it.'

'Then they can lump it.'

'They'll go for you — not red in tooth and claw, but just as unpleasant.'

'If they do I'll throw it wide open. *Der Spiegel . . . The Morning Star*, or whatever the rag is. Perhaps *The New York Times.* And the French — they'll love it, *France Soir. Perfide Albion* . . . '

'Sleep on it. I'll give you time — and then, my dear Andrew, I frankly don't care a damn. And between ourselves if I were the man I used to be — I still wouldn't care a damn. I'm a stand-in messenger boy, and even at that I'm long tired of standing unless it's on the banks of the Test and there's a good hatch of fly going — and then in a few years as Izaak Walton once said — *A quiet passage to a welcome grave.*'

'Bloody nonsense. You'll still be dining in here when Arabia is dry of oil and the Arabs have folded their tents and gone back to a wholesome diet of goat's milk and dates. Tell them from me the answer is no let-up. Caesar insists on his tribute. Now I must be off to pick up Christine from her beauty parlour. Some women never give up you know — and damn right. And neither do I.'

Warboys watched him go, signalled for more brandy and, smiling to himself, let his fancy roam. Quint would have loved it. He might tell him some time. And that Johnny-come-lately, Kerslake in Birdcage Walk, jerking as the strings were pulled from above, how would he take it? Well, for one thing, not entirely like a gentleman. Not that he was a bad chap — time and tribulations would shape him.

★   ★   ★

When Carla left her boutique Aldo was standing outside on the other side of the road. He signalled to her and — typical, she thought — waited for her to make her way between the traffic to him. After he had greeted her with a brotherly kiss, as automatic for him as probing at his teeth with a *stuzzicadenti*, she said, 'You have come to see me safely home? Ah, *caro fratello* — my knees go weak at such attention.'

'Shut up. We walk back to Maurice's place. You have the key?'

'Yes, of course. Why do you want to go there?'

'Because, little sister, I can't wait for him to come back. I must get someone else to finish the cleaning of the Zais.'

'And the copy?'

'No — how could I? There is no one but Maurice could do it. I write it off. In all businesses there are losses. One must be philosophical.'

'*Certo* — and now I know why you look different. Suddenly you are a philosopher. And Aldo — how it suits you. Though I do not think the toothpick sticking out of the corner of your mouth is the right touch.'

Disdainfully Aldo spat the toothpick into the road and with a surprising gentleness said, 'Now you tell me . . . do you think Maurice will ever come back?'

'How should I know?'

'Women should know about their lovers.' He thumped his chest. 'The heart. The heart is supposed to tell them.'

With a gentle exaggeration and flickering her eye-lids, she said, 'My heart says nothing. Though it aches with love for him — even though he is pig of all pigs.'

'You find nothing in the flat about him? No letters, no nothing?'

'I've told you already — no. Maurice leaves nothing. No letters, nothing. How do you think I can find him if I know nothing?'

'There are telegrams he has from Switzerland. What about those? You never find any about the place?'

'You think I go round looking for something which is not there? Always they come over the telephone, and no confirmation. Or if they do come when I am out — then he destroys them, burns them. He never keeps anything like that. All I know is that they come from Switzerland where he once worked. What do you want me to do

— go along to the *maestro delle poste e telegrafi* and say please go through the records and find out — '

Aldo laughed suddenly. 'Carla — you are brilliant. Why did I not think of that?'

'You mean you would do that?'

'Why not? But not to the top man — but I have friends who have sons or mistresses who work there. I must have — and then it is so simple . . . ' He rubbed the thumb and forefinger of his right hand together in an expressive gesture.

'That is your business. But why on earth do you want Maurice so badly? You have made enough money out of him. Forget him.'

'Can you forget him?'

'That is of the heart — not the purse. What is there so special you want him for?'

Aldo beamed slyly. 'Let us say there is a picture coming to be cleaned soon. *Magnifico* . . . and already I have a customer. More I cannot tell you. It would be indiscreet.'

'Oh, please don't be that, Aldo. Think of your reputation as an honest man. Did you say something about buying me a drink?'

'I did, my dear sister — but the need for such generosity has now evaporated. But when I get what I want I will pay for a nice trip to Switzerland for you.' His face suddenly changed and he said soberly, 'He would come back if we find him, surely? He loves you and wants to marry you and have his hands on your money. He would come back surely?'

They were crossing the Arno now and Carla stopped and nodded over the parapet at the waters below, saying, 'You see the river that runs to the sea. You think it can turn and start to run back to the hills? You would like to make a bet on it? I tell you, I would sooner bet on that than on anything Maurice might or might not do.'

'And this is the man you love?'

'Why not? Married to someone as predictable as you I would grow moss in a fortnight. *Ciao*, Aldo. I go now to buy myself a little blouse I fancy, and I shall charge it up to your account. They will not be surprised. They know how generous you are to your family . . . '

★   ★   ★

Two days later Sir Andrew and Lady Starr returned to Avoncourt Abbey. Sir Andrew went up to his bedroom to change his London clothes and the first thing he noticed was that the Augustus John painting of himself was missing.

He stood in silence for a moment or two,

staring at the space where the picture had hung, noticing, even in his surprise and pleasure, that the wallpaper where the picture had been still retained much of its original colouring whereas that of the rest of the room had faded. Well, he would have to put another picture up. Then suddenly he began to laugh long and loudly.

The noise brought Lady Starr to him from her adjoining room.

'Andrew, what on earth is so amusing? And, dear, you do guffaw in the most common manner.'

'Never mind the way I laugh, my love. It comes from the heart and the humour of it all. Do you see what he's done?'

'Who?'

'Our son, my dear. Our son. He's gone — and he's done me the greatest favour in the world. He's taken the Augustus John.'

'Then you must put the police on to him. The wretch — after all our kindness.'

'Don't be an ass, love. I told him he could take any picture he liked. And the sentimental lad chooses dear old Dad. By God — that rhymes, or does it?'

'Well, I must say I never really cared for it much. He'd given you a queer sly look about your face. Oh, I know you get it at times — but it's not characteristic. Not at all. You really have a quite noble face when you try.'

'Bugger my face, love. All I'm concerned with is that he's done me the biggest favour in the world. Oh, God — I can't wait to let Warboys know. He will laugh his head off. Cheer up his dotage. Short of bringing the colour back into his cheeks it'll do wonders for him. Make him a new man.'

'Well, I'm glad to hear that. He really has been such a miserable washed-out misery these last few years. Have you ever suggested he dyes his hair?'

'I could never do that.'

'Why not? You were at school together, and all through the war and then — '

Sir Andrew turned, smiled and gave a little sigh. Then he kissed her on the cheek and said, 'The lad has the true Starr touch, you know. Not for him one of the Canalettos. But his Dad's picture — not out of sentiment, I swear, but because he knew that it did neither me nor John credit. But there's far more than that he's done for me . . . '

'Well, I'm so glad to hear that. And don't forget we're dining with the Armstrongs tonight. Informal, nothing elaborate — that means she's probably lost another cook and that bean-pole of a daughter of hers will do it and come rushing in oven-hot, breathless and awkward. They've quite given up any idea of getting her married, you know . . . such a shame. She really has a quite nice skin and there are times — '

'And there are times, my dear wife, when even unknown to you the gods smile on us.'

'Good. That's nice to hear, dear.'

When she had gone Sir Andrew made a brief call to the Red Lion Hotel and then sent for his chauffeur.

When the man came, Sir Andrew said, 'Have they got the station wagon fixed up yet, Lloyd?'

'Yes, Sir Andrew.'

'Good.' Sir Andrew pulled out his wallet and handed him a ten pound note, saying. 'Take yourself off in it to the Red Lion in Salisbury tonight. Have a few drinks and a bite of food. Keep sober, and find out for me all you can about that French chap — Monsieur Crillon — who's been up here lately doing the pictures. He's probably left by now — but you know the kind of thing I want. Asked the desk about rail times or boat sailings, has he? Local girls up in his room, eh? You know the kind of stuff. The dirt, they call it.'

'Yes, Sir Andrew.' He put the note in his pocket and then went on, 'Would it be all right if I take the wife, sir? She's got a better way than I have for that kind of thing. Knows a couple of the girls down there, too, I think. Also, sir, she don't drink so could drive back.'

'Excellent. Do that. Nothing like a well-organized marriage.'

When his chauffeur had gone Sir Andrew locked his bedroom door and then picked up the telephone by his bed and lay back on the pillows prepared to enjoy himself. He dialled Warboys' home number.

When Warboys answered, Sir Andrew said, 'Good — I thought you might still be at the Birdcage Walk offices tunnelling away at the foundations of ill-ordered civilization.'

'My presence, unlike the figure-head of a ship, worm-eaten as I may be, is not mandatory each day. Only when some knot of Gordian nature turns up and there's no one there with courage and common-sense enough to take a knife to it. Has some petrol lorry fallen into the lovely Avon and polluted and ruined your fishing?'

'No. But I expect it daily. I'm calling apropos of our little chat, hinting that I might be about to have my arm twisted by the high gods, my birth-right taken from me, my family bereft. Always liked that word. Sounds like linen tearing.'

'Shroud cloth — is that why you're so cheerful?'

'In a way. You must be psychic. You can

forget any idea of my handing over the original stuff you — or rather the pretender to the throne about to unseat you — wants. At least as far as I am concerned.'

'Of course, you don't mean you've destroyed it?'

'Good God . . . my dear Warboys, that's not my style. Burn money, even though I no longer lack it? Destroy a set of character references to some of the highest in the land? Good God, no, old chap. I am nothing if not reasonably honourable. Anyway I've had all I want out of it.'

'Does anyone ever have enough?'

'Of money, yes. Of power, no. There's the true drug which can never be forgone once taken. Thank God, I was happy to make no more than colonel. Field marshal — and there was one among them, as you know — was a rank I never coveted.'

'My dear Andrew — I love the way you never spit out the pips until you've sucked all the juice out of the orange. I'm delighted to hear you so happy. Let me share it. Bodily appetites decline, but intellectual joys endure as long as we do. Some of the nicest things have been the last words of worthy and unworthy people. *Between the stirrup and the ground. Mercy I askt, mercy I found.*'

'Nice — *inter pontem et fontem*. And

probably a four-pound trout scared by the splash. But do you want to hear this or not?'

'Of course. Brighten the tag end of a dull day for me.'

'Well . . . ' Sir Andrew hesitated for a moment between truth and fiction and then decided — since no one could foresee the future — to stick to fiction.

'Well, what? Are you having second thoughts?'

'No, taking a long breath before going in off the deep end. Well, you see, it's like this. Some time ago I met a young French chap — well young by our standards — who'd been going round the galleries and about the gardens. Saw him once or twice and then we struck up this acquaintance while talking about my paintings. Knew his stuff . . . turned out to be a bit of an artist himself, but more than that a first class restorer. So I got him to do one or two jobs . . . you know, touching up and cleaning and — '

'And a long preamble, so I presume I'm not getting the full truth. Can I hope for it some day?'

'Possibly. Anyway, I gave him the run of the place and a room to sleep in if he chose — though most of the time he preferred the Red Lion, and I don't blame him — cistern noises all night here and bird banter from five o'clock on. And — '

'And when you got back you discovered that he had decamped with the under house-maid and the family jewels?'

'Far worse. He's pinched the painting of me that Augustus John did — the one of me in my near twenties. You know it, don't you?'

'Of course I do. And I never believed it was by John.'

'Oh, it was all right. But I agree far from one of his best. So I'm not really sorry to see it go.'

'Quite right. But don't tell the insurance adjusters that.'

'Of course not. But that isn't the point. Tucked away in the back of the picture are the originals of the stuff Birdcage now say they want to have and destroy. Splendid, isn't it? Now they can't wipe the bloody slate clean because the other side will — '

'Insist on the originals or nothing. That's what they want to see destroyed before their very eyes.' Warboys laughed. 'Intriguing. Did you think that one up on the way home? *Zwischen uns sei Wahrheit.* Appropriate language, too.'

'Damn the damned language. Yes it's *the* truth. I say it to you.'

'Then I believe. Odd place to keep it, wasn't it?'

'It was as near as I could get to keeping it

under the bed mattress. So if your people want their dirt they've got to find him and get the stuff back. But I want to make this clear — so far as the picture is concerned I make no charges. He's welcome to it. I make it a retrospective gift.'

'Odd. You might tell me why one day?'

'Could be. I think you'd enjoy the joke. But that's for later. You want the original documents then you must get them to find Maurice Crillon. They'll mean nothing to him. He'll be quite reasonable.'

'Does he read German?'

'I've no idea.'

'Could he still be at the hotel?'

'No. I phoned. He's gone.'

'When he signed in did he put his address in France?'

'I didn't ask.'

'Why not?'

'Because unless ordered — I don't intend to do any work, however slight, for Birdcage.'

'Something like the faint tinkle of a High Mass bell rang in my ear then — or did it?'

'It was a bird outside the window.'

A long sigh came over the line, and then, 'We'll find him, you know. Could be he might write to you?'

'What for? The man's just pinched a bloody picture from me. But I have to admit

126

that I'm enjoying the piquancy of it all. Will your bright boy at Birdcage still want to see me?'

'Oh, I'm sure. Didn't I tell you? He's got this uncanny knack of being able to tell fiction from truth. Anyway, dear man, it's nice to hear you sounding so happy over the loss of an Augustus John.'

★   ★   ★

When Sir Andrew's chauffeur reported to him the next morning his — or rather his wife's — gleanings from the Red Lion Hotel were brief but not without considerable human interest. His son was clearly a chip off the old block. Maurice Crillon had left the hotel at quarter-past two the previous afternoon in his car, after taking lunch with a young lady as his guest. The young lady was fairly well-known to one of the waitresses — a friend of Mrs Lloyd — for she now and then had the habit of coming into the hotel for a bar snack lunch. Her name was Miss Margery Littleton and she worked for one of the town's solicitors. She had left in the same car with Maurice Crillon.

And Lloyd added, 'I got his address from the register — and of course we know about his car, sir, from his coming up here. I wrote it all down for you.' He handed his employer a piece of paper with the number and make of the car. Underneath this was also written — *No.2. Rue de Belfort, Bordeaux* — which surprised Sir Andrew a little since why should Maurice not have used his Cragnac address? However . . . it was not his business to worry over that. The days ahead were going to be full of heart-warming piquancies. Birdcage could do their own dirty work. And he hoped that they fell flat on their faces. Perhaps — after a while — he might go and have a private talk with Margery Littleton. Shouldn't be difficult to find her. His own local solicitor knew all the others and would trace her, no questions asked. It wouldn't surprise him to learn that she had gone back to France for a while with Maurice — chip off the old block. See that with half-an-eye. Then a thought suddenly struck him for the first time — Maurice had taken the Augustus John out of sentiment and as a compliment to him, but suppose some day, sooner or later, he should take it out of its frame, say, to clean it — which it needed — and found the documents, the originals which Birdcage now so avidly desired for some dirty, cover-up deal of their own with the ageing bastards who wanted true peace of mind and, probably more so, release from their yearly tribute to him? Well, if he couldn't read German and just chucked the stuff into the fire as back packing needing renewing . . . well and good. But if not — and he started something on his own. God help the dear man — he would be walking into a jungle full of tigers. Though . . . thinking that over, he realized at once that Maurice Crillon was not the kind of man who would risk his own neck by coming into the open too soon. There was that about him which in some indefinable way was apparent to him — perhaps because he himself belonged in the same category — that marked him as a survival man. *Cher* Maurice could well take care of himself.

That noon the telephone rang and a prim, dehumanized voice enquired whether it would be convenient for Mr Kerslake to call and see him the following afternoon, and whether he could kindly indicate a convenient spot in the grounds of the Abbey where his helicopter might land?

Sir Andrew said, 'The Abbey's not open to the public that day. He can land in the small paddock to the south of the chapel of the Knights Hospitaller.'

Putting down the telephone he gave a shrug of his shoulders, thinking how the old crusading knights had gone all the way to Jerusalem on horse-back. Those now who defended Church and Establishment dropped out of the skies like marauding locusts. The world was becoming overstuffed with hundreds of means of annihilating time and distance. Oh, brave new world . . . and how nice that it had Maurice Crillon in it to complicate things for Birdcage . . . dear Maurice, he really had thrown a spanner in the works. No doubt about his blood lines — travel your comforts with you. Sometime he must find out about this Margery Littleton . . .

★   ★   ★

At that moment Margery Littleton was lying on her back on the edge of a small copse of aspen trees on the right bank of the river Dordogne. Chiff-chaffs and willow warblers filled the air with song. From beyond the trees came the sound of traffic. She was drowsy from the wine of an early lunch to which had now been added the smooth ecstasy of recent love-making. Maurice, she had soon learnt, was, when desire took him, heedless of risks or embarrassment. He was sitting now farther up the bank talking to an old man who had bicycled into view when their passion had been recently spent and respectability was — like heaven, she wondered — all about them. The old man was using a twenty foot fishing pole which he occasionally jerked to mark a bite and then lifted absurdly small fish free of the water to go into his keep net. Some time that evening they would be in his good wife's kitchen . . . *frits en brochettes.* For a little while she let herself imagine she was Maurice's wife — not seriously, but for the fairytale pleasure of it. There was no harm in it. Nothing was going to mar or mis-shape this glorious break in her humdrum life. When the great firework display was over, the ground littered with the broken and charred rocket sticks, she would only have to close her eyes and the whole episode would be in her memory, unmarred, unmarrable . . . She closed her eyes now against the sun and drifted into a deep sleep which heralded itself by a long sigh of contentment.

★ ★ ★

The next afternoon, a blue helicopter came in low over the elms that crested the hills behind Avoncourt Abbey, did a close circuit over the chapel, and then settled to the ground in the small paddock that overlooked the river.

Kerslake got out of the machine, turned and said something to the pilot, and then walked across to where Sir Andrew Starr waited for him, leaning on the paddock gate.

He had met him before briefly at one or two conferences of no importance and doubted very much whether the man would remember him, except by name.

Sir Andrew pulled the gate back for him to leave the field and said, 'Kerslake?'

'Yes, Sir Andrew.'

As they shook hands, Sir Andrew said, 'Nice to see you. Met you last a couple of years ago. You were minus the moustache then. Suits you. Not me, though. I tried it once and Lady Starr said it made me look like some ageing walrus who'd just lost his last cow to an up-and-coming young rival.'

Kerslake laughed, a thin, dry sound though it came from genuine amusement, and said, 'I don't care for it much myself. But when they pushed me upstairs Warboys suggested it. New office, newer responsibilities needed a slightly newer persona. Somehow I got attached to it — or it to me.'

Sir Andrew laughed again and shook his head. 'They told me you were as dry as a stick, tough as nails and as ruthless as a broker's man. You'd like to come in and have some tea — or take a walk along the river?'

'The river, I think, if that suits you, Sir Andrew. I was born by a river. The Taw — Barnstaple.'

'Ah, yes. Do you fish it?'

'No. I poached it until I became a police cadet and had to be respectable. And then . . . well, where I sit now there are bigger but less noble fish to go after.'

'Bloody sharks most of 'em.'

They went down the hill path and when they came to the stile leading on to the river bank they both in silent accord — which moved some memory in Sir Andrew, though it was too foggy to be captured — sat on it in unspoken agreement.

After a moment or two Kerslake said, 'I don't want to go into the bigger issue at this moment, Sir Andrew. Warboys has briefed me on your feelings about that. I think we can leave all that until we get the original papers back. I'd just like to know all you can tell me about this Frenchman, Maurice Crillon.'

'Damned little, really. Said he was over here on holiday. Staying at the Red Lion. Noticed him coming up here three or four times — used to see him in the picture galleries and then walking down here sometimes. Fact, it was right here that we first got talking — about paintings. Knew his stuff all right . . . ' He went on, telling the story, editing it where necessary.

'So, in a sense, he finished up working for you?'

'Yes — but not for cash. Just for pleasure.

He was passionate in the truest sense of the word about paintings.'

'Did he ever see the Augustus John in your bedroom before he took it?'

'Oh, yes. I took him along once to ask him if he thought it needed cleaning. Know what the cheeky sod said? He said it was a lousy painting — right to my face — but it could do with cleaning. Actually between ourselves it wasn't the best Augustus John in the world. Homer nods occasionally and portrait painters more often.'

'What kind of car did he drive?'

'Renault. But don't ask me the number. Never look at that kind of thing.'

A kingfisher went down stream fast and a distant cuckoo soothed the afternoon with a few lazy notes.

Kerslake said, 'Seems odd he should take that picture?'

'Damned odd. But there you are. But I could cite you plenty of other things in my life which were just as damned odd. And, let's face it, there wouldn't be any need for all that set-up in Birdcage Walk if there weren't even odder things in life.'

'Did you ever gather whether he spoke German or not?'

'No idea.'

Kerslake suddenly smiled and said, 'Proper

up a gum tree, aren't we, Sir Andrew?'

'Perhaps. But only for you and all that lot you've suddenly decided to do a deal with. You aren't going to expect me to be broken hearted over all this, are you?'

'Far from it. I should think you're really enjoying it all. And personally I don't blame you. But in my official capacity — well, you know how that must be.'

'Yes. Well, you've got all I can give you. What will you do?'

'Trace him. It shouldn't be hard. The French authorities will help one way or another.'

'And what about the other side? Tell them the original documents have been pinched — or some politer less brutal story?'

'Tell them the truth, I think.'

'That'll be a change coming from Birdcage.'

Kerslake smiled. 'Why do you pretend to despise us, Sir Andrew? You know better than most the need for our existence — and once you worked for us.'

'So I did, Kerslake. So I did. But that was during a time of national peril. The Sermon on the Mount was put away for the duration.'

'And afterwards . . . Sir Andrew Starr went into business on his own account.'

'Damn right. Couldn't resist it, not with those bastards. And, of course, needs must when the Devil drives. If things had gone their way what would have happened to England's green and pleasant land? Sure, I blackmailed them privately for years, and then I began to sense that they might try and take me out . . . shooting accident, car crash, something that wouldn't raise a stink or publicity. Just a brief obituary notice in *The Times* for Sir Andrew Starr . . . *et cetera* and so on . . . So, I decided to go to my old firm and take out some insurance — and as a *quid pro quo* you got the photostat copies.'

'And now we want the originals.'

'To burn on the kitchen stove?'

'Just at the moment there is a division of opinion about that. After all these years some of them have worked their passage back, seen the light and wish to be shrived. Barefoot to Jerusalem and back.'

'Aye — and that a pilgrimage they would have denied many others. Barefoot and ragged-arsed to a gas chamber was what they had in mind. So, Kerslake, you know my position. The documents have gone — and now the ball is in your court. Exit Sir Andrew Starr — laughing.'

Kerslake smiled. 'I don't blame you. I fancy we'll be able to manage without you.'

'Good. Now can I offer you a drink before you take off?'

Kerslake hesitated for a moment or two, and then said, 'That would be kind of you. Perhaps, too, I could take a look at your bedroom and the maintenance room where Crillon worked.'

'Finger prints and all that stuff?'

'No.'

'Why not?'

'Because I don't think Birdcage will be doing any serious chasing. And like you I don't owe the other side any favours — despite official policy. I just wanted to have the picture in my mind of an itinerant Frenchman, working at the Abbey and then for some quirky reason making off with an indifferent picture when he had so many others of far higher quality to choose from. You must have thought that odd?'

'My dear Kerslake, I thought it was bloody odd — and also bloody amusing. Fact, I've an idea that the gods with endless Time on their hands had decided to set up a completely random set of circumstances so that they could sit back and watch the show — hoping that it would turn out good and run for a long time. Perhaps steal the record eventually from *The Mousetrap*.'

★ ★ ★

137

Now and again, in the late afternoon on her way back from work, Carla went up to Maurice's flat to see — though with not any perceptible stir of hope — whether he had written to her. He would never have sent anything direct to the family home, knowing that Aldo would have no scruples over opening and — if necessary — destroying any communication from him.

Today her hope was rewarded. Nestling in the wire letter box behind the door was a picture postcard of the view from the Domme ramparts, the great, lazy snake of the river Dordogne coiling along the valley below.

He wrote:

Briefly here on business. Sorry so long no word, but my thoughts are almost always of you. I am lost without you. Can't say when I shall be back. My mother died and I have to clear up affairs.

Love Maurice.

She dropped the card on to the table and was about to pour herself a glass of Cinzano Bianco when the door bell rang. It not only rang, it went on ringing — which told her all she wanted to know. She opened it to find, without surprise, that Aldo was outside.

She said, 'How did you know I was in?'

'The *portinaia* told me.'

Carla eyed him for a moment or two, smiling, and then asked, 'Why are you so happy? Your face looks quite different when you are in a good temper.'

'Why should I not be happy? You have made me so.'

'Me?'

'Yes. My clever sister. I did as you suggested about the telegrams from Switzerland. Antonio Maratino — you know who has the *trattoria* at Fiesole — well I discover he has a friend who works in the Post Office, who owed him a favour, and from this friend I find out about the telegram from Switzerland. It is good to have friends who are always ready to help and ask no questions — '

'Mafia?'

A shade offended, Aldo said, 'I talk of friends. Anyway, I find out. So now you can go to Switzerland and have a little talk with this friend.' He handed her a slip of paper which she glanced at briefly and felt no surprise. Even if she had she would not have given Aldo the pleasure of knowing it. She reached for her bag from the table and put the paper in it.

Enjoying himself Aldo said, 'Your face shows nothing.'

She gave a long mock sigh. 'Ah, but Aldo in my heart there is deep sorrow. Always the woman pays, is that not true?'

'That I have always told you.'

'But this time it is the man, you, who begins to pay. If I work for you, you must pay me. Before I go to Switzerland you settle one half of my money on me. Without that I do not stir.'

'One half! I could go for myself.'

'Then do that.'

'How so? I do not speak German. And, anyway, *cara*, these things arrange themselves better between women. One quarter, I pay. Is that not handsome?'

'One third is handsomer. You have no thought for my feelings? You would send me to talk to this Fräulein. Can you not imagine why she does a thing like this for Maurice? It is not a nice situation, my dear brother.'

Aldo threw up his hands. 'Now — you become all sensitive because Maurice has other women?'

'We will not discuss my feelings. One half.'

'One quarter.'

'One half — and paid into my bank before I go.'

'One quarter and I lend you my car to drive there and pay your hotel bills.'

'That you must do anyway. One half.'

Aldo was silent for a while. Then he suddenly smiled, reached for her hand and kissed it, and said warmly, 'You are my sister. Pappa dies too early to bring you up, but I have done it for him. And why not? I am a good son. All right — I make over one third.'

'Tomorrow. Then I leave when the bank confirms it — in your car, plus all expenses.'

'Agreed. Oh, you make me so happy. When he comes back you shall have the rest of your money and you shall be married and Maurice will become one of the family and stay for ever — like a brother to me.'

Carla smiled and shook her head. 'Aldo — do not run too far ahead. Maurice is like a rainbow. Now you see it and now you don't.'

'And you would be happy married to a man like that?'

'I would be happy, yes. But I cannot give you the reasons for they are not to be laid out like the clauses in a business contract. God gives men and women love to make of it what they will. It is a contract with no small print at the bottom for the lawyers to worry over. Naturally you will see the car is full with petrol before I go. Also here is a postcard which I have just had from Maurice.'

Aldo took the card and read it. At once his gross, dewlapped face fell into the conventional lines of polite solemnity and his words

141

matched the falseness of his appropriately masked face. '*Ah, mia cara sorella* . . . it is now he needs you. To lose a mother — that is terrible! We must find him. He shall come back and have happiness in our family, and he and I shall work together like brothers — '

'Cheating and forging and stealing. Oh, Aldo you are impossible.'

Aldo straightened his fat shoulders indignantly and said with a sudden intensity of feeling, 'In that you are wrong. One day he will do big work. His own — he has that gift in the eyes and hands which God gives only to a few.'

'Yes, he has that. But God — for some reason — gave him something else.'

'What?'

'There is no name for it yet. Eve was tempted and from that moment it was doomed that from time to time some of her children should reach for the forbidden fruit despite any gift God had given them at birth.'

'You talk nonsense again. Sometimes I think you are a little *pazza*.' He put his forefinger against his head and turned it with a screwing motion.

'Maybe — but not in the head. In the heart, Aldo.'

5

Standing at the window of his room in the Birdcage Walk building, his back a little obliquely set to Sir Julian Markover, Warboys watched a mallard drake take off from the lake in St James's Park. It banked up into the strong, almost gale-force wind and then turned to glide high and easily along the front of the Foreign Office windows and over Horse Guards Parade and then was lost beyond the ivy-green top of the Fortress, heading north, perhaps for a change to sample the summer delights of Regent's Park. He said over his shoulder, 'That's all I can tell you at the moment, Sir Julian. It's all we know. The stuff you wanted — the substance of the settlement that has been agreed in principle — has gone. It's somewhere in France, hidden in the back of a picture in the boot of a car.' He turned, smiled and went and sat down behind his desk.

Sir Julian said, 'You will pardon me if I say that this has happened at a very inconvenient time, my dear Warboys. The thing was all settled and now there is this hitch. For whatever was done and would have been done, we have suffered and paid. I agree that the paying was no problem — and the suffering . . . well in life there is always that. But now I have children who have children who know nothing of the sins of their father and grandfather. The others, too . . . We have always been frank, you and I. The tribute has always been paid regularly to Sir Andrew — and our services have always been at your disposal, and have been used many, many times. When I die — I want no skeleton in my cupboard or that of the others. You tell me this has happened — all out of pure chance?'

'You have my word. But we shall find this Frenchman and recover the picture and then you shall have what you want. We shall find him.'

Sir Julian was silent for a moment or two, and then he shook his head. 'No — that is not how it can be.' He smiled broadly, and for a moment or two Warboys found him almost likeable.

'Why not?'

'Because this affair is now no longer an official one. Oh, naturally you can go through the motions without enthusiasm and, of course, if with luck, you get the picture — then we shall both be happy. But in the meantime those of us who are still concerned must also take steps. You have an organization which is excellent — but in times of crisis conscience sometimes mars it, or a new expediency. But we have an organization, too. In life the Fates throw up situations which make it necessary sometimes to apply drastic and terminal solutions from which you people here would turn away, knowing that this is not a commitment to which you are utterly dedicated. Do I make myself clear?'

'Absolutely. If the need arose you would kill this Frenchman to get what you want. Whereas, here, well . . . no. After all he is completely innocent of the situation he has caused. The picture he took was a gift. We shall find him.'

'And we shall also look for him. We need nothing from you. Already you have told me enough to begin with. And if you so wish there is no reason why this conversation should ever go further than this room.'

'I make no promise, Sir Julian.'

Sir Julian rose. 'Naturally.' He moved to pick up his hat and the stick which he used to ease his limp and, glancing for a moment out of the window, he turned to Warboys and said almost wearily, 'All men of vigour and ambition have dreams they strive to bring true. I had one and it was held quite genuinely — this country gave my grand-father a home and through his work a great

145

fortune. Long before Dunkirk I could see its downfall coming — and with a few others I planned to save what could be saved. Why resist when defeat is inevitable? And it was — should have been, had not Hitler hesitated and then lost his chance after Dunkirk. Better to eat the dry crusts of shame than to die fighting a battle which can never be won. I know better now. Can God or Man blame us for being what we are? Historically, too, this country has always in the end come to accept what we would have — the Romans, the Saxons and Danes, the Normans. I see you smile — perhaps you find some fallacy in my thinking which escapes me?'

'Surely, I do. In times of war all men change. The prospect of defeat becomes a challenge and pushes logic — the kind you have just instanced — into limbo. First they are enraged and then they are inspired, some. Others lie down and feign death, hoping to escape the thundering hooves and iron wheels of the chariots. The British in crisis seldom act with logic — they become intoxicated with an arrogance which bereaves them of the power to think straight but they know — without questioning — from their own private line to God that all is not on the side of the big battalions. I am sure that it pleases the Almighty when such men defy the inevitable and turn irrefutable logic upside down. Mind you, God does not always allow this to happen. Every so often He disappoints them for their own good — what fun would there be for them if they were always betting on a certainty?'

Sir Julian laughed, and said, 'Most of you are convinced that the map of paradise — unlike that of the world — is still largely coloured red.'

'Well, why not? A nation without irreverence is a police state. But now — ' he broke off for a moment, rubbing a lean forefinger over the morocco binding of his desk blotter, '*revenons à nos moutons*. If you can find what you want in your own ways, remember that an innocent Frenchman now has what you want. Find him if you can — we shall be trying, too. Get what you want from him, but leave him free. We shall be trying to do the same thing. If we get the documents — you shall have them.'

'I give you my word. No extreme measures — unless unavoidable.'

'Thank you.'

★ ★ ★

They spent the last few days of their time together at a small hotel on the outskirts of

Les-Eyzies-de-Tayac. They had a room at garden level. They went to bed late and rose late. The weather was good and they breakfasted in the garden. Then — neither of them concerned with the curiosities and sights of the area — they drove out on excursions, buying themselves a bottle of wine and a picnic lunch, and ate *al fresco* wherever the fancy took them. Margery had no interest in tourist sight-seeing. She was content to drift through the days at his side. Though 'drift' at the end of each day seemed a misnomer to her. The days passed too swiftly. At night they dined on the hotel's wisteria-canopied terrace and talked, but in all their talk she learned little of him and his past, and what she did some instinct told her was not to be trusted. Once she caught him out on a contradiction and the love and wine in her prompted her to point this out. At this he laughed and said easily, 'There is no contradiction. I am a man with many pasts — and sometimes I get them confused. It is not a good thing just to live one life. It gets so boring.'

His obliquity left her unmoved for she had no desire to mar her present happiness. She knew she was being silly and romantic, and had no qualms about it. One day soon he would put her on a plane at Bordeaux and it would all be over, except the glorious memories of these days. And those she knew would be enough. At dusk a nightingale sang obligingly for her and, since they left the garden door part open for the air, the hotel cat came each morning to curl up at her feet and wait patiently for the remains of their breakfast milk. Only one thing loomed ever nearer each day — the return to Bordeaux. She closed her mind to it — or for the most part succeeded in doing so.

It was during this time that Sir Julian Markover flew to Paris and arranged through his contacts there to put out the word for Maurice Crillon, painter and picture-restorer, description and estimated age, likely make of car. He knew that it would take time, but it would be done. He was content to wait. Birdcage too went to work — more on a point of professional pride than anything else. There was nothing more satisfying to Kerslake and Warboys than a completed file. Also — since no man could read the future and the exigencies it might throw up — they acted from a sense of duty, that duty to which everyone in the organization was in his or her way completely dedicated.

Sir Andrew Starr, indifferent to all this, gradually let the whole thing slip from his mind, except for the occasional moment or

two when memory was triggered by sentiment after a few drinks and he found himself
thinking how damned odd it all was. He had
a son and he didn't have a son. And the
damned odd thing was that he damned well
didn't know what he thought about it all. And
more than that he didn't care a sparrow's fart
any longer. He had collected the last of the
tribute demanded for treachery and was tired
of the whole business, had no interest in it
— except he hoped they would never find
Maurice Crillon.

★　★　★

The information which Aldo had obtained
through his friends simply read — Trudi
Keller, and then gave a Gunten telephone
number. Carla, arriving in the early afternoon, booked in at a lakeside hotel and then
telephoned the number.

A woman's voice answered her call and
when she asked for Trudi Keller she was told
that Fräulein Keller was at work. Carla asked
where this would be since she had an
important message to pass to Fräulein Keller.
She was given the number of the school at
which Fräulein Keller worked and its name.

Carla telephoned the school and talked to
Trudi Keller. Carla's German was good since

Aldo, though mean over many things, believed in a liberal education and when he had become unexpectedly early head of the family — and Carla then only fourteen — he had seen to it that she had learnt French and German for in his business there was a need for them and, looking to the future, he had already planned that she should work for him as a secretary, part-time, after finishing whatever regular work she decided to take.

With little preamble Carla explained that Maurice Crillon had until recently been working for her brother in Florence but had left some time ago, and that her brother was anxious to get in touch with him.

A cool voice at the other end of the line asked, 'Did Maurice give him my name and address?'

'No. We got it from the telegram you sent Maurice about his mother's death. I could explain more if you would be kind enough to see me. I have my car with me. Perhaps I could meet you after school, Fräulein, and we could go to my hotel in Gunten and talk?'

There was a long silence at the other end, and then Trudi Keller said, 'You know Maurice very well, *signorina?*'

Carla laughed. 'Who knows Maurice very well?'

There was a long pause again, and then

151

Trudi Keller said, 'I think I understand. Yes, please, if it is your wish. I finish here today at four o'clock.'

'That's very kind of you.'

'It is less kindness than curiosity, *signorina*.'

When they met Carla was a little surprised. Knowing Maurice, she had no doubt that they had been lovers — but she was such a big girl. Not heavy or fat, but an abundant Rubensesque type, placidly good-looking and she had a deliberation of movement and speech as though, Carla thought, everything worked well but she cautiously watched herself in case she did or said something wrong.

But after a little while, during which time coffee and cakes were ordered, Carla recognized that there was no reluctance in her to talk. It was as though she had been waiting with longing for someone from Maurice's life to come and widen the horizons of her knowledge of him. For Carla this increased her sympathy for this large, Amazonian beauty. Sympathy because, she sensed, this woman's defences were far less adequate than her own for dealing with the arrogance of Maurice's nature. Understanding and sympathy for one another rose spontaneously — they both loved him (there was no jealousy in Carla about this) and he treated them as pure conveniences for his own purposes. The bond was soon recognized and a relationship established but with unspoken reservations on both sides. Carla told her how she had first met Maurice and his pursuit of her, and Trudi Keller laughed.

She said, 'So it was with me in Zürich. My father has a monumental mason's business there. One day Maurice comes into the yard — I am in the little office where I worked part-time on the books and my father is with me. Maurice says to my father does he want a designer . . . '

Her father had said he did not. Undeterred Maurice had opened his brief case and pulled out a portfolio of drawings — architectural and sculptural. Her father had been impressed, but said that he had not enough business to employ a full-time designer. Maurice had said that he could also sculpt and work headstones and memorials and her father — who she sensed had taken a fancy to him — passed him a design for a Madonna and Child and told him to see what he could do with it — pointing to a small block of white Carrara marble in the yard.

Trudi said, 'Signorina, he worked three weeks on it — almost day and night. It was of a beauty and craftsmanship never seen in my father's yard before. So he came to work for us. And my father said to me that same day, 'Trudi — you must watch him. I have met his kind before. You must keep yourself distant from him for his hands have other magic as well for a young girl! So I tried for, though I love my father, I was very much afraid of him then . . . But when Maurice wants something there is no stopping him. I am very fond of amateur dramatics — so, he also joins the society so that he can be with me. And when he is with me . . . ' She spread both hands in a gesture of capitulation.

As she talked on Carla had already anticipated her story. She had fallen in love with Maurice. They became lovers, and eventually the father found out. He dismissed Maurice . . .

Trudi at this point gave a little shrug of her statuesque shoulders and said, 'I went with him. For five months and then it all finished. I became sensible. I still loved Maurice but I knew it was not a good thing for me or for him. So I left him and went back home — which was terrible for a while, then, when things were quiet again, I came here to teach in the school. At home I was always thinking of him. But we kept in touch . . . and from time to time we have met here in Gunten. He is not a man easy to cut out of one's life. I think, maybe, you know that, no, *signorina?*'

'I know. Oh, yes I know. And I can understand too why you still do things for him — like being a letter box.' She laughed wryly. 'Once you have given him your love he uses you — and you do not mind. Why is that? Some magic? A spell he casts?'

Trudi shrugged her shoulders. 'He takes and gives love — and then uses one if it suits him. And when I ask him once about all this and why I should still do things for him, like being a letter box, you know what he says — 'If a good fairy promised me any wish in the world do you know what I would ask for?' When I shook my head, he said, 'The gift of walking across sand without leaving any footmarks.' So now you know. Do not let him do it to you.'

'He already does.'

'Ah, so. And that is why you are here?'

'Partly, yes. I love him but expect nothing from him. It is my brother who wants him to come back and finish his work in Florence. He was cleaning and restoring a very valuable painting for him. All we have had is a postcard from France — with no address — saying that his mother has died.'

'Yes, I know that. I send Maurice the news. He gives my address for his people in France.'

'And you know his address there?'

'Of course. Very early I knew that from him.'

'Could you give it to me?'

'Would that be right?'

'Why not? It is not to make trouble for him. Merely to ask him to come and finish his work.' Seeing the hesitation on Trudi's face, knowing its provenance, she added. 'I would like him back, too — for my own reasons. But I have no hope, Fräulein. When he has finished his work he will go — and I shall stay.' She reached out and touched the other's right hand. 'We both know that. He is a little mad, you know. How true what he said to you about leaving no footprints. Joy and great pleasures one can have with him — but no real happiness. We both know that.'

'True.'

Trudi pulled a pocket book from her bag, tore a leaf from it and wrote the address. Handing it across she said, 'I am glad to have met you. If you are in Switzerland again some time perhaps we can meet. You see — meeting you is like finding a sister I never knew I had.'

Carla laughed. 'Oh, I wish I'd said that first.' Then her face clouding, she went on, 'What will happen to him in the end?'

Trudi shrugged her shoulders. 'What must happen to anyone who thinks he can walk across sand without leaving prints, walk through life without real concern for anyone else? God will become angry with him.' She crossed herself and stood up. She held out her hand and Carla took it briefly, saying, 'Sometime we shall meet again, I hope.'

★ ★ ★

Kerslake, deep in the great leather armchair facing Warboys' desk, uncomfortable with his semi-foetal position, holding his glass of dry sherry on the arm of the chair, wishing it were a pint of draught bitter, hearing the slick of car tyres on the wet roadway outside, and a little angry at the belated news which Warboys had just given, said, 'Oh, they can do it — in some respects better than us. But I don't like it.'

'You think it gives them a semi-official position?'

'Perhaps, sir.'

'Let them do the hard work and, if we find it expedient, at the end we can step in. Think of the economies, too. Our budget is already over-extended.'

'They'd cut his throat without a qualm if they thought it would get them something.'

'Time has modified their procedures — a little. But let us forget them for the moment.

What have you got?'

'I've had a man down there. There was nothing much to gain at the Abbey. However, the Red Lion turned up something. The day he left he had a guest to lunch. Waiters have long memories when they hear the rustle of a fiver. A Miss Margery Littleton. Took a bar lunch there two or three times a week. Solicitor's private secretary. Three phone calls tracked her down. Or rather her office. She left the same day as Maurice Crillon — to go and look after a sick aunt in Scotland.'

'Ah, the sick aunt — what would life, leave alone fiction, do without her? So?'

'No point in phoning a sick aunt who might not be sick and so make her sick with anxiety or curiosity. Our man went to the block of flats, rang the bell, got no answer and the caretaker kindly obliged — '

'Spare me the rest — unless it's particularly piquant.'

'Traditional. Young chap spent the night with her once or twice. She told the caretaker to keep an eye on things since she was going off for some days, and he watched her drive away in a Renault 14 — '

'Flushed and happy as a bride. And now nothing to do until she returns from her sick aunt in France. She seems a girl of some spirit.'

'I don't understand some of these girls.'

'My dear Kerslake, you sound positively upset.'

Kerslake laughed. 'Well, they take risks, don't they?'

'We all do every time we cross the road. Anyway, enough of this. You've got nothing germane.'

'No. But we've asked the French to check Renault 14 car registrations under Maurice Crillon — that'll take some time. Longer, perhaps all eternity.'

'Don't be depressed. She'll be back, dewy-eyed and full of fond memories. I really do admire the girls of today. When she does come back, perhaps you might see her yourself — and be gentle. And don't upset the apple-cart for her at the solicitor's office. Let her sweet memories remain untarnished. And remember — there's really no hurry about any of this.'

'May I ask you why not, sir?'

The now rare 'sir' amused Warboys. He said, 'If you'll excuse the cliché — there's more to this than meets the eye. I wonder if you got that feeling when you were at Avoncourt Abbey?'

'I got the impression that Sir Andrew was enjoying himself. Some private joke?'

'His life has been full of those — and

griefs. But one mustn't imagine for one moment that he is an entertaining buffoon. You know his record — open and closed. A gallant soldier, and then an ardent Gaullist with the Resistance Movement. One of our on-and-off irregulars whenever we needed him. I never censured him because during the Rommel advance pure luck dropped something into his hands which he kept from us for his own private use — vendetta, you might say — against the Sir Julian Markover types. Did you know that his son, never seen, a few weeks old, was killed in the first bombing raid by the Italians on Toulon in nineteen forty?'

'No.'

'That leaves the kind of emotional scar which never quite heals. And its memory works a strange yeast in a man's attitudes. We should never have known about the business of Markover and the others, had Markover not taken the deliberate risk of coming to us eventually.'

'Preferring official to private blackmail?'

'And thereby opening up the prospect of eventual re-establishment.'

'And Sir Andrew's private joke?'

'Ah, yes — that. Until we know better then it's a case of . . . *He only does it to annoy. Because he knows it teases.*'

'More likely *pleases* as well. You think?'

'Oh, yes — but us, too, when the day comes that we see the point of the joke. Of that I am sure.'

* * *

The end came as she knew it had to come, but she found herself — and was pleased at this, for she wished to have nothing mar her paradisiacal interregnum — without high emotion, or tearful regrets and longings. She made it that much easier for herself, too, by cosseting the simple fiction in her mind, though more banally expressed, that though man proposes, God disposes. There was no law against hope. Some day he might come back for her — the too short idyll would be renewed on a much longer tenancy and — stretching it over far — though she did not insist on this element — the wedding bells would ring. And, anyway, if it were all girlish nonsense and she wished to encourage it in herself, no one could say her nay. Though she was sensible enough to keep her dreams unexpressed to him.

They drove to Bordeaux on a Saturday, lunched on the road in a vine-arboured garden, held hands across the table, denying nothing of the romance fleeting so fast from

161

them — and perhaps, though not openly expressed — each one (for there are some situations which suspend time and suppress mercifully truth long known) giving temporary living room to the *if-onlys* and the *wouldn't-it-be-wonderfuls* which make the coarse inevitabilities of life bearable by temporary remoteness. Playing her game, Maurice, to his surprise, found himself pleasingly deceived too by the romantic handful of days passed and now and again giving house-room to thoughts which had long been strangers to him. She was so good and beautiful and bountiful it seemed a shame for the curtain to fall and no cries of *Bis! Bis!* ever able to raise it again.

They came in to Bordeaux over the Pont d'Aquitaine and the Garonne and booked in at an hotel in the Parc des Expositions overlooking the lake. She would have liked to have seen the art school in which he worked, but was easily steered from this wish.

Their last night was pure Paradise Sustained, though she wept a little, silently, after he was asleep, and — an odd thought in her drowsy drift to oblivion — wondered if she would ever tell her aunt about it all . . . not the full truth, for that was hers to cherish, but an expurgated edition, enough to reward her for making the past marvellous days possible.

He drove her out to the airport at mid-morning, leaving the barest but comfortable time to catch her plane — and this, part of his kindness, she knew — because there is no agony on earth more rending for lovers than to spend an eternity of two hours in an airport lounge, bereft of real speech, denied privacy for true embraces, waiting for the tannoy to call the boarding warning and the fall of the curtain on over-prolonged and inhibited farewells.

She was back in Salisbury by seven o'clock.

Maurice Crillon was in Cragnac by half-past three. He unloaded his car and for the first time took out the Augustus John painting of his father from its brown paper wrappings. For a while he was undecided what to do with it. There was little room on the sitting room walls for it. He took it upstairs to his bedrom and hung it on the far wall from the window where the light fell evenly on it. He had no sentimental feeling about it, only an odd conviction that from his mother — no mother, but deeply loved and respected — there had come to him his own love of secrecy, of protecting his true emotions, and the almost mystical passion he had for giving no more of his true self to anyone than absolute necessity demanded.

Straightening the picture a little, eyeing it

now with professional regard, he thought that some day, when he had the time, he might clean it. A little act of unnecessary tenderness towards Sir Andrew . . .

★　★　★

Told on the telephone the next morning — a Monday — by his man in Salisbury that Miss Littleton had returned to her flat, Kerslake, less out of tenderness for the woman's feelings than from a need first of all to consult Warboys, told him to take no action until instructed. Warboys, coming in late from a weekend fishing on the Test, was pleased to hear the news of the return, but asked, 'Why are you holding your man off?'

'Because of the other side. They're working on it too. What's the poor girl going to think if first we go in — and then Markover's people follow suit?'

Warboys smiled. 'Never did I think to have such compassion demonstrated by you. But you're right. Two visits from different people. She's going to wonder what on earth it's all about and maybe — all her passionate protective instincts roused — then neither side will probably get much from her — if there is anything useful to get. And come to that — just one visit will seem strange. People she doesn't know, or know about — pumping her about Crillon? Oh, yes — you're quite right. Well, I can fix it with Markover. He'll understand and trust us. But it's still going to be a strange somebody who walks in on her. How do you get over that?'

Kerslake smiled. 'I'm thinking of somebody she knows about and will respect, and who already has a valid connection with Crillon. I think he'd enjoy it — and do it as well as anyone. If he will do it, that is.'

'I think he will. But do we trust him? After all Sir Andrew isn't a bit interested in whether we get the painting and its contents back.'

'I'm glad you said it and not me. But it presents no difficulty. She's out all day. I'll get the flat bugged. When Sir Andrew gives us his version of their talk we can check it against the recording.'

Warboys shook his head with mock sadness. 'That I should do this to one of my best and oldest friends. Still in different circumstances he would do it to me. That's what friendship is all about — understanding. Nothing is dearer to a man than a serviceable friend. Not my words: Plautus. All right, I'll get in touch with him. Markover won't mind. His fraternity works on different lines from us.'

So it was that two days later Sir Andrew Starr saw Margery Littleton. This took place not, as had been expected by Warboys or Kerslake, in her already efficiently bugged flat, but at her place of work — a slip-up unforeseen by Kerslake and not catered for in Warboys' talk with his friend, since both had assumed he would seek a private meeting.

At eleven o'clock in the morning Miss Littleton was called into her employer's room and introduced to Sir Andrew and her employer insisted on leaving them alone as a mark of courtesy to Sir Andrew, who soon put her at her ease.

'Nothing serious, my dear. Just wanted a chat about someone we both know. Maurice Crillon. I thought you might be able to help me.'

The adrenalin charge in her beginning to ease, Margery said, 'If I can, Sir Andrew. How did you know him?

'I had him up at the Abbey — cleaning and restoring some pictures for me. Damned cheek my coming here like this. But it seemed the only way. He mentioned once that he'd made friends with a Miss Littleton who worked in a solicitor's office. So I tracked you down. Damned cheek again. But there it is . . . '

'Well, Sir Andrew . . . if I can help . . . '

166

'I'm sure you can.' He gave her a reassuring smile. 'I hear you've just got back from nursing a sick aunt in Scotland.' There was a warmth in his slight roguish half-lift of an eyebrow. 'At your age I used my aunts in the same way. Fact is one way and another I was very impressed with Maurice Crillon. Comes from good stock . . . ' he rattled on, putting her at her ease. 'But the point is that he started this cleaning work for me at the Abbey — and now he's popped off into the blue. And I want him back to finish the work — wouldn't trust anyone else. You wouldn't know where I could find him, would you, my dear?'

Suddenly the tension in her was gone and confidence in this man spread through her like a slow balm. Added to which she knew that here was a man of long experience to whom she could talk in confidence. Perhaps the only person in the world she would ever want to talk to in such a way.

Smiling, she said, 'I've got an aunt in Scotland but she's not been ill — though she agreed in case — '

'Say no more, my dear.'

'We went to France together. It was something . . . well, I never imagined I could or would ever do.'

'Good for you. Gather ye rosebuds and all

that — but no need to tell me anything more on that side. I can read it in your eyes. Also — ' he put out a sun-browned hand and touched one of hers ' — I admire your spirit. But the point is — do you know how I can get in touch with him? I could give him six months' work at the Abbey, cleaning and restoring.'

'Oh, that would be wonderful . . . but I don't really know, except that he said he worked in an art school in Bordeaux. That's where he put me on the plane. I don't even remember the names of all the places we went to.'

'Why should you — paradise isn't a place. It's something you suddenly find all around you. Well, don't worry. If he's in Bordeaux I'll find some way of getting in touch with him and — ' he was silent for a moment or two, eyeing her with a fatherly tenderness, ' — when I do I'll let you know.'

'Oh, that would be lovely, Sir Andrew.'

'And don't worry about things here. The firm handle quite a few of the Abbey affairs.' For a moment or two he wished that he could tell her Maurice's address but rejected the temptation. For himself he was only going through the motions demanded of him by Birdcage. Common sense told him that to trust her with it was too dangerous. Other people would be watching her — and he did not mean to help either Birdcage or the other damned side. In his heart of hearts, too, he guessed that Maurice would have given him no thanks. They had had their time together. Leave it at that. Memories unmarred, the red hot coals greying to ash which the winds of Time would finally and gently scatter . . .

That afternoon he telephoned Warboys and told him that he had got no joy from Margery Littleton. But since he knew it was a lie he did tell him about the possibility of a Bordeaux address . . . the more false scents the better. So far as he was concerned Maurice could run forever . . . dear boy — a chip off the old block in so many ways. Damned fine girl, nice — but a bit on the emotionally stupid side, God bless her. One day, of course, they would catch up with Maurice — the odds had to be that way. What would they do? Sneak in at night and pinch the Augustus John? And that would be that. *Finis*. And the dead would go on sleeping . . . and he one day would join them. But not too soon . . . there was a great deal more yet left to live for.

★   ★   ★

Maurice was lying on his bed in the late afternoon after working for a while on a pen-and-ink drawing he had been doing from

169

memory of Margery Littleton, naked, but transposing her into the attitude of Goya's *La maja desnuda*, raised a little against a pile of pillows and giving her face — in contrast to the original — a look of pure innocent joy. While doing it, remembering that Goya had died in Bordeaux, he had smiled to himself and had written underneath in English — Souvenir of the Hotel Aquitania, Bordeaux. Sometime perhaps he would send it to her. It was the kind of thing she would love ... Just for a moment or two he regretted that she was no longer with him ... undemanding, trusting, and loving. Thinking of her and of Salisbury and Avoncourt Abbey, he looked across at the painting of his father. He still didn't like it very much. Perhaps one day he would clean it and send it back to Sir Andrew. Perhaps ...

At this moment someone banged the heavy knocker on the front door three times loudly. He went downstairs unhurriedly and opened the door. Carla stood outside and across the road was parked Aldo's Alfa Sud.

'Maurice!' Her arms went round him and her mouth found his and without hesitation his own knew his hunger for her. Still embracing her, he drew her inside and put out a foot and shut the front door.

She laughed then, and drawing back from

him said, 'Oh, *caro* Maurice . . . always Maurice. I do nothing to compromise you, you beast. There was an old man working in the garden when I first came by. I wait until he goes for I say to myself maybe here my dear Maurice has a reputation to guard. After all it is your home. Are you not glad to see me? You want to talk first. Or we go upstairs — or maybe you have some little visitor there and I go away and come back after? Such good news that I have will keep — '

He laughed, sat her down in a chair, and holding her face in his hands, kissed her lips lingeringly and then sat down himself. He said, 'My heart when I saw you leapt for joy. But now joy must wait a little while. My head is full of questions.'

'Are you angry that I find you?'

'No. I knew you would one day. You are the one from whom final escape is not possible. This you have always known. Now from the beginning. Take your time and I will get you a glass of wine. *Mamma mia* — things must have changed with Aldo since he lends you his beloved car.'

'Many things have changed — and more will if you are sensible. Still we leave that for the moment. I will tell you everything from the beginning.'

She did, but still restless with happiness,

she reached out and held his hand now and again and the thought passed through him that not even the greatest artist in the world could ever truly and fully catch the linked moments of joy passing across a woman's face, for they defied the eyes of mortals. Maybe the gods looking down saw them fully.

When she came to Trudi, she said, 'I like her and we are at once as sisters so she tells me everything.'

'Everything?'

'About how you run away together. And then how you leave her . . . poor Fräulein Keller. She is not the type to know you for what you are. And then to use her as a letter box — oh, Maurice you are wicked.'

'Who is not?'

'Ah, but yours is true wickedness. But I understand and accept that and can deal with it. All you have to do is to come back and do a little more work for Aldo . . . poor Aldo — it would be a kindness for he is very worried for his obligations to the Mafiosi. And think — a few months and then I get the rest of my money and we are married. It is true — Aldo has promised. Before I leave I make him swear it with his hand touching the robe of the Blessed Virgin in the dining room. And after we are married but not too soon . . . well, I shall be very understanding.'

'We are not married yet. I have to think about this.'

Carla stood up. 'Oh, no. You have had long enough time for thought. Now, you have to say *Yes* and swear it.'

'At this moment. This very moment?'

'You need time? You do not know in your heart already? You think I have changed since you left? I have thought much about this. Now I, Carla, take charge. Everything is *Yes* or *No* and black or white.'

He grinned suddenly, and said, '*Cara mia*, you have changed. You are a different woman. How am I to know that I shall love this different woman?'

She smiled and shook her head. 'Always you joke. No matter — I show you that I am still Carla. But different. You would like that?'

'As a man dying of thirst in the desert yearns for water.' He reached for her hand and they went upstairs.

Later, lying together on the bed, she reached out a hand and took his Goya-type drawing from the bedside table. She studied it for a while and then said, 'Who was she?'

He shrugged his shoulders. 'Someone I met in England. And parted from in Bordeaux.'

'*Bene* — for that I care nothing. But from now on you will keep your little mementoes somewhere discreetly.'

'Don't worry. There will be none. You have changed me. And now we get dressed and go and find a hotel for you — '

' — but I already have a hotel. I have been here some days waiting for you, praying for you to come.'

'That is good, then, You cannot stay here. Not now that we are going to be respectable. What will the villagers say? And monsieur le curé? And the gardener? Gaston will leave and my dear mother's garden will become a wilderness — '

'*Basta* — you are right. A hotel still, *caro mio*.' She sighed happily, stretched her arms so that her breasts rose proud and firm, and then said, looking at the painting of Sir Andrew Starr, 'What is that? Not something you have done?'

'No. Not mine.'

'That I can tell with one eye. Who is it?'

'Some young Englishman. I picked it up in Bordeaux. It needs cleaning. One sees that from here.'

'Then you should do it before you sell it. You will get more money. Now that we are going to be married I shall be very careful with money so that one day we shall have a villa on Capri. Ah, there is so much to come.'

'At the moment the next thing is back to your hotel for you.'

'Good. You begin to have the sense of things. In your own village we must be properly behaved. In Florence, well . . . we can stay the same since everyone knows.' She raised herself on one elbow, looked down into his face, and said firmly, 'You are sincere, *caro mio*? About all this?'

He nodded gently.

'Say it with your mouth, not your head.'

'I am sincere. I say it.'

She laughed then and said, 'You would say anything to suit yourself with others. But between us, remember — always the truth.'

'Even if it is bad?'

'Even. Now I get dressed and go respectably to my hotel. It is good to get accustomed to that sort of thing. With me you will become somebody. I shall see to it.'

Smiling, loving her, but knowing she had no power over him at all — only at this moment a desire to please her — he said, 'Yes, we must get accustomed to a lot of different things. But I do not need to become somebody. I am somebody already — and I like what I am.'

Later, on his return from taking Carla to a hotel in nearby Cragnac, Maurice was just in time to catch monsieur le curé who had called to see him.

They went inside together and, when the

priest had been settled with a glass of wine, he said, 'Well, my son?'

Maurice smiled. 'I have been to England and seen my father and my mother. They are nice people, my father nearly seventy and my mother a little younger. I could have claimed what was mine and they would have accepted it. But I could see that it would never have given them real happiness — nor me. So I told them that I wished to remain Maurice Crillon.'

'It was a good and wise thing to do. And now?'

'Oh, I shall leave Gaston to look after things here. From time to time I shall come back. But I must go back, too — to my work.'

'And where is that?'

Maurice shrugged his shoulders. 'Wherever I find it. But you can always get me through the Swiss address. I have told Gaston that you will let him have it if he needs it.'

The curé allowed his right eyebrow to rise a little and said, 'And anyone else who needs you? Am I to tell them?'

Maurice hesitated briefly, and then said, 'Yes, of course.'

The curé said quietly, 'Tell me, my son — why do you like to stand so far apart from people? Is it because you have a troubled conscience?'

Maurice shook his head. 'No. It is a matter of my nature which I could not explain to you because I do not understand it myself.'

'Perhaps I do — not the underlying reason, but the practical one. No animal — to which I do not liken you, of course — is so stupid as to approach its hole, or earth or burrow always by the same route.'

Maurice laughed. 'We live in a dangerous world.'

Monsieur Bonivard rose to go and said, 'We live, my son, in God's world and that is not always easily understood by us. We can only have faith and trust in His purposes and His wisdom and try to resist temptation. If we try honestly and fail and then try again and again He is never unaware of our efforts.'

He raised his hand and blessed him.

6

Kerslake knew that the man was upset at not being able to talk to Warboys personally. When he wanted something he was accustomed to go right to the top without let or hindrance.

Kerslake said, 'I'm sorry, Sir Julian, but he left yesterday by air for America. A conference in Washington. He won't be back for four or five days. Perhaps I can help you?'

Sir Julian sat on the other side of the desk, black-haired, black-suited, his hands clasped on top of a heavy walking stick, gold-banded but, thought Kerslake, hiding no rapier to be drawn quickly for defence or attack. If such were ever needed others would do his work.

Grudgingly Sir Julian said, 'Well, I suppose so. You're fully briefed about this Crillon business?'

'Yes, of course.'

'Well, so be it. Take a look at these.'

He drew a small, rubber-banded package from his jacket pocket and dropped it in front of Kerslake.

Kerslake slipped the rubber band free and spread the six photographs before him on the table, neatly as though laying out a hand of cards. He took his time and a little more over each — knowing he would be touching the raw of the man's impatience. He was professionally interested in and emotionally disdainful of all that this man represented and would have represented if the German Panzer divisions had come rolling up the beaches of Southern England all those years ago, and was thinking, too, of the Dunkirk beaches where he had lost an uncle in the Navy — destroyers — and where his father had the fingers of his right hand blown away so that his life work as a sign-painter and decorator had come to an end. Turning each photograph and reading the details on the back, he knew where they had come from . . . In fact he, himself, still waited to receive a similar pack for Birdcage. It was no surprise to him that Sir Julian had more influence with some of the French authorities than Birdcage. His *pourboire* sweeteners in the right places were ethically denied to Birdcage. Finishing with them, he said, 'Six Maurice Crillons. All the right age group and all artists, art masters or connected with the art world.'

'They are. One of them could be the man I want.'

'We both want, Sir Julian.'

179

'Don't trifle. The man could be among them.'

'He could — and even if you checked them all in France you wouldn't know which was the right one unless you could establish that he has or has had the portrait of Sir Andrew.' Enjoying himself behind a slow bleakness of dislike for the man, Kerslake went on. 'Even if they were laid out in front of Sir Andrew you know he would give no help. His position has been defined. For him the game is over. But not for us. Do you have any suggestions?'

'I understand from Warboys that this Crillon picked up a local Salisbury girl and took her to France.'

'So he did. But, I gather that she is a very sentimental, romantic type. She'd do the same thing — but for a different reason than Sir Andrew. She'd just say the man she knew was none of these? Or am I wrong?'

'No. I think you're right. I want this thing cleared up quickly.'

'I'm sure you do — and so do we, believe me.' In the meantime, Kerslake thought, face unmoved but the imp of joy teasing his spirit, there was a great deal of pleasure to be had from Sir Julian's concern. He saw his father with one of his beloved pigeons sitting on his stub of a hand. But despite that he knew that nothing could alter his commitment to

Birdcage. He went on, 'If the man we want is amongst these I can have him identified for you quite quickly.'

'How?'

'If I asked you, Sir Julian, how you can get these photographs more quickly from the French than we can . . . I expect we'll get them in a week's time . . . would you tell me?'

'Of course not.'

'Then you must trust me. If one of these is the Crillon we want then I can isolate him. Let us say, through channels which are not open to you.'

'I don't care a damn how you do it as long as you let me know — and as soon as possible.'

'If he's one of them — you shall know. We want this business closed up as much as you do, Sir Julian.' He gave the man one of his rare official smiles, and added, 'It will take two or three days. Of course, I shall want to keep these.' He swept together the photos laid out neatly like a disclosed hand of cards before him, tapped and tidied them into order, and put the rubber band round them.

Sir Julian stood up and, resting both hands on the top of his stick, stooped forward a little, black-garbed, vulture-poised, the menace and drive of the man momentarily — and deliberately — exposed, and then the illusion

181

suddenly destroyed by a warm, friendly, yet slightly mocking smile as he said, 'I could find a place for you, Mr Kerslake, in my organization if ever you felt that Her Majesty really was most grossly under-paying her servants.'

Kerslake laughed. 'I'll bear it in mind. Thank you, Sir Julian. I'll be in touch with you about these.' He tapped the neatly stacked pile of photographs before him.

★ ★ ★

It was done quite simply and officially. Kerslake flew down and had a meeting with the Chief Constable of Wiltshire. On the way back he was minded to call on Sir Andrew Starr, but resisted the temptation. For some time now an odd feeling had been growing in him, from an almost unregarded source ... as from a wet patch in high meadow, masking the true source of the stripling river miles distant, a winter-bourne that only once in every four years ran true from its mother spring. Put finally into words, as though he needed the direct stimulation, it came vaguely to him as he directed the helicopter pilot to take a flight line above the upper Avon on the way back and for a few moments distantly glimpsed Avoncourt Abbey and its gardens. From the flagstaff on the western side of the

Abbey roof the fresh breeze was streaming out the Union Jack that flew from its tall white flag-pole. For a moment or two he wondered why, for what saint's day, what celebration? And then it came to him. Today was the third of June — the last day of the distant evacuation from Dunkirk. No matter what the rest of the world might think — no matter the strict military interpretation — for this country it had been the beginning of victory. Sir Andrew had had a long run for his money — until now, in fact, the money meant very little to him. Why, then, at the moment when Birdcage was insisting that he should quit and he had agreed, had it happened that this Frenchman should so conveniently have come along, gained his confidence and friendship, and then so conveniently again have left taking with him the Augustus John — and from his bedroom? Surely, the worst type of Frenchman — or any other man for that — would never have repaid kindness with such an odd choice of gift taking? At the moment he didn't know why. But it would bear thinking about. Something was wrong somewhere. With a free choice of all the other and mostly far more valuable paintings — why the Augustus John? Damned odd. Well, maybe something would turn up to throw more light on that.

That evening a plain-clothes detective of the Wiltshire Constabulary visited the Red Lion in Salisbury, had a word with the manager, and then had a few moments in turn with the reception clerk, the head waiter and the permanent bar keeper. Each when the photographs were laid out and asked which resembled the Monsieur Crillon who had recently stayed at the hotel picked out the same photograph — on the back of which was written — Maurice Crillon, Rue des Glycines, Cragnac, Dordogne. This information, together with the photographs, was sent back the next day by special messenger to Kerslake. On that day, which was her half-day, Margery Littleton went into the Red Lion for a bar lunch and it was not long before the snack bar waitress gave her the news that the police were making enquiries about the Maurice Crillon who had stayed there. She went back to her flat and sat in some agony of mind and confusion until she remembered the kindness of Sir Andrew Starr and his warm understanding of her attachment to Maurice. After half an hour of indecision she made up her mind and found the courage to telephone Sir Andrew.

He was kindness itself, put her at her ease, and finally smoothed away her anxieties.

'There's absolutely nothing to worry about,

my dear. I should think your Maurice committed some motoring offence over here. Or was wanted as a witness to one and they just had his name and car number and the hotel address. Something like that.'

As he spoke he knew that a moment or two of real thought on her part would shred to pieces the logic of all this . . . but, dear creature, she was in no state to apply logic when her romantic head held only anxious and sentimental thoughts about her beloved Maurice. To calm her completely, he said, 'The Chief Constable is a near friend of mine. I'll give him a ring and find out for you. But don't worry — I'm sure it's some minor thing.'

Half an hour later he called her back and eased her fears completely, though he had not in fact rung the Chief Constable.

He said, 'It was nothing, my dear girl. As I thought — he witnessed an accident and gave his name and address at the hotel — very properly too. I told them that he'd gone back to France — and that he lived in Bordeaux. I gathered, this being so, they wouldn't bother him to be a witness, since there were others. Don't give it another thought, my dear girl. Nothing to worry about.' He paused, waiting for her to ask the one question which would knock his story to bits, but the question . . . dear, love-hazed child, bless her heart . . . never came. To ease her mind further, spurred by a genuine emotion, after all she was in love with his son, he said, 'Matter of fact, my dear, I was thinking of giving you a ring. Wondered if you would like to come up and have tea with me sometime . . . see the pictures privately.'

'Oh, I'd love that, Sir Andrew.'

'Good — we'll arrange it soon.'

Alone — Margery Littleton's anxieties calmed — for good, he hoped — he took the dogs for a walk and considered his own situation. Birdcage and Sir Julian Markover were both working in their separate ways — but with a common end, at least so far as could be conjectured at this moment. You never damned well knew with Warboys. But with Sir Julian there was no doubt. He wanted the promised documents in the back of the Augustus John so that he could destroy them and have final peace of mind and all possible threat of some future tribute being levied on him and his kind denied. Dear . . . dear . . . Maurice had stirred up a hornet's nest by taking the Augustus John. However, the real point was that he must be relieved of the documents . . . Composition of the Provisional Government of the United Kingdom . . . Swastika stamped . . . Der bloody Führer signed and all the bloody traitorous names appended, with Sir Julian Markover's heading them. And, on them still, the bloody finger prints of the man he had killed to get them, scrabbling at them in his death agony, the two of them alone in the big apartment high above the Boulevard Haussmann. Dear, dear, so long ago and far away. And now here was the whole thing breaking into life again simply because that dear boy of his had made a sentimental choice of pictures. Well, he himself would have to do what he could to clear up the mess.

That evening he made an international telephone enquiry for the number of Maurice Crillon at Cragnac. He was told that no number was listed. A further enquiry got him the number of Monsieur Bonivard, *le curé*. What secrets the Church had known in its time. His call was answered by a housekeeper. He was told that the *curé* was away at a conference and would not be back for three or four days at least. Sir Andrew gave up — a move he found which with age came easily to him. God's will would prevail.

That evening, too — after receiving confirmation of identification from the police — Kerslake telephoned Sir Julian Markover and told him that the Maurice Crillon he wanted lived in the Rue des Glycines,

Cragnac, in the Dordogne. Their civilities were brief.

The next morning Maurice and Carla left Cragnac in the early morning to return to Florence in their separate cars, Carla leading. After some while Carla realized that Maurice had lost touch with her. Unworried, she kept on driving. Maurice was firmly hers now. She had no fears that he would desert her. In Florence late that evening she went to Maurice's apartment. They had agreed they would spend the night there. An hour after her arrival Maurice telephoned her.

He said, 'Cara mia — I am so sorry but I have had trouble with the car. I'm stranded in this little hole until the garage gets it fixed. I'm afraid I've got to stay the night here.'

At once she was suspicious. She said, 'And where is it you are?'

He gave her the name of the place which was on their route, though she only had a vague recollection of it. She said, 'Have you got a place to stay yet?'

'No — but I will find somewhere. I will be with you tomorrow, cara — and a new life begins.'

She was silent for a moment or two and then said, 'Maurice — you are not beginning to play games again, are you?'

'Why should I? It is not my fault that the

car breaks down. I shall be with you tomorrow. My heart is broken that I am not with you now.'

'Good. That I will believe because I love and trust you . . . with all my heart. But my head is a different matter. That is always logical. So, *caro mio*, you will give me the number you call from, and then wait for me to make a call back to you.'

Maurice laughed. 'All right.' He gave her the number. She rang off, waited a few moments and then called back. Maurice answered her. 'So you see — I tell you the truth. That is how it shall always be between us now. Tomorrow I shall be with you and then we go to Aldo together. Is the Zais still there?'

'Yes.'

'Good. Then I can finish it for him. Sleep well, *cara*, and dream of me.' He rang off.

Carla walked to the window and stood looking out over the river and the lights of Florence, remembering how he had insisted that she should go ahead of him on the road back so that if she broke down he would be following up to help her. A lover's fond concern . . . ? How could one know with Maurice? But if one could not know it was not right to think the worst.

Two mornings later, when Gaston came to

work in the garden of the Crillon cottage, he found that the side entrance door to the house had been forced open. He went inside and looked around the rooms. There were the remains of a meal which someone had eaten in the kitchen, together with an almost empty wine bottle. But everything else was in place downstairs and upstairs so far as he could see for he knew the place well from often having cleaned it when Maurice's mother, ailing fast, had been alive. It was no fault of his that he did not realize that the painting of Sir Andrew Starr in Maurice's bedroom had been taken, for he had never known of its existence. He reported the break-in to the gendarmerie and also to Monsieur Bonivard when he met him later that day. The priest told him that he would let Maurice know of the break-in. Which he did when he returned to his house, sending the letter to the Swiss address.

★   ★   ★

Alone in the study of his apartment overlooking the Avenue Foch, Sir Julian Markover — who had flown over from England that morning in his private helicopter — laid the large, brown-paper-wrapped parcel on the low window table, slipped a

190

penknife from a pocket of his double-breasted black waistcoat and cut the cords holding the paper in place.

Freed from its wrappings — no hurry in him now, the prospect of permanent ease from old and lingering guilt imminent — he propped the painting up on the arms of a Louis Quinze chair and studied the youthful features of the man who had held so much power over him for so long. And this a rare circumstance for him, he who had long known power and its pleasures and not the least of the pleasures the moments when some arrogant opponent faced with the moment of truth suddenly became a beggar, suppliant and willing to do his bidding. But this man — youth here with the future to come — had never been his. The tables had been turned by events and for years and years he had been a victim — justly or not made no difference. The pain of a wound received honourably or dishonourably remained the same.

Without hurry he cut free the top layer of thick backing paper and then eased away two neatly folded layers of newspapers and then a final layer of thick porous cardboard so that the back of the canvas on its stretcher was exposed. For a moment or two his disappointment was frozen. He walked to the window and watched the traffic moving down the avenue, marked the flight of a handful of pigeons circling and then coming to rest on the roof of a building opposite, and then the movement of a high-heeled girl tapping her way up towards the Arc de Triomphe, one hand swinging in that of the young man who walked with her, and then slowly felt the bite of his face muscles tautening as anger and bitter disappointment possessed him.

He turned and went back to the picture and picked up one of the newspapers which had backed it. It was a month-old copy of *Le Monde*. Below it were some spread-out pages from *Paris Match* of a more recent date.

The following morning he was with Warboys at the Birdcage Walk office. The canvas had been propped on a chair in the window, the sheets of backing material spread on a nearby table.

Warboys, straightening from looking at the painting and then picking up the loose pages of *Paris Match*, said, 'The painting has also been cleaned quite recently.'

'By this damned Crillon fellow?'

'Who else?'

'Why should he bother to do that?'

'God knows — perhaps he was bored and had time on his hands. I don't suppose Sir Andrew had ever had it cleaned since it first came into the family.' He paused and shrugged his shoulders, enjoying himself but giving no sign of his pleasure at Sir Julian's discomfiture. 'What do you propose that we can do for you? Crillon could have burnt the old back packing and the documents on the fire or shoved it in a dustbin.'

Angrily, Sir Julian said, 'You're enjoying this, aren't you?'

'Hardly. But I must admit that there's a certain irony about it which I find piquant.'

'Does this Crillon understand German?'

'I've no idea. I could give Sir Andrew Starr a ring and see if he knows. You won't mind my telling him what has happened?'

'Tell him what you like. In the meantime — '

'You will be looking for Crillon?'

'And I shall find him.'

'And then?'

'How can I say? If he has no German and says he has burnt the old backing . . . well that might be an end to the matter.'

'And if he knows German — and says he has burnt the documents?'

Sir Julian was silent for a moment. Then hunching his shoulders, he said, 'You expect me, after all these years, to change my nature? What Sir Andrew and you have known for years is one thing. Ironically, we trust one another. But this unknown Frenchman . . . No. For years I have waited for true peace of mind. So, I shall have to — '

Warboys interrupted him. ' — I think it better if you don't spell it out to me.'

Sir Julian laughed dryly. 'Don't play act with me. If this were all the other way round, I know exactly what Birdcage would do. Make sure the only way one can make sure.'

'Do you want me to approach Sir Andrew?'

'You do whatever you like. The thing now is out of your hands. I shall find Crillon — and unless I'm absolutely convinced that he knows nothing . . . well, then.' He paused for a moment, looking down at the painting, and rubbing a well-manicured hand over his chin, said pensively, 'Why do I get the feeling that Sir Andrew is hiding something from us both? Why do I find it a little disturbing that he suddenly takes a fancy to this Crillon, gives him work when he appears out of the blue and then makes a present of a picture to him? He's an odd bird, near eccentric, I know . . . but something smells wrong. Have you considered that?'

'Frequently. But as we all get older I think we all get a little odd — or odder. However, I'm not prepared to advise you either way. So far as we are concerned the whole matter is now out of our hands.'

'You mean you're withdrawing — completely?'

'Possibly. Your documents are either destroyed or kicking around somewhere disregarded — or regarded by this Crillon. Of course — if you wanted us to join in the hunt we would — for old times' sake.' Warboys smiled broadly, enjoying himself.

'What you do — or don't do — is of no significance to me now.'

'Well, that's refreshing. It's not often we can close a file here and write — *Finis* — on it. *Post tot naufragia portum.*'

Sir Julian was silent briefly, and then shook his head, sighed, and said bitterly, 'You people, and Sir Andrew, have harried and bedevilled the best years of my life. But if a list of sins and evils were made — then yours officially would far, far outweigh mine.'

'Take comfort from that then.'

'I will — and do.' Then indicating the Augustus John, he went on, 'I've no further use for that. Perhaps Sir Andrew would like it back.'

When Sir Julian had gone, Warboys called Kerslake to his room and explained what had happened and finished, 'Perhaps you will call Sir Andrew and ask him if he would like the picture back? Tell him exactly what has happened and then I think it would be a good idea if you arranged for a little surveillance of his mail. I'll get the necessary authority for you. The post-van always collects his outgoing mail when it delivers in the morning. A small concession and convenience owed to a former sheriff of the county.' He paused for a little while, regarding Kerslake with distant eyes, though fragmentarily wondering what it was about the clothes which the no-doubt future head of the organization wore that always betrayed some touch of provincialism . . . sometimes a clearly made-up bow tie, sometimes a shirt, beautifully laundered, but which had never come out of the Asher and Turnbull stable and sometimes nothing but a general impression of being 'not quite' as his old friend Quint would have put it. He went on, 'I presume you are with me?'

Kerslake said, 'I think so. He has a regard of some kind for Crillon and relishes the irony of his taking that particular painting. Clearly Crillon must have taken the documents out to do the cleaning and has either destroyed them or — if he knows German — has read them and may have kept them. Sir Andrew might well decide to write and give him some kind of warning — possibly obliquely — of the position he is now in. But — '

'Ah, yes. The intriguing *but*.'

'According to him — he does not know Crillon's address.'

'And what do you think?'

'I think maybe he does.'

'Then why keep such an innocuous secret from us? There is no touch of the 'willing to wound but afraid to strike' in Sir Julian's philosophy. Maurice Crillon, one way or the other, unless the gods take his side, is probably not destined to grow old and retire to Provençal bliss with his easel set up under a vinecovered courtyard while his mistress, now fat and comfortable, sings in the kitchen as she prepares the vegetables for the potage.'

Kerslake smiled. 'Perhaps we should ask Sir Andrew that question directly. No? Unwise?'

'Let's try his mail first.'

'Let's hope that in his old age he has forgotten — if he has anything to hide — some of the simple rules of security.'

'You hope for too much. Some habits acquired young are only cured by death. Somewhere in all this, you know, there is a factor which is escaping us. Happily it is a common occurrence in our work so that we have long lost the habit of being surprised. I'll bet you that no letter to Crillon turns up in his out-going mail. Yes?'

Kerslake smiled and shook his head. 'No.'

Later, when Kerslake telephoned Sir Andrew at the Abbey and told him about the cleaning of the painting and the new backing which had been put to it, Sir Andrew was pleasantly indifferent.

'Well, there's a dear chap. Can't think why he bothered though — unless he's going to sell it and turn a bob or two. As for the original backing and the stuff Sir Julian wants I don't care an onion-eater's fart. I've no concern with all that now.'

'Sir Julian is going after Crillon, Sir Andrew. Would you like me to give you Crillon's address? A word of warning from you might be appreciated.'

'No. I don't want his address. If you want to warn him that's your business. You get in touch with him. That bastard Sir Julian must have his address since he got the painting. I want no more to do with the whole affair. The last thing I want at my age is to be drawn into any Birdcage business. I worked my passage years ago and, to mix the metaphors, I'm too old a horse to be led out of the green pastures of retirement to be put between the shafts of anybody's cart. The day will come when you will feel exactly as I do now.'

But immediately after speaking to Kerslake, Sir Andrew went to his study and wrote a letter to Crillon in which he explained in general terms the importance of the document which had been in the back of the picture and asking him to send them back to him at once or — if he had destroyed it with the rest of the back packing — to write to him immediately and confirm this. He posted the letter himself in Salisbury that evening on his way to a choral recital in the Cathedral. He had lived and worked too long with his dear friend Warboys not to know the way his mind worked. He was not over-worried about Maurice Crillon, for in the course of their acquaintance he had learnt that the man had no German. He had probably burnt the document with the rest of the old back packing. Nevertheless there remained an itch in his mind which he knew would take some days to pass.

★   ★   ★

It was true that Maurice Crillon had no German. In the restoring of his father's portrait he had found the document hidden there. For a while he was undecided what he should do with it, discounting almost immediately the obvious course of sending it to Sir Andrew. Things hidden must always have some importance. It was not in his character to subdue his curiosity — or the thought that, perhaps, somewhere there might be gain for him in knowing what its exact nature was. So, on his way back to Florence he had decided to make a detour to visit Trudi Keller in Switzerland — after making the appropriate excuses over the telephone to Carla.

He had spent the night with Trudi — always eventually ready to succumb to his desires — at a lakeside hotel, given her the document and asked her to make a translation of it into French — which she knew well — and to send the translation and original on to him at Florence.

Shortly after this a man called on Trudi one evening at her lodgings and asked her if she could let him know where he could find Monsieur Crillon. He had enquired for him at his home in Cragnac, been referred to the local cure, and had been given her address. Before she could ask him why he wanted Monsieur Crillon he told her that he had heard of his skill as an expert restorer of paintings and wished him to do some work for a client of his. Maurice had once said firmly that only letters were to be forwarded to Florence. If personal enquiries were made he could be contacted by letter addressed to him *poste restante* at Bologna. Only twice over the years had she had to do this, then writing to Maurice telling him and never knowing whether he ever did anything about collecting letters from Bologna.

When she told the man this he said, 'He seems a very elusive type, Fräulein Keller. This could be a very profitable job for him. My client is very generous.'

Trudi shrugged her shoulders. She did not like the man or the way he looked at her, and, moreover, she felt a sudden irritation at herself for still being Maurice's pawn. It was all right when he came to see her personally ... all feeling except her love for him shredded away in the joy of his presence. She was a fool to be so biddable to him. But there was nothing she could do about it, since she still nursed the slim hope that one day he would return to her so that things could be as they were when they had first fallen in love.

She said, 'I can tell you no more.'

The man was silent for a moment or two and then reached out and briefly touched one of her hands. saying, 'He seems a very odd sort of man. Why do you do this for him?'

She had had this question before, and she gave the same answer as she had given in the past. 'That is my business. Not yours.'

To her surprise the man suddenly smiled and said, the quality of his voice quite different, even having, she thought, a touch of long-borne weariness in it. 'I'm sorry. But I think I understand. In some ways it is the same with me. I am paid to do as my clients wish and, more often than not, I do not understand what lies behind their wishes. Though in this case, I assure you, it is a simple matter of restoring a painting. However — ' he stood up ' — thank you for your help.'

When he had gone Trudi took from her bureau the document in German which Maurice Crillon had left with her and went on with the translation which he had asked her to do. She was completely uninterested in what she was doing, and only minimally curious as to why Maurice required it. But then with Maurice nothing was obvious — often puzzling, yes. Sometimes she even felt that he was a little touched in the head and all this business of using her as a post-box sprang from some elaborate fancy he had created in his mind . . . a fancy which she dimly apprehended. He was a man who hated to leave footprints behind him. God knew why. Walking on sand without leaving a mark. This document was donkey's years old. Something about the war which had all happened before she was born. Perhaps she was a fool still to be his creature. The man who had just gone was personable and towards the end he had shown a touch of warmth and kindness.

And there had been other men from whom she had kept herself . . . for what? An adventurer, possibly a scoundrel, here today and gone tomorrow, using her, baffling her with his little quirks of secrecy? Maybe it was time she learned sense and found a new self-respect and broke free from him. A half resolve leaped into her mind then: she would do this translating for him and when she sent it would tell him that she could be his creature no more and, when he came to charm her back, would deny him, stone-hearted and cold-faced . . . Suddenly tears came into her eyes and a few dropped on to her translation, blurring some of the words . . . *et les soussignés, ayant accepté les conditions stipulées ci-dessus, sont nommés par la présente Ministres du Gouvernement Allemand d'Occupation en Grande — Bretagne* . . .

She let her pen drop and said aloud suddenly, 'I must. I must. I will . . . '

★   ★   ★

Signor Mario Andretti was — though without showing it — resentful. He was old and old-fashioned in his private life, and he had known power too long to welcome being summoned, no matter how politely, to a meeting with Sir Julian Markover in Paris. To him the man was a *parvenu*. The Andretti family could trace their ancestry back to the Sicily of the *latifundia*. An Andretti had died fighting against Napoleon's invasion of Italy. *Omertá* to him was an almost sacred word — never to apply for justice to the legally constituted authorities. Though in this day and age, he agreed, it was easier to work sometimes through the courts of justice. His own father, in 1927, at Termini Imerese, had been given a life sentence by the Fascist régime and had died in jail. From the age of thirteen he had become a man. Now, almost seventy, he was old-fashioned, intolerant, gently devious, and privately contemptuous of the Johnny-come-latelys like Sir Julian Markover. The old order had changed, was still changing, and many of the changes he spat upon. However . . . he kept most of his old-fashioned thoughts private. Sir Julian was not and never could be a member of the Mafia. Now and again, however, they helped one another. Even so, he would never have come to France at Sir Julian's bidding. It had just so happened that he had been taking the waters at Vichy while one of his mistresses was shopping in Paris.

Sir Julian, who knew the man too well not to know his thinking, said, 'I would, of course, have come to you in Italy but hearing you were at Vichy . . . '

Signor Andretti waved a large, veined hand and said, '*Far niente*. What can I do for you?'

'I want to find a man.'

Signor Andretti laughed. 'Well, that makes a change. And what man — and why?'

'The name and such details of him that I know I can tell you. But the reason . . . well, it is very, very personal.'

'You have to be so vague?'

'The man almost certainly has some papers of mine of the highest importance. I want them back, and for this I must find him.'

'And when you have them — what about the man?'

'It will depend.'

'On what?'

'Whether he has read them or not.'

'So you ask him — and he lies. How will you know truth from falsehood?'

Sir Julian said, 'How would you know if it were your situation?'

'The days of the rack and the thumbscrew are over. And men still in this age go to their death sometimes without speaking. It is the last gift they can take from life — leaving one not knowing whether one's secret has not already been shared with others.'

'I do not care whether he has spoken or

not. So long as I get my papers back I shall be content.'

Signor Andretti shook his head. 'It must be a strange sort of secret that a man could talk about to the world, and no one would pay attention.'

'If a man calls you a thief — he must have proof for the charge to hold.'

'But the damage could be done. However, this is your affair. And what happens if we find this man for you and he says he no longer has your papers — maybe has not but maybe has?'

'Is it so hard to bring a man to the point of truth?'

'Some no. But a great many, yes. Among them have been many an Andretti. To live is beautiful; to die a martyr is more. I think the heavenly Father, no matter the moral sentence passed, has a certain sad respect for them. Is there any man who comes to the judgment seat without sin? However, you clearly are in no mood for a theological argument. Give me the facts you have about this man.'

He pulled from his breast pocket a crocodile-skin bound notebook and drew from its spine a silver pencil. As Sir Julian gave him the details he wrote them down with an unhurried, meticulous hand. When he had them all, he said, 'So, he covers his movements behind this woman in Switzerland, and a *poste restante* address in Italy. She probably knows more but it would be stupid to put pressure on her. Women, you know, are the most difficult creatures to deal with in this sort of affair. Their loyalty comes from a different source than man's. Many more have gone to martyrdom, I fancy, than men — holy or otherwise. But if he is an artist and picture restorer in Italy and lives under the name of Crillon, I can promise you that it should not be difficult to trace him. We shall try this first.'

'I shall be very grateful.'

'And when we have found him? You wish more?'

'You would do more?'

'Have we not in the past? You for us — and we for you. You have but to say.'

'It depends. To begin with I want only to know where I can find him.'

Signor Andretti rose to his feet. 'I ask no more. We will help you in whatever way you wish.'

★　★　★

Changing from casual into formal clothes — Carla had insisted on this — to go to a family dinner with Aldo and his wife and children, Maurice Crillon was uneasy. Ever since he had returned to Florence and taken up his work for Aldo again — the Zais was finished and gone, but fresh commissions had already come in — Carla had changed. The simple fact that they were soon to announce their formal engagement had brought out an unsuspected regard for propriety in her. She came still to clean the apartment and to look after him, and most days they made love in the afternoon. But she now refused to spend the night with him as before she had frequently done. She had, she said, her reputation to consider, and anyway — they had the afternoons — what did the nights matter? It was good that now he was working again he should get his sleep at night and be fresh for the coming day. She had also become a little critical about his dress when she went out with him. He was to become her husband, and she wanted her friends to be impressed by him — despite the fact that all her friends knew what had been going on between them for so long.

At first he had been tempted to rebel and carry on as before, coming close to saying that if it was not respectable to sleep with him some nights, it was no more respectable to sleep with him in the afternoon . . . but the temptation had not lasted. And now he was unworried, accepting her new régime, because — and how often had it happened in his life before? — he knew that the time had come for him to pass on to some new venue. To reinforce this feeling, he had recently met a dealer who did business with Aldo occasionally, a Spaniard, who had privately said that if he ever wanted a change from Italy he could give him all the work he wished in Spain . . .

'My dear Maurice, there are old families and jumped-up industrialists who own the most marvellous stuff but would never know the difference. Their eyes are full of dust. The only things they look at and understand clearly are either their overloaded family trees or their bank balances. Here, in France and Italy and Germany, you know, even the parvenus are beginning to see with true eyes and the old families are turning schloss and château into hotels and selling their stuff to finance them. Aldo is working a gold mine which is almost finished . . . Any time, just give me a call. Think — when have you had anything as good as an El Greco or a Goya to do?'

Maurice was not deceived by the statement. There was plenty left for Aldo and for others after him — but the prospect of change was enticing and would bear thinking about. There was only one true doubt in his mind. Cleaning and restoring he liked doing. It was a service he did gladly — but now not so much for Aldo and the money (after all he had money now, safely lodged in Switzerland). He did not want to go to Spain or anywhere else just to carry on doing the same thing. He wanted to be on his own and turn out Crillons. It was a bit late in his life, he acknowledged, to become ambitious, but not so late that it could not be done. And to his surprise Carla recently had said to him, 'You know, *caro*, I do not wish to be married for too long to a man who one day may be picked up by some *agente di polizia* to be questioned about art forgeries, and lose you. Aldo and his kind . . . oh, when the weather is fair they smile. But you are not of them. They would sacrifice you, and Aldo would weep real tears for you for a week and then forget you. Always they work like that — with someone in front. No, the time is soon to come when we must be respectable, and I shall have all my money so that we can afford it. You owe it now to me and the children we shall have to become an honest man. Though, mind you — there is no rush. We bring Aldo round to it softly, softly . . . '

Sitting at dinner that evening — with Aldo

at the head of the table, himself at the far end with Carla on his right, and Aldo's wife, mid-table, schooling the children, and pleasantly bullying the maid and shouting orders and comments through to the cook in the kitchen — Maurice, although enjoying himself, for it was not in his nature to let worries over-trouble him, saw the future ahead and wondered a little how he had come to be careless enough to let himself be drawn so firmly into the life of the family. Nevertheless he showed no signs of his rising unease. The *minestrone* came, and the *spaghetti bolognese* . . . dish after dish . . . lobster with a shrimp sauce . . . roasted song birds . . . an enormous *pasticcio di carne di vitello* . . . and the wine flowed, Orvieto, Chianti, and Asti Spumante. Laughter and banter filled the room, and Crillon began to feel that he was a drowning man slowly being sucked towards the whirlpool centre of the family, to be swallowed up for ever in its vortex . . .

Afterwards, when the children had gone to bed and Carla and her sister-in-law had retired to the sitting room together, Aldo and Maurice remained at the table with their brandy and coffee.

Aldo, beaming and flushed behind his balloon glass and a big cigar, was full of bonhomie. He said, 'After the wedding and you are one of the family, we talk real business. I have seen a place just off the Piazza della Vittoria which we can buy cheaply — so we go in together, half my money and half yours and Carla's and we open it . . . *Mamma mia,* not trash stuff for the tourist trade. But good paintings, and no funny business. No, no, that we keep to one side still — and just now and again you do something good like the Zais.' He laughed, double-chins shaking, his face wreathed in a roguish grin. 'I no tell you yet how pleased they are when I take the Zais back? *Il Conte* is so happy. He says, 'But it has come back to life. It blossoms again. I see it now as must my great-great-great-grandfather.' Maybe I do not get the number of great-grandfathers right, but of his joy there is no doubt. Mind you I would not try to cheat him over a horse or at cards. Those he knows. He pays well — and soon we shall have our settlement for the real Zais . . . Ah, *caro* Maurice, how pleasant life can be with the right friends.' He paused for a moment or two to finish his brandy and refurnish the glass, and then said more seriously, 'Never I ask you the indelicate questions about yourself. Never I am curious about where you come from and why sometimes you go off into the blue. A man, I know, must have some part of his life only to himself — like when I go to Roma. These things we understand as men. All this Carla understands too. One day she will have *bambini*, and a place of her own, and she will grow plump and full of understanding. And you will be kind — for that is your nature — and make her thank the good Lord in her prayers for guiding her into such a happy marriage. If one has understanding of women it is so easy to keep them happy and docile. The first time I am with Mamma, when we are both young, I wake with her lying naked by my side, she is so beautiful . . . Giorgione could have used her for his model for the Sleeping Venus. Today, for the eyes, the magic has gone — but there now is something else which only the heart can understand . . . '

Maurice listened, liking Aldo. Rogue or no rogue, the man had an eye for beauty and a reverence for all those who could capture it on canvas. There was no need for him to make more than perfunctory answers to Aldo. Aldo was content to talk and not be inter-rupted.

As he was leaving that night, Carla came to the door of the apartment with him, shook her head when he would have kissed her good-night and slipped on a light summer coat which she had over her arm, smiling at him.

'Tonight, I come back with you. Today is

special, even though you did not ask Aldo formally for permission to marry me. But he understands.'

Waking early, morning sunlight falling across the bed, he looked down at her as she slept, uncovered and naked beside him. Giorgione, he thought, would have liked her a little plumper, but that would come. So, he thought, he had awakened on many mornings in the past to look down on sleeping women . . . their beauty delighting the eye and the senses . . . Trudi and Margery the English woman . . . Stay long enough, he thought, and they all want to hold you down . . . a business in Florence . . . a monumental mason's yard in Zürich . . . all with no true love for vagabondage . . . always wanting to settle. What would Margery Littleton — had there been time enough for the desire and hope in her to arise — have wanted? Some picture shop, some art school post in some English town where everybody knew everybody, knew all about them except their secret dreams. And himself? Well — he knew all about himself, but had yet to fall asleep and be captured by a secret dream. With luck it might never happen. One thing, however, was clear — very soon he would have to move on. Poor Carla. She would weep her eyes out — and then after a while find someone else, and then after a further while realize that it had all been for the good. Héloïse and Abélard . . . Dante and Beatrice on the bridge below his windows, the bridge where he had first seen Carla . . . It was all the stuff of dreams. And himself? Well, one day the itch to move, to call no place or woman his for good, would go and he would have to think again. But such a time had to be a long way off yet.

That morning after Carla had left he had a letter from Trudi, enclosing the document he had found in his father's picture and its translation into French and the information that a man had called upon her — having been given her address by Monsieur Bonivard — who had wanted to find him to discuss some picture commissions, and that she had put him off by giving his address as *poste restante*, Bologna. She then went on to say curtly that she had decided to act no longer as a letter-box and go-between for him, and that she never wished to see him again. She would mark all letters — *Unknown at this address* — and put them back into a post box.

Maurice was not unduly upset at this. Once or twice before she had written in the same vein — and had changed her mind on his going to visit her. Well, as things were here in

Florence now, that visit would not long be deferred. Distance made women adamant — it was another matter to defy a lover to his face . . .

He tore the letter up and flushed it down the lavatory. Carla regularly went through all his apartment hunting for hidden correspondence or anything which would give her some clue to his private life or his past. He read the translation of the document and it conveyed little to him. The war had meant nothing to him. He was scarcely learning more than his alphabet at his mother's knee when it had ended. However it was possible that it was not just back packing, but meant something important to Sir Andrew . . . might have been hidden there . . . But hardly since Sir Andrew, knowing his French address, would only have had to write and ask him to return it if it were important. Some time he would send it back to him . . . Perhaps better, for he knew he had to move on from here soon, he would go back to England for a visit . . . Yes, that sounded pleasing . . . Margery Littleton would be happy to see him and a little more of Sir Andrew's company would be refreshing. At the moment though . . . well, what was he to do? The signs all clearly read that the time was fast coming when he must leave Florence.

7

Sir Andrew Starr, sitting on a fence a little downstream from Warboys, and well clear of his back cast, the two dogs at his feet, watched his friend and past colleague put his fly over a rising fish under the far bank. Time and time again the trout ignored the offering and — perhaps out of contempt — refused to be put down.

Sir Andrew said, 'What fly are you using?'

Without turning Warboys said, 'A Black Gnat.'

'Useless — fish here won't touch 'em.'

'They should today. If only to indulge my whim.'

'What's so special about today that the trout should know?'

'It's St John's Day. Midsummer.'

'I'm still not with you.'

Warboys laughed and reeled in his cast. He came back and sat on the fence. '*Bibio johannis* — that's what the real fly is called. And if you want to be really critical go on and tell me that the real fly is not black but a dark brown. Fishing is not an exact science. It is — as Doctor Johnson once said of marriage

— the triumph of hope over experience.'

'Mine's all right, thank you. Though, without irreverence, I must say there's a different kind of blessed peace about the place when my dear wife takes off to our place in France for a while. Will you be staying the night? You're more than welcome.'

'No, I have to get back.'

'You've come a long way to fish a fly that won't take a trout. Are you fishing for something else?'

'No — but there is a touch of troubled waters about it.'

Sir Andrew sighed and began to pack a pipe. 'You know that is one of the things that always made me glad I was never officially Birdcage. Just an outside man, openly wearing — when circumstances permitted — the king's uniform. You chaps always talk as though you're giving clues to a crossword puzzle.'

'Would that it were so. If the world were just plain black or white — how easy. Do you know Maurice Crillon's address in France?'

'That's plain enough. And the answer is No. Do you?'

'No.'

Sir Andrew laughed. 'Well, that could — I don't say it does — make both of us liars. You know why you play this kind of game, don't you?'

'Tell me.'

'Because the chaps in the field, as I used to be, have few options. Kill or be killed. Fail or succeed. It was no game in those days. If you thought there was the slimmest chance of Hail and Farewell — you put the knife or the bullet in first. It was all good clean fun with rules you could count on the fingers of one hand — you might already have lost the fingers from the other. But really, my dear Warboys, why don't you take a deep breath of this lovely country air and speak plainly to me.'

'All right. As plain as I can be. Sir Julian knows his address, and — as you know — they found the painting of you, but without any document in the back. From the *curé* where he lives they got a forwarding address in Switzerland. It was that of some woman who still, as they say, carries a torch for him, and acts as a post-box for him. Seems he likes to hop about from place to place. He has a *poste restante* address in Italy — Bologna to be exact.'

'You got all this from Sir Julian?'

'Oh, yes. He's got the bit between his teeth and needs no help from us. Maurice Crillon, painter and picture-restorer, height, age, description — photo enclosed — possibly Bologna area, but almost certainly living in

219

Italy. Shouldn't be difficult to find — if you go to the right enquiry agency.'

'Mafia?'

'Yes.'

'Well, bad cess to them. Anyway, why are you telling me all this?'

'I thought you'd be interested. You took, as they say, quite a shine to the chap. Why?'

'Because he knew his stuff about art.'

'And pinched a portrait of you. Odd — and no offence meant, but why not pinch something of real value . . . something he could sell easily on the black market?'

'Good question. But the answer rests with him. Your guess is as good as mine.'

'It would help if we could take it out of the realms of guesswork. Confidentially, the matter has escalated somewhat.'

'You intrigue me. What are you silly buggers up to now?'

Warboys was silent for a while. Then with a shrug of his shoulders said, 'Well, why not? Above and beyond Birdcage — you know — there sit the curators and custodians, the recorders and collectors of historical documents. The hoarders of State secrets. The Public Record Office. Probably there's a hell of a lot they hold going back to the Norman Conquest which still hasn't been made public. What can't be told now can be turned into weighty tomes of scholarship in a hundred or more years and then with a few more years the literary hawks and sparrows take their pickings and possibly some lady romancer turns Sir Julian — surprise, surprise — into the hero of the piece. Today's arcana become next century's torrid best sellers. You'd be surprised how jealously the State regards its family papers, its record of political squabbles and royal scandals. How else would we have known which of Henry the Eighth's queens suffered, not just from the pox, but from a delight in the pleasures of Lesbos? Do you or did any of your ancestors ever throw away the Abbey rent rolls, the details of new buildings and — more piquant — the letters or diaries of ancestors? So with the State. The historians of tomorrow must not be disappointed. So, although Sir Julian is off the hook, all forgiven, it has now been decided that the State should keep the original document. Birdcage has been over-ridden by the Master of some Oxford college. Sir Julian must be content solely with his absolution.'

'All this has come a bit late, hasn't it?'

'Well, perhaps that is how the best things come. Though often the feast is disappointing. *Sero venientibus ossa.* But then historians are well used to licking over the old bones of long dead scandals.'

'Sir Julian will be livid when he finds out.'

'He will learn to live with it. The thing is that we now want the documents back. And your help to get them.'

'How can I?'

'Perhaps by telling us why with such insouciance you accepted the theft of your portrait by an itinerant French artist whom you knew for only a handful of days? Is there some skeleton in the Starr family?'

'Dozens. And they all rest in the Crusaders' chapel.'

'For an old friend you can say no more than that?'

'As an old friend I can only tell you that I took a fancy to the chap. If you want him, find him. You know where he lives, clearly. Send someone down to look in the outside loo. He probably tore the document into neat squares and hung them there. My father, bless his parsimonious soul, always had that done with his old newspapers here at the Abbey. Sometimes an odd scrap — from the *News of the World* — made interesting reading and it was fun searching for the missing pieces . . . '

'Well, well . . . then there's an end to it. And now would you like to bet me that I can't catch that trout within four casts?'

'A fiver. And you can change your fly.'

'I will.'

Warboys walked up the bank a little, changed the fly on his cast, and began to fish. At the third cast the trout took and was quickly netted.

Sir Andrew pulled out his wallet and handed over a five-pound note, saying, 'What fly did you put on?'

Warboys grinned. 'Who said anything about a fly? I said I would catch the trout. I put on a maggot — always carry a few to avoid disappointment on a bad day. What the eye doesn't see the heart doesn't grieve over. Nice fish. I shall call on old Quint on the way back and present it to him. He'll probably fancy it up into *truite aux amandes* for one of his lady friends.'

★ ★ ★

Two days later Trudi Keller received in her post a letter from France. The handwriting on the envelope was familiar to her, though she could put no name to it, for she had seen it often on the envelopes forwarding Maurice's mail from Cragnac. It was in fact that of monsieur *le curé* at Cragnac. She opened it to find a single letter enclosed, a letter bearing English postage stamps. Embossed on the

223

back was a little coat of arms with a motto underneath it reading — *Sic itur ad astra.*

She had no interest or curiosity about it. She had passed too many letters to Maurice now to find temptation in herself to open them. Everything was now finished between them. This was the moment when she had to begin to make her vow a material fact. She marked the envelope — *Unknown at this address* — in German and put it in a post box on her way to school in the morning.

With this act she felt herself at last finally breaking with Maurice. But, though his visits had always been brief and widely spaced since the day he had left her, she knew that it would take a long time for the memory of him to rest undisturbingly in her mind. Maybe, she thought, it would be a good idea to give up her work here and go back to Zürich. And the thought, she knew, sprang from her own weakness. If she stayed here and Maurice came to see her she doubted that she could long resist him. The one thing he would never do, she knew, was to search her out at Zürich.

At this moment in Florence in Aldo's apartment the telephone rang. Aldo sitting over his breakfast coffee and rolls called to Carla to answer it. She came from the kitchen and went through into the little study off the big sitting room which Aldo used as an office. After a moment or two she came back and said, 'There is a Signor Andretti wishes to speak to you.'

Aldo looked up, his fat face suddenly creased and set with surprise. He gaped a little and then said, 'You are sure of that name, *cara*?'

'Signor Andretti. That is the name. Personally.'

Without a word — though his consternation was clear to Carla — he got up, wiping his mouth on his napkin and then, giving the lapels of his jacket a mechanical tug, went by her and through into his study, closing the door behind him.

Carla, knowing her brother, went back into the kitchen where her sister-in-law was kneading the dough to make fresh pasta for the evening meal. She said, 'Who is Signor Andretti?'

'That was the telephone?'

'Yes.'

'Probably some customer.'

'When was there ever a customer of Aldo's whose name could make him jump like a cat off a hot brick?'

'You ask too many questions.'

Carla laughed. 'I see.' Then, her face suddenly taking on a serious cast, she went on, 'You do not get worried sometimes?'

'I am in his house and in his bed — but more often in his kitchen. Also, I think, I am a little bit in his heart. Not so much as once. But I am content — because I do not let myself get curious. With men that only leads to trouble.'

'And one day . . . say, something goes wrong? What will you do then?'

'It is arranged. I shall be patient until he comes back. But he is no fool. He has good friends in the right places. One day it will all happen to you with your Maurice. But you need not worry. Aldo's friends will be his friends.' She began to roll out the pasta mixture, readying it to be cut into ravioli shapes for the evening meal.

'And you are content?'

'I am content. Is it any comfort to be anything else?'

'And love — does that not die a little with absence?'

'Love — ' she laughed, ' — that is the bait put in the trap at the beginning. Once you are in the trap you must learn to live there. It has its comforts.'

Carla shook her head. 'Sometimes I think that I shall never marry Maurice. Never be in the trap.'

'So? What does it matter? You know our

saying — One nail drives out another. By the way, have you reminded him that it is little Marco's birthday in three days' time? Since Maurice is soon to be his uncle — '

'There is no need to remind him. With children he forgets nothing. Only with his women he is careless.'

At this moment Aldo came into the kitchen. He was smiling and seemed to stand a little taller than he usually did.

He said pompously, 'That was Signor Andretti at Fiesole. *Mamma mia* — you should see that villa, and the stuff he has there. Also — ' his face momentarily was stern, ' — he is a man with whom I could only ever do straight business. His eye is that of a hawk. In all the years, sadly, I have never done business with him. He is an eagle that flies high over sparrows like me . . . but not now. You know what he wants?'

To tease him Carla said, 'A copy of Botticelli's *Birth of Venus* to sell for authentic in . . . well, say, South America. And you would have Maurice do a copy for him.'

Unperturbed Aldo said good-humouredly, 'You do not touch me. And you should be pleased. He wants Maurice to go to him and advise him about his pictures. For cleaning. There is nothing wrong with this business. It is of Signor Andretti that we speak.'

'Mafia?'

Aldo looked shocked. 'Carla, to speak so is an insult to a fine gentleman. Not in my house do you ever say anything like that again. Where is Maurice?'

'How do I know — since I am forbidden to sleep overnight with him?'

'Go find him and tell him I want to see him. And say nothing of Signor Andretti. To please him with this surprise must be my pleasure.' He drew in a deep breath and then let it go from him, saying, 'Such a day . . . to be called by Signor Andretti. I know now how my beloved father felt the day he was called to see the great Bernard Berenson. Now go — go find Maurice. Tell him I want to see him. At once.'

Carla smiled. 'Never say — *At once* — to Maurice. There is a devil in him which will make him take an hour to put his shirt on.'

Aldo snorted. 'Maurice . . . Maurice! One day he is going to learn to be a man like other men. To marry and to be a good husband. To stop wondering what is over the horizon because there is only more of the same. In the end all men come, sooner or later, to learn that foolish dreams are of no comfort in old age. To learn that what I have here with Mamma and my family, and with my good business, is paradise.' He rubbed his hands together. 'Ah, when the world knows that Aldo works for Signor Andretti — then you shall see how my enemies and those who have tried to cheat me will come crawling.'

'And what will you do?' asked his wife.

It was no surprise to either woman that Aldo took the question seriously.

He said judicially, 'Some, because of my Christian heart, I shall forgive. But for a few — the door closes in the face. Like this — *Piaaf!*' He clapped his hands together and blew a great breath.

* * *

That morning, while Aldo was basking in his pride at the call from Signor Andretti, Warboys — wearing a red rosebud in the lapel of his black jacket, purchased in Shepherd Market on his walk to the office, and placed there by a charming girl assistant who, had it happened for him to be twenty, possibly ten years younger, would have soon found that with time this slight familiarity would have led to greater ones — called Kerslake into his office. In a little while now, he thought, he would be gone and Kerslake would be beyond calling for he would sit here as Supremo, though not — he allowed himself a mild touch of vanity — with such distinction of appearance as himself. But, dammit, give the man his due, probably rather more competent, if not so imaginative as himself. Life was full of ironies, and he personally relished them. Kerslake had no such predilection for them.

Kerslake gave him a good-morning and took the chair he was nodded to and Warboys, knowing that the man had no time for obliquities of approach, chose deliberately to start with one, and said, 'A few days ago — coming back from an afternoon's fishing on the Avoncourt Abbey water — I called in on your old mentor Quint — he who chose to quit early instead of soldiering on in the hope of occupying — and I may say certain hope — the chair in which I am now sitting and which will be yours when *the book of Nature Getteth short of leaves*. Did I catch the breath of a sigh? Such confusing allusions so early in the morning?'

To Warboys' surprise, and he had to smile good-humouredly, Kerslake said, 'The not unpleasant disease which Quint has always suffered from is catching. After he left it took me a while to rid myself of the milder form I had begun to adopt in self-defence. But I was hampered because I had little Latin and less Greek. I presume, sir — ' the last word was faintly emphasized, ' — that you discussed Sir

Andrew with him? The odd fancy he took to Crillon. The odd fancy Crillon took to his Augustus John portrait, and the odder fact that the document it contained was not found in it after Crillon cleaned it.'

'To some extent all those. He said that the important one probably was not the odd fancy he took to Crillon, but the odd fancy that Crillon — with so many far more valuable paintings to chose from — took to the Augustus John.'

'Just that? No more?'

'Well, yes. I'd taken with me the photograph of Crillon you got rather belatedly from the French authorities and he had a good look at it, front and back with the details on it. He really made a meal of it. And then he said, like Sherlock Holmes rather, 'The odd thing, you know, is that I've never really fathomed the meaning of — *Plain as a pikestaff. Penny plain and tuppence coloured,* yes.' And then rambled on . . . he'd finished nearly a bottle of Petit Chablis before I arrived . . . talking about Chesterton and The Man Who Was Nobody. But I had a distinct feeling he had his nose up into the wind and some scent was coming down it to him. But I couldn't get more from him. Why is it that when men leave this place they become so unco-operative?'

'Well, sir.'

Smiling, noting the rare *sir*, Warboys said, 'Ah, yes, of course. If the reason is to be known, I shall know it soon. Only a few more weeks, my dear Kerslake, and you will sit in my place. And I can think of none better. However, all this by way of easing my irritation with Quint. The real point is that there is other game afoot. You know that Sir Julian handed over the search for Crillon to the Mafia?'

'Yes.'

'Well, just to complicate things, and very delightful I find it, I had a visitor call at my flat last evening late. Would it surprise you if I said that hagiologically speaking he made clear that he stands on the right-hand side of Signor Andretti's throne?'

'Nothing surprises me with them. And I don't care for them much . . . at all.'

'Ah, there speaks the Barnstaple boy. But well you know that here we subdue . . . better, forget . . . our prejudices. He that sups with the Devil must have a long spoon. But this particular Devil has his uses. Signor Andretti, I am told, has found and will shortly be picking up our Maurice Crillon and hopefully the document also so ardently desired by Sir Julian — and those same papers also now so ardently desired by our

232

State archivists . . . so, to be vulgar, I was offered a deal.'

Kerslake smiled. 'Instead of going to Sir Julian they come to us — and what do we have to do . . . or give?'

'It seems that Signor Andretti has a nephew or a cousin — or probably someone of no relation at all — who cares? — and this gentleman is on the verge of deep trouble, his arrest is imminent.'

'Gaming casinos? Vincente Paraccini?'

'Ah, you read your papers. Yes. We arrange that all charges likely to be made be withheld. The police won't like it — they've been trying to get him for a long time. But they're used to disappointments. Would you have any objection?'

'Do I have any choice?'

'No. But if you had?'

'I would have none. My father lost the use of one hand at Dunkirk — and my uncle was killed there. But what of Sir Julian?'

'You are concerned?'

'No. Curious.'

'He will learn to live with it. Does he deserve more?'

'If things had gone his way — do you think that the flag would be flying over Buckingham Palace to show that the Queen is in residence?'

'Ah, a nice touch. Rugged sentiment. 'Take 'old o' the Wings of the Mornin', An' flop round the earth till you're dead: But you won't get away from the tune that they play — To the bloomin' old rag over head.' Splendid stuff. So we consign Sir Julian to the wolves?'

'Why not? And what happens to Maurice Crillon?'

Warboys was silent for a moment or two and them said with heavy banality, 'Do you think anyone really cares? But, of course, yes. Someone must. No man can be so forlorn. It is a state Nature abhors.'

★   ★   ★

Aldo — sitting sideways at his desk in his little room overlooking the Piazza Santo Spirito, part of the façade of Brunelleschi's church just visible, Brunelleschi one of the first men of the fifteenth century to establish the laws of perspective — as Aldo well knew, but who was now much more interested in the new and long reaching perspectives pointing to the future — gave Maurice Crillon the benefit of his warmest smile.

'*Amico mio* . . . this could be the moment when life begins to change for us. Once the world knows we are being patronized by

Signor Andretti . . . ' He rolled his eyes heavenward and closed them, the prospect as yet too dazzling to behold. He opened them and then said sternly, 'Of course, you know who he is?'

Maurice said, 'I've heard of him. An industrialist, isn't he?'

'That — and much more. And the paintings he has! Mamma mia! As we talked, there staring me in the face from the opposite wall was a marvellous *Adorazione dei Magi* which could only have been a Leonardo. I swear.'

Maurice smiled. 'Then don't do it too loudly — unless he has lifted it from the Uffizi Gallery and they have not yet missed it.'

Aldo said indignantly, 'There is no fake in his house, I swear. Leonardo was very prolific.'

Maurice laughed. 'Come to the point, Aldo. All right, this man has some beautiful paintings — but he has to have more to make you so good-humoured and over-awed. What does he want from me?'

'Did I say that?'

'Do you have to — calling me over here like this? Carla twittering like a swallow, and you with the Chianti flask open at this hour of day. But most of all . . . your eyes. Ah,

Aldo, your tiny little eyes . . . they are full of the love of *lire* light.'

'Maurice, I beg of you — when you go to see him — do not talk in this fashion. I warn you — he is a man who by lifting a little finger could put me and thousands of other honest business men in this country out of work tomorrow. *Aie!* — and more. Out of life were it necessary. Now when you go to see him — dress soberly and talk with respect.'

'Mafioso?'

'Maurice — keep such a word from your tongue and your mind. He is a gentleman and an upright man.'

'Like you. Like me. And if I do not wish to go?'

'Maurice — it is unthinkable! If he likes you and gives us work and his patronage, we are made for life.' He straightened himself in his chair, bulking out his fat chest, and went on soberly and with an incongruous dignity, 'Just think — if his light shines on us — we can become honest men and, more important, prosperous too. Never, you know, have I liked this faking and cheating. It does not become our talents — mine for business and yours for your genius. Ah, perhaps now and again — if it is necessary — we relax a little. But on the whole if we can get Signor Andretti's patronage we shall be men of worth and standing. And you, you will paint pictures under your own name so that people will walk into galleries and say at once — *That is a Crillon. Can only be a Crillon.* And should I be standing behind I would be forward enough to step up to them and say — *It is a Crillon, and he is my brother-in-law and if you wish I will take you to see him in his studio. You will find him the most charming and delightful of men* — senza orgoglio.'

'Many thanks.'

'So you will go?'

'Why not? The gates to a new world will open.'

Aldo was so overcome that he jumped up and embraced Maurice. Then stepped back and said, 'He will see you at half-past one today.'

'He takes no siesta?'

'He is a man who needs none. Already there is not enough time in his day for all his affairs. Be prompt and — Maurice — be polite.'

'I will.'

Maurice that afternoon drove up to Fiesole. A manservant led him through the house and out on to the terrace, which overlooked Florence, and then down a wide flight of balustraded steps, graced at intervals with figures of life-sized scantily draped goddesses, and so to a small enclosed arena. Close-clipped myrtle hedges fringed a maze-like arrangement of paths that held at their centre a sunken pool patterned with water lilies and the movement of white, silver, orange and gold-coloured carp. A fountain stood in the centre of the basin, water spouting from the mouths of three leaden dolphins. By the side of the fountain, at a marble-topped table, under the shade of a large beach umbrella, sat Signor Andretti reading a book. From this spot the garden and hillside fell away to give a magnificent view of Florence in the valley below.

When the manservant had gone and Signor Andretti had greeted him, the two men sat at the table and the Italian carefully placed a marker in his book and laid it down. It was somewhat worn with use, bound in tooled and embossed leather, and entitled — *La Pittura Italiana dalle Origini al Novecento.*

Seeing his eyes on the book, Signor Andretti asked, 'Do you know it?'

'No, Signor.'

'It is not much to be regarded by today's standards. It was published here in Florence in nineteen hundred and thirty. My father gave it to me when I was not yet twenty. I have a sentimental feeling for it since it started my love for paintings. Aldo Pandolfi tells me you have that same love — and more, that you are a painter of genius.'

Crillon smiled and shrugged his shoulders, saying, 'Aldo exaggerates everything.'

'I wonder? However, perhaps to your disappointment, I have to tell you that I wish to speak to you of other things. After that — if you wish — I will show you around my little collection. You see I am very direct. It is my wish that you be the same with me.'

'But, of course, Signor Andretti.'

'Good — then I speak frankly. Your real home is in France?'

'Yes — at Cragnac.'

'I understand that from there not so long ago you made a visit to England. Why did you go?'

Crillon, covering his surprise, paused for a while. He had no idea where this line of questioning might go — so he decided not to commit himself until forced.

'My mother had recently died. I thought a holiday in new surroundings would . . . well, take my mind off things. My father is long dead — and I have no other family left.'

'Ah . . . so. I am sorry. I had no idea. To lose someone so dear . . . Forgive me.'

'How could you have known? There is nothing to forgive. I went back to the South

239

of England where I had once studied English.' He paused for a moment, well aware now that Aldo in his simplicity had mis-read this man. What was to come he had no idea, but he decided to fall back on a mixture of truth and fancy. 'I had been happy there and felt I might . . . well, come to my happiness again.'

'And did you?'

'In a way. I met a *signorina* who was kind to me and we went on excursions around the country. You must know how these things are, *signore*.'

'It is natural. Now tell me how you came to meet an English milord called Sir Andrew Starr.'

The question surprised Crillon, though he gave no sign of this. But at once he sensed that this man's interests were far from solely concerned with paintings. He said, his voice casual, 'My friend took me to his home. It is called Avoncourt Abbey and is open to the public on some days. He has a very fine collection of paintings which are also on view. By chance I met him in the gallery and we began to talk. I told him that one of the paintings was a fake. There were others, too — but I did not wish to over-embarrass him. No collector likes that.'

Signor Andretti laughed. 'When you look

around mine I hope you will be completely honest.'

'Does it always pay, signor?'

'With me, yes. How has this gift come to you, to be able to tell?'

'I don't know. It is just there. I suppose, *signore*, it is as if you sleep with a girl who is one of identical twins and one night in the dark her sister takes her place . . . *Magari* — you know at once.'

Signor Andretti leaned back and laughed and then said, 'But you say nothing and let her stay, eh?'

'With a woman, yes. A picture, no. With men also, no. It would be kind of you, therefore if you were to speak frankly to me. I know my dear friend — and brother-in-law to be, Aldo — is at heart a simple man. I am different. So, at the risk of annoying you, I say — why do you not be frank with me? You want something from me? Then ask me.'

Signor Andretti reached out a hand and fingered the leather-tooled cover of his art book, his face heavy and brooding for a moment or two — and then a warm smile took its place.

He said gently, 'You are a good judge of character. And so am I. So, you ask me to be frank and I will be. *Mamma mia* — but you are wasted with Aldo. So let us be frank, and you will not suffer by it. You became friendly with this Sir Andrew Starr. And you worked for him?'

'For a little while. I cleaned some pictures for him. He took to me and quickly we became very friendly. Sometimes friendship is long coming, sometimes it flowers fast. You must have known this at times in your life, *signore*.'

'Possibly. But we speak of you. You know who and what I am?'

'Aldo told me.'

'It is no secret. But there are secrets which are not told until a man has proved himself. I can help you great deal. But first I want you to help me. It is known that before you left England Sir Andrew made you a present of any picture of your own choosing.'

'You are well-informed. That is so. He is a very generous man.'

'Why — when you had so much to choose from — did you take a not too good painting of him?'

'Search your own heart, *signore*. You would have done the same. It would have been unseemly and greedy to have taken a Rubens or a Canaletto. I am a simple man — what would I have done with such? I have no gallery. Only a cottage in France. So I chose to take a little painting of Sir Andrew Starr. Not a good painting. But one which would always remind me of my holiday and a man I came to call my friend.'

'And when you got back to France you took it out of its frame and cleaned it?'

'Yes, I did. It needed cleaning — which I have to say did something for it. The artist was — '

'I know, Augustus John. I met him once in the Camargue. But it is not the painting I am interested in.'

'Then what, *signore?*'

'In the back I am told — where Sir Andrew had hidden them — were some pages of a document in German. Do you read German?'

'No, *signore*. Italian, Spanish and a little Greek.'

'What did you do with this document?'

'I kept it.'

'Did you not think these papers might be important to Sir Andrew — since he had hidden them there? You could have sent them back to him.'

'He knew my address in France, *signore*. He had but to write. I would have sent them back.'

'So you kept them?'

'Yes.'

'Why?'

'Because I was a little curious about them — and also because I wanted to make sure that they were of no importance. On my way back to Italy I left the document with a friend in Switzerland and asked her to translate it for me.'

'And has she done this yet?'

'Yes, *signore*. I had it a few days ago.'

'And you have read it?'

'Naturally, *signore*.'

'And what was it all about?'

'Well, I do not properly understand. It was old stuff about the last war, and something to do with a government that the Nazis would have set up in England if they had won the war. And then a list of names of people who would form the government.'

Signor Andretti smiled. 'You do not remember the war, of course?'

Crillon shook his head. 'I was only four or five years old when it ended. My father was killed in it. But, am I right in thinking now that, maybe, these papers are of some importance?'

'They could be to some people.'

Disingenuously Crillon, now well aware that the document had to be of real importance to someone, went on, 'To Sir Andrew Starr?'

Signor Andretti shrugged his shoulders. 'I doubt it. Or otherwise, as you have said, he would have got in touch with you and asked for it.'

'Yes, that's true. But to you or someone

you know it is important?'

'It's possible. One cannot tell until one has read the document. I would like to see it.'

Deliberately, Crillon put on a doubtful look that masked the rise in him of a slow current of excitement. The papers were obviously of importance — and they belonged to Sir Andrew Starr, his father who had been good to him. This man had power and influence. When he wanted something he got it — by fair means or foul. He felt the biting edge of a challenge which he welcomed because he knew it was the spur to movement which his whole spirit had been waiting for. He realised that he was going to play with fire, but he could not deny his nature which instinctively prompted him to outwit this man — despite the fact that he had taken quite a liking to him, which was natural since they clearly had much in common. For all his wealth and outward respectability he was much the same as himself. And, anyway, the document belonged to his father — though why he had not asked for it back he could not understand — and to his father it should go. But, above and beyond all this was the knowledge that now he had no need voluntarily to burn his boats here in Florence. Now — and the prospect filled him with joy — he *had* to go a-wandering again, but this time he would be backed by a more than substantial bank balance in Zurich.

He said, 'I will get them for you, Signor Andretti.'

'Good. You are being very helpful, Signor Crillon. You will not be unrewarded. But, of course, all that has passed here between us remains between us. Aldo, as you know, has a loose mouth.'

'As you say, *signore*. And now, is it permitted to look at your paintings?'

Signor Andretti hesitated for a moment and then smiled. 'I think we will leave that to some other time.' He laughed. 'If I am to be told that my *Il Ciarlatano* by Giandomenico Tiepolo is a fake I would rather defer the disappointment.' He gave Maurice a sly smile.

Maurice laughed. 'If you have it, Signor Andretti, then it must be a fake, since the original is at Venice in the Papadopoli collection.'

Signor Andretti grinned. 'Ah, we are going to get on well, you and I. Though, mind you, it would be some time before I would buy anything from you and Aldo Pandolfi without being very, very careful. Some other time we will go round together.'

'I look forward to that, *signore*.'

Signor Andretti pressed a little electric call button on the table before him, and said, 'You will be kind enough to take one of my men back with you and hand him the document and also the translation which has been done for you. He will get a taxi back.'

Without hesitation Crillon said, 'But of course.'

Within a few moments a man — introduced to Crillon simply as Berini — soberly dressed, in his forties, running to fat, heavily jowled, but with a humorous glint in his dark, almost olive green eyes, arrived.

Signor Andretti said, 'You will go to Florence with Signor Crillon and bring back some papers he will give to you. You will, of course, seal them first, Signor Crillon.'

'As you wish, *signore.*'

Berini laughed. 'He is my uncle — and still he does not trust me. What would you do with an uncle like that, Signor Crillon?'

Crillon smiled. 'Obey him, respect and love him, for uncles are always more forgiving and generous than fathers. I am myself to be very soon an uncle to Signore Pandolfi's boy Marco.'

Signor Andretti nodded, pleased. 'You are to marry Aldo's daughter, Carla?'

'Yes — *signore.*'

'Good. I will find you both a nice wedding present.'

Crillon drove Berini back to Florence and, when they were in his apartment, he waved the man to a seat and poured him a glass of marsala, saying, 'Now I will get the papers your uncle wishes.'

When he came back it was to find Berini, glass in hand, standing by his window work table, looking at a painting which he had been cleaning.

Without turning Berini said, 'This is surely a Sernesi?'

'Yes, a lovely little country scene.'

Berini sighed. *'Un' opera di sublime bellezza* . . . The scene is Tuscany, is it not?'

'So you know about paintings?'

'Why not? My uncle loves them but knows nothing about them really. But with me . . . they are more than food, drink and women. You are cleaning it?'

'Yes. And now, Signor Berini — turn round very slowly and do everything exactly as I tell you — then no harm comes to you.'

Berini turned and a look of surprise spread slowly over his face. Crillon was facing him holding a pistol in his right hand and Berini — who knew as much about guns as he did of paintings — recognized it at once for what it was — a 'Manurhin' Walther, Model P.P.K.

He said, 'This is very unfriendly.'

'I have no choice.'

'I see. Perhaps later we shall be making you explain that. It will not be a happy occasion.'

Crillon smiled. 'I like you. Under other

circumstances we might have become friends. Now you will turn round and walk into my bedroom and do exactly as I shall tell you.'

'Since you say so — *bene*. I suppose it is no good offering you some good advice?'

'None whatever. I shall stand at the door and give you certain directions which you will obey without question.'

'Certainly. I have no option.'

Ten minutes later, without bothering to pack a suitcase, taking with him on his person his passport and a few other items which he knew he would need, Crillon locked the bedroom door and sat at the main room table and wrote two notes. He left the bedroom key with them. Whistling he left the apartment and slammed its self-locking door behind him. He went down the stairs in a light-hearted mood. He had out-worn Aldo and Carla and Florence. A little sadness and some occasional nostalgia would linger — but now the world was before him and somewhere in it would be a new place for him to find and call for a while home.

★　★　★

Early that evening when Carla returned from her work in the boutique — until she was married Aldo had insisted that she stay there

— Aldo, worried and restless, came out of his room and said, 'You have called to see Maurice on the way home?'

'No. Why should I? I go round there later as usual.'

'I ring and ring him and I get no reply.'

'Then he is not there.'

'Then, Mother of Jesus — where is he?' Little beads of perspiration dewed Aldo's forehead.

'How should I know?' Carla smiled. 'Dear brother — not since your lovely new car was stolen last year have I seen you so upset.'

'This is no matter of a car. He goes today to see a most important customer, and I wait for him. This customer means the beginning of great things.'

'Good. I like to see the money look in your eyes. So you are both to be rich — honestly I hope?'

Angrily Aldo said, 'Were you not my sister, you should feel the back of my hand across your face. Can you not see that this is a matter of great importance to me? I sit here waiting for him to bring back good news for us all.'

'Good news, dear Aldo, will always keep. But if you would like a little now I can give you some. The wedding will, I think, have to be brought forward.'

'Impossible — the date is fixed, all is being

arranged. But do not bother me with that kind of talk when you can see that I have more important matters on my mind.'

'Ah . . . in these charming moods I can see how my dear sister-in-law found you irresistible. You do not wish to have my news?'

'I wish to have Maurice. I ring and ring — and no answer.'

'Sometimes I have been there and it rings and rings and I want to get out of bed and answer it but he keeps me with him, saying, 'Who would leave paradise to answer a wrong-number call?' Once I insist and it was a wrong number. So I learn.'

'You think he is in bed with . . . ' He exploded. 'And I am here burning for news! And you do not care that he may be with another woman?'

'I care. But no other woman can change matters now. Maurice is mine. I am going to have his baby. Is it not splendid news?'

'*Putana!*'

'I knew you would be pleased. Come — we go together to see if he is there and to give him the good news. Which do you fancy, dear Aldo, a niece or a nephew?'

'Have you no shame?'

'No — only happiness. Now he cannot escape me. But to make you happy we will go together. I have my key and if there is some other woman there — naked — you make no fuss. After all he can no longer use me for a model since that would not now be proper.'

Some minutes later they were in the apartment. Propped against a vase of white roses on the studio table were two notes. One for Carla and one for Aldo.

Aldo's note read:

I did not care for Signor Andretti — and so I must go. You are at liberty to show him this. Thanks for everything. Maurice.

Carla's read:

Although you would never speak your thoughts you knew it would never last with a man like me. Put me from your mind and find someone worthy of you. For all the happiness you have given me I kiss your hand. All the fault is mine. God did not make me for staying or true loving. Maurice. P.S. I have left little Marco's birthday present by the Sernesi painting. I hope he will like it. Tell him it was very useful to me.

Automatically, scarcely knowing she was doing it in her grief, Carla went to the Sernesi painting in the window. Alongside it lay a heavy-weight replica model of a Walther pistol and the presentation box which had held it.

At this moment came Aldo's angry voice, 'Who does he think he is, that he can fly away like a bird? *Santo Gesú* — we could have made a fortune! Pray God that Signor Andretti does not hold me responsible for then I am a lost man . . . a lost man.'

Carla turned and said hoarsely, 'You were lost a long time ago. For me it just begins. For me the fear I have always had is a truth. What is left for me?'

Suddenly, surprising himself, Aldo was entirely aware of Carla's grief and loss. He put an arm around her comfortingly and said, '*Cara sorella mia* . . . begin now to put him out of your mind. He was not worthy of you. In a little while I find you a man who will be understanding and gentle. It will be arranged and you will be married. Aldo will make everything right for you. Your child will become respectable — and think — ' his voice rose with a note of hope, ' — he may inherit his father's genius. He will do big things.'

At that moment there was a banging on the inside of the bedroom door and a man's voice called. Aldo gave a worried look at Carla and then went to the door, turned the key which was in the lock and opened it. On the threshold stood Berini, whom Aldo knew.

'Signor Berini — how come you are there?

And without your trousers?'

Berini smiled. 'It is a long story which I will tell you later.' Then seeing Carla, he went on, 'Signorina, I apologize to appear before you in my underclothes. Perhaps you will be kind enough to call the *portinaia* and ask for my trousers. Signor Crillon said he would leave them with her.'

Aldo let out a long, slow wail and raised his hands to heaven. 'He has done this to you? *Mamma mia* — your uncle will kill me.'

'I think not — since he will understand it is not your fault. In fact, he will laugh at the whole thing — at first. But then later . . . *Dio mio* . . . already I am beginning to be sorry for Signor Crillon.' As he spoke he walked to the Sernesi painting and picked up the Walther. 'So . . . you know, it did cross my mind. But then when it is a matter of life and, maybe, death one falters to trust entirely one's judgment.' He turned and smiled at Aldo, and added, 'I am embarrassed that I should meet your charming sister so attired. Perhaps you will ask me to dinner one night?'

Aldo beamed. 'But, of course, Signor Berini. Oh, of course.'

At that moment, the car radio playing gently, Maurice Crillon was driving along the autostrada northwards, heading for Milan and then Switzerland.

8

Sir Julian Markover, having asked to see Warboys, was surprised and annoyed — though he covered both emotions — when he was shown into Kerslake's office.

Kerslake said, 'Mr Warboys is in Downing Street at the Cabinet Office. He was called there unexpectedly this morning.'

Sir Julian, without rancour, said, 'Sometimes Warboys has the most convenient early morning appointments. However . . . '

'Is there anything I can do?'

'Possibly. I want some information. You're briefed, of course, about this Crillon business?'

'I am.'

'You know that Signor Andretti is handling it for me?'

'I do.' Kerslake was taking a mild pleasure in the brevity of his replies.

'Are you aware of the latest development?'

'No, Sir Julian.' He was, however, well aware, for Andretti had telephoned Warboys late the previous evening and he had been fully briefed by Warboys this morning.

'Well, yesterday Signor Andretti found Crillon in Florence, saw him, and sent a man

with him to his apartment to pick up the
. . . well, my property.'

'Signor Andretti has worked fast. So now,
as far as we are concerned, the whole thing
can be forgotten.'

. 'Not at all. At the apartment Crillon gave
the man the slip and made off with the
documents.'

'Indeed?' Kerslake widened his eyes, letting
false surprise take his face.

'Yes, indeed. I see your surprise, and I
share it with you. I would never have thought
that Signor Andretti would ever have let this
man slip through his fingers.'

'Nor I, Sir Julian.' Kerslake's eyes marked
the movement of a blue-chequered cock
pigeon that had just settled on the window sill
of the room. The bird was in poor condition.
Not like the birds which had once graced his
father's lofts.

'The thought occurs to me that there may
be something not quite genuine about this
story.'

'In what way, Sir Julian?'

'Ways might be a better term. Signor
Andretti could be lying. He has the papers
and has let Crillon go.'

'Why should he do that? You took
everything from our hands and put it all in
his. Why should you doubt his word?'

'I am not doubting — merely keeping an open mind.'

'For what reason?'

'I see that Warboys has trained you well.' Sir Julian permitted himself a rare and bleak smile.

'Naturally — but the imputation escapes me.' The small curl of a wave of pleasure broke in Kerslake's mind and, since secretly he had long been filling some blanks in his education, he let the word *imputare* float gently on the crest of his hidden bonhomie. He could never replace the lack of a classical education but at least he might come to the stage when he would be far from a complete Boeotian . . . Greek though that might be and for ever out of his reach.

'I doubt it. But I will make myself clear. The master of a certain Oxford college — for which at times I have made available considerable gifts and donations — had dinner with me recently. He has a weakness for port which makes his brain and his tongue work uncontrolled at times. He let slip the suggestion that soon there might be available — not for public perusal, of course — certain wartime documents detailing the constitution of the government which the German Reich would have set up here when they took this island.'

'Not knowing, of course, your involvement?'

'That is so. And not to be made public for many years. True or false?'

'I would have no idea.'

'And Warboys?'

'You could ask him.'

'And get no satisfactory answer. So now you see.'

'What do I see, Sir Julian?'

'That I trust neither you people, nor Andretti.'

To his own surprise Kerslake heard himself say, 'Did you ever?'

Sir Julian gave a dry grunt. 'No. I just wish to say that I am now taking things back into my own hands. Andretti I now trust no longer — and you here I have never trusted.'

'So what will you do?'

'I think when you report this conversation to Warboys that he will be able to give you the answer to that.'

He rose, picked up his hat and cane, and departed without another word.

A few minutes later Warboys came into the room, smiling, a rosebud in his lapel, expertly filched as he had come across St James's Park that morning, since it was a Sunday and his Shepherd Market source was closed, and through the part-open window now came the sound of church bells making the morning sweet.

He said, 'You handled that very well.'

'Thank you, sir.'

'Ah, the rare 'sir'. And to which party now do you think Sir Julian has turned?'

Kerslake smiled. 'All governments cherish State papers and have scholars and archives.'

'Breeding places for . . . what? That persistent little beast — *der Bucherwurm?* And let's face it — the document is still legally the property of the Germans.'

'Poor Crillon.'

'Yes, poor Crillon — poor in prospects, but rich in interest. David faced now with more than one Goliath. Birdcage, the Mafiosi, and the Federal Republic of Germany, maybe even the German Democratic Republic . . . However, for the time being, he has given everyone the slip. Where do you think he's headed?'

'A fox has more than one earth. I think we wait until we get a full report from Signor Andretti. And in all this — what about Sir Andrew Starr?'

'Ah . . . yes. Yes, indeed. I wonder why I still get that — towards an old friend — reprehensible feeling that he is leading us up the garden path? So easy for him since he has so many to choose from. However, I think

259

he can for a while be left to his rustic delights. By the way . . . I feel I must tell you how pleased I am that so late in life you are now decided to enjoy the delights of Virgil and Horace.'

Kerslake smiled. 'Waste paper basket in my office?'

'Yes, indeed. Quite by chance. My eye was caught by *amo, amas, amat.* Keep it up and remember — though I think Pliny said it of some painter — *Nulla dies sine linea.* Translate?'

'No day without a line?'

'Splendid.'

★   ★   ★

Maurice Crillon stayed the night in Milan. The next morning he sold his car cheaply — a fact that came to Signor Andretti's ears within twenty-four hours — and then rented another from the Hertz Company. He then drove to Zürich, where he made certain arrangements with his bank there. He knew quite well that Carla, willingly or not, and probably the former, would be milked of all the information she had about him. And he guessed, too, that Trudi Keller would either be approached for news of him — or watched to see if he made contact with her. He was in Zürich for two nights and during that time

260

took a walk along the street in which Trudi's father had his stonemason's yard — this an indulgence of pure sentiment and nostalgia.

Leaving Zürich he made his way leisurely southwards through Lucerne and so down to Brient at the head of the Brenner See. Thirty odd miles away lay Interlaken and the easterly end of the Thunner See. He stayed in a small hotel in Brient, bought a sketching pad, and went for walks, and sometimes, giving up walking and drawing, would sit and consider his future. Time, he knew, was a great healer. Once or twice he considered the possibility of being unchaste with a pretty Swiss girl in the hotel's reception office, but resisted the temptation. He had arrived in Brient on Tuesday. He had decided — and there was an important reason for his wanting to do this — to get in touch with Trudi on the coming Friday.

During this time, unknown to her, Trudi's movements were being monitored by three men of different nationalities . . . a German, an Italian, and an Englishman who, had he so wished, could have passed comfortably as a German or an Italian. All three of them were soon, in their different ways, well aware of the little unholy trinity which they formed though none made any sign of it. All three, too, were considerably bored because from the limited information they had been given they felt that Maurice Crillon would not be fool enough — even if he had reason, and reason here seemed a frail flower — to try and get in touch with Trudi. These three each day checked Trudi's movements to and from school. It was high summer, tourists and holiday parties bathed and boated and some climbed the nearby small alps to catch the tinkling of cowbells and to exclaim with delight over the profusion and beauty of the Alpine flowers. And, although Maurice Crillon guessed they would be there, he had had no curiosity to establish this for himself. They had to be there. When the scent goes cold it was, if a forlorn hope, common sense to hark back and wait to see if the gods of chance would be kind. He guessed that the same thing would be happening at Cragnac and, indeed, might be happening, too, in Salisbury ... somebody shadowing sweet Margery Littleton to and from work ... somebody keeping an eye on Sir Andrew Starr ... his dear pappa.

Meanwhile, on the day that Maurice Crillon arrived in Brient, Warboys motored down to Hampshire to spend the night at Avoncourt Abbey. He was a self-invited guest, but that was not unusual or unwelcome.

After dinner he and Sir Andrew took their

coffee and then port on the small balcony outside the dining room on the first floor of the Abbey.

Looking out over the public-free gardens and parterres, the fountains in the sunken gardens playing late in his honour, the butler given his congé and gone now to his own parlour to drink port from the same bin as that which rested between the two men, Warboys said, 'I thought you might be interested in the latest of the Sir Julian saga.'

'My dear chap, of course I would. Don't tell me you've come all this way just to keep me abreast? Damned decent. What do you want from me in return?'

'Nothing. Nothing tangible, that is.'

'Good. This is no night for the tangible. Fairies and Queen Mab . . . perhaps the ghost of one of our old Knights Templar, leading a shagged-out war horse across the lawns, finally back from Acre or Jerusalem. Or maybe out of his chapel tomb to stretch his legs. No horse, of course. The Church for some odd reason denies the holy precincts. Can't imagine why when you think of some of the sods who get the psalms and the sprinkling of holy water. However — don't let me stop you in full stride.'

'I thought, too, you'd like to know the latest news of your Maurice Crillon. He's leading everyone a bloody dance.'

'Ah, the dear chap. Who's everyone, though?'

'Us. The Mafia — '

'For Sir bloody Julian?'

'No — they parted company.'

'Good for them. Who's he using now? Not back with you, I hope?'

'No. The Germans.'

Sir Andrew laughed. 'Well, well, back in the same old nest. Their archives, I suppose? Well, if they get it he can be sure it will never cause him any trouble. Safer perhaps than if you had it. So what's dear Maurice done?'

'Ditched the Mafia in Florence. Left one of their respected members trouserless and took off. Left also his girl friend in the family way.'

'Oh, bad show — but boys will be boys. He must have had good reason — for running, I mean.'

'Yes, he did. He'd got a Swiss girl friend to translate the stuff you'd hidden in the Augustus John.'

'Did he now. Well, that rules out looking behind the bog door to check the toilet paper. Well, well, the dear boy. Why should he be making all this stir?'

'Your guess might perhaps be a bit better than mine.'

'And what's yours?'

'Cussedness. Some people are like that. They don't like being pushed around.'

'There should be more people like that. Everyone is being pushed around in this fart-ass country. Pickets outside factories, societies for this and that, fill up the bloody census form or else. Don't park there — don't park here. Keep off the grass, block up the bridle paths . . . You want me to go on with the list?'

'No thanks. But what's your guess?'

'Haven't one. I ran out of guesses years ago. Have you forgotten that for a damned long time I lived and survived by them? What's A going to do if B does something and C does nothing and I've only got one shell up the spout and another in the chamber. Now, was that a mouse behind the arras or just the old house creaking or something that's going to end up — if you're quick enough — by your having, to corrupt the Old Bard, the job of lugging the guts into a neighbour room?'

'Andrew, in some way, to be crude — I think that you and this Crillon are deliberately buggering us about. I don't say without reason. But you know how I hate mysteries. Here's a chap who is cocking a snook at all comers over these papers of yours — and he knows what they are. His girl friend translated them for him. All right — if he regards them, and quite rightly, as your property why doesn't he just send them back to you? It would be the straightforward thing to do. Why doesn't he do that?'

'I've no idea — and that's God's truth. Still, as you say — it is a bit odd, ain't it?'

A little crossly for once, Warboys said, 'You must have some idea.'

'Sorry. I'm too old. I don't deal in ideas or ideals any longer. I just rise each morning with the sun my daily round of duty to run — and that takes all my time. I tell you this stately homes business is worse than Barnum and whoever the other was.'

'Bailey, I think.' Warboys laughed.

'Do you know what happened the other morning? A fair old gypsy type turns up here. Splendid face he had — Rembrandt would have gone crackers over it. Nobbles me in the sunken garden, pulls out a fistful of hundred pound notes. Fans them in my face as though he was showing a Royal Flush and wants to buy the centre piece of the fountain for some customer he's got living up in Golders Green. I had to make up my mind quickly about kicking his arse out of the place or liking him. Chose the latter on humanitarian grounds and we ended up having a nice chat and I took him in to the kitchen for a bottle of

Guinness. He told me he had eighteen children — not all by his wife — and God knows how many grandchildren. Then he pulls a bottle from his pocket and offers it to me for a fiver. He said two spoonfuls at night, no matter what your age, would work wonders when you bedded with your woman.'

'And you bought it?'

'No. But I think Lloyd, my chauffeur, could have done.'

Warboys laughed and then said gently, 'Well, we do seem to have strayed from the point. Would it have been deliberately on your part?'

'The question direct. And the answer truthfully. I haven't the faintest idea what this Crillon is playing at. You have my word. But whatever it is, I hope he is enjoying himself while he can. By God, I wish I were his age again — no need for any bottle of buck-you-up-oh then!'

'Odd you should have taken a great fancy to him.'

'I've taken fancies to all sorts in my time. Cheeky buggers and sneaky buggers. Good, sound, solid upright types make dull company. That's why for years I've enjoyed yours. Nothing penny plain about you, dear Warboys.'

'Or you — I think you're holding

something back from me.'

'Well, I've done that before as you know. But it's always been for your own good.'

'Thanks. Now come clean. What is or has been going on between you and Crillon?'

Sir Andrew laughed and raising his port glass rubbed it gently against the side of his nose, starlight brightening his eyes as he regarded Warboys. He said, 'Nothing. What could?'

'That's what I'd like to know. I think, maybe, that this is the first time in my life that I have showed the quick flirt of the underskirt of frustration.'

'Something wrong with your metaphor. But I get the meaning. If there is any answer it is that I'm enjoying myself. Here's a rather wayward, brilliant Froggy, with the eyes and the hands of a great artist, a law unto himself, a dealer in magic and spells who's got everyone at Birdcage and beyond with their knickers in a twist. He's an adventurer and a rogue and has a silver tongue and a silken touch with women — and he's got the Establishment, Birdcage, the Mafia and God-knows who else all running round and tripping over one another for no reason at all on God's earth that any of them can think of — and all over a few sheets of paper with a list of names of bloody-would-have-been traitors most of whom now are pushing up the daisies. Of course, one of that lot will get him in the end.'

'And that doesn't worry you?'

'Not in the least. Why should it?'

'I can't think.'

'Then give it a rest.'

Warboys smiled and shook his head. 'As far as Birdcage is concerned there can be no burial without the body.'

Somewhere in the far woods a bird called and Sir Andrew said, pleased, 'Did you hear that? A bloody night-jar calling. Haven't heard one around here for years. In my father's time there were plenty. Night hawks he called 'em.'

Warboys, later in the main guest room, lying under the canopy of the Elizabethan four-poster bed, the mattress offering only lumpy and Spartan comfort to the body, pondered Sir Andrew's obvious evasions — knowing, too, that Sir Andrew knew he knew that they were evasions — and knew more, that nothing could extract from this man anything he wished to keep secret. He understood, too, that he was gone beyond all claims of loyalty to his old service. Curiosity inhabited his mind like some sylph making nudity more apparent by its absence as, dancing, her draperies swung about her like wood smoke in the wind.

He shrugged his shoulders and gave up, reaching for his bedside book — Gibbon's *Decline and Fall*, volume two, knowing that he was never in his lifetime ever going to finish the complete work — but it was a healthier way to court Nature's soft nurse than taking sleeping pills.

★   ★   ★

It was Berini, by nature a lazy man though very far from unintelligent and certainly absolutely diligent in his commitment to Signor Andretti, who proposed the arrangement with the other two, the Englishman and the German. Each of them, for some days, had monitored Trudi's movements to her school and back from it in the afternoon. Inevitably they had become aware of one another. Once she was at her school they were free. Contact with the Englishman had been made easy since they both now worked towards a common purpose — to find Crillon, obtain his document and see it safely to Birdcage Walk. This link was, however, unknown to the German, since he had not been briefed with the full past history of the affair, or the nature of the document which Crillon possessed. After two days of monitoring Trudi from her lodgings to her school and then picking her up again as she left for her lodgings and then hanging about until the light went on in her bedroom or, sometimes, following her evening stroll to the lakeside before she retired, Berini approached the Englishman as the light went out in her bedroom and said, '*Signore*, what we are doing is completely *pazzo*.'

'*Pazzo?*'

'Mad. I am from Signor Andretti and you are from Signor Warboys. Why we not share our work?'

'Why not? The whole thing is daft anyway. I'm only here on a flier. From what I know it seems to me unlikely that Crillon will show up. For what reason?'

'Ah, *signore*, I feel that too. But such are my instructions. Wherever this Crillon has had contacts then there is someone waiting for him. In Cragnac. Also in England, in Salisbury with this Sir Starr.'

'What about the Kraut?'

'He is — as you say — a different pot of tea. I have no warmth in my heart to spare him his fatigue.'

So it was arranged that one day the Englishman would do the morning to the late afternoon when the school closed for the day, and then Berini — who loved his siesta — would take over until Trudi was safely in

271

bed. After two days it was noticed that the German had been given supplementary help. Two Germans now shared the vigil.

Through all this Trudi pursued her well-regulated life and all the watchers were content that, if Crillon made personal contact with her, or by telephone or letter arranged a rendezvous, then they would be aware of any deviation from her routine and could act accordingly. Personally the Englishman, knowing that Birdcage had swamped every possible venue where Crillon might show, thought the whole thing was a waste of time. Still the weather was good and the food at his hotel excellent. He had had such assignments before and knew how to make himself comfortable — the car radio, a supply of books, and the correspondence course he was taking in Hebrew in the hope of getting a Middle East assignment which would take him away from the English winters. And Berini, when on school duty, just sat in his car with his mind a pleasant and restful blank except for the recurring phases when he thought of the way Crillon had treated him — though these tended to become wider spaced as the days passed and he concentrated more and more on his feelings for Carla who in a very long session had told him all she knew of Crillon and so some yet-to-reach-ripeness accord had been born between them. And how Aldo — his eye always on the main chance — had encouraged this to the point of hinting that the baby she carried could . . . well, there were ways. But Berini had been in his own mind firm about this. Life was sacred — unless of course someone had crossed his uncle — and that of a child doubly sacred. But anyway . . . one would see.

★ ★ ★

On the Thursday morning of that week Maurice Crillon left his hotel at Brient for good, with a few slight regrets about the receptionist, and motored down the lake to Interlaken and then took the north shore road along Lake Thun a few miles to Merligen — some four kilometres from Gunten. He booked into a lakeside hotel — taking a double room — in his own name and saying that his wife would be joining him late on the evening of the next day for the weekend. That evening before, during and after dinner he drank heavily and quite genuinely so that the staff and the other guests were well aware of it. He slept late the next morning and came down with a hangover which was yet far from abandoning him.

Just before lunch he drove off and took the road back to Interlaken and then around the far shore towards Spiez. Some way from Spiez he pulled off the road and slept again for a couple of hours and woke feeling more his old self, though still tender-headed, but with a growing lift in his spirits. At about the time that the watchers outside Trudi's school were anticipating her leaving for the day he drove into Spiez.

That afternoon the Englishman was on duty, parked a little way beyond the school, listening to a reading from Goethe on Zürich radio and wishing he were back home in Hampstead waiting for his own children to return from school. Children he loved because they were genuinely unpredictable. The unpredictability of the adults he so often shadowed always had an artificial air, never entirely natural . . . borrowed suits he called it. The creases made by others never fitting those of their temporary hosts. The tubby little Fritz down the road had turned up this day in a battered old van and was wearing — perhaps simply to give himself a change of personality, or was he an amateur dramatic following a hobby in his employer's time? — workmen's overalls and a black beard. A zealous servant he thought, remembering his days in Birdcage's Berlin office, but

— *Blinder Eifer schadet nur.*

After the children had come scattering out of the school, a colourful noisy flock to be met by parents on foot, in cars, and two or three to hang around the request stop to wait for the Beatenburg — Thun bus, the Birdcage man kept his eye on the bicycle stand to the side of the main entrance steps where Trudi's machine stood with others belonging to teachers.

He waited and saw the teachers emerge until there was only one bicycle left — Trudi's. He waited another hour and there was still no sign of Trudi. A little later an elderly woman whom he had seen before and had placed as probably the headmistress of the establishment came out wearing a hat and a light summer coat, got into a Volkswagen parked in the forecourt and drove off and — to his relief — was waved away from the top of the steps by Trudi who, as the car disappeared, turned and went back into the school. A little sigh of relief escaped him. Friday night, the end of the working week, and the good *Direktorin* was probably off for dinner and bridge with a covey of other headmistresses while Trudi Keller held the fort in charge of the few boarders for whom the notice board at the entrance gate said the school catered. The poor little brats whose

275

parents were glad to be shot of them, telling themselves without guilt that absence makes the heart grow fonder. He thought back to his own miserable days at boarding school. Well ... Berini would turn up in due course, wondering what had happened, and he could take over the all night shift if it came to that. After all *die Direktorin* might have some cosy friend whose Friday nights she brightened. Male or female he wondered, but not with any great degree of concentration.

He sighed and turned on the radio to be met by the sound of a set of Swiss handbell ringers. He reached for a bar of Toblerone chocolate and wondered briefly whether it was a Pavlovian reaction.

★ ★ ★

Maurice Crillon ran the nose of the motor boat which he had hired in Spiez into the soft sand of a tiny beach two hundred yards east of the school and jumped out, taking the anchor with him. He jabbed one of its flukes deep into the soft turf of the low bank which backed the beach and then, in the fading light of the warm July night, he began to walk along the narrow strand towards the lakeside garden of the school. A little mist was rising over the lake, distorting the lights of the waterside houses and towns and the air was full of the scent of unseen flowers.

The first few moments he knew would be difficult, but after that she would crumple. She always had and she always would. Often before he had come to her this way of a Friday night when she stood in for the headmistress. She would be sitting in the little garden room, windows and door open to the night, knitting or reading or doing both. The blonde *Hausfrau* . . . once loved, still loved in a way . . . who had loved and still loved him . . . finding resolution to discard him only when he was absent. He had treated her badly, like so many others. But could the leopard change its spots? Anyway, he was coming bearing gifts.

He came to the waterside steps that led up to the garden. Going up them he saw the light through the open door of the garden room, the phantom movement of moths making a moving mist around the outside door light. The air was full of the richness of the night-scented stocks that bordered the path between the play-scuffed grass of the lawns. Children, she loved them. Himself? No — he always had the feeling that they looked at him with wiser and more discerning eyes than any adult. Grown-ups were fools — only looking for what they wanted to see. Children saw things as they were.

She heard him coming for he deliberately scuffed at the gravel. He had no wish to alarm her. He needed her — perhaps now more than he had ever needed anyone. Another paradise lay ahead but she had to help him reach it . . . would do, he knew, because he could make it worth her while. After all, his role was a new one . . . a kindly magician, opening up an Aladdin's cave for her. She had to help him because for the first time in his life he knew he was in deep, bad trouble. Some people, most people, were born to be made fools of. But not the likes of Signor Andretti. What devil in him had made him think he could pull the nose of such a man? Perhaps the simple fact that the temptation to play David with a Goliath was irresistible. After all, David had got away with it . . .

When he stood just outside the garden door she looked up at him without surprise, and then she said calmly, 'I must tell you, Maurice, that I had a funny feeling that something like this would happen. Always, when you are in real trouble you come back to me.'

'How would you know I was in trouble?'

She dropped her knitting to her lap, pushed the ends of the needles into the ball of wool, and said, 'At this moment there are men out on the road, put there to watch me. But not because they want anything from me. They are hoping I might lead them to you. And this is what I shall do in a few minutes unless you can give me good and honest reasons why I should not.'

'This I swear to God I will do. When are you off duty?'

'At ten-thirty when Frau Schliegel returns.'

'I have a boat along the beach. I will wait for you at the bottom of the steps.'

'I may not come.'

'Then I am destroyed.' But in himself he knew that he was not. In her mind, he knew, was the wish to abandon him, but in her heart there was the other thing which had no true name. It was a thing, he knew, which had been from birth forever denied him. God, for some reason, had not made him that way.

She said, 'I make no promises.'

'I shall be waiting below the steps.'

He turned and went away down the path and on to the little strip of strand and sat down.

Trudi picked up her needles and returned to her knitting.

Outside the school the watchers watched. Just after half-past ten the school principal's car came up the road from Gunten and turned into the courtyard.

The watchers waited for Trudi to come out and take her bicycle to go back to her lodgings. They waited an hour and one by one the few window lights in the school went out and, last of all, the light over the main entrance.

Seeing this, Berini, who was sitting with the Englishman in his car said, 'Friday night — and she stays the night. So?'

'So,' said the Englishman, 'you take the first part of the night and I'll be back at four to relieve you. You know, when I first got into this game I was young and looking forward to all the excitement. Now I know that excitement is only one-tenth of the business — the rest is tedium.'

A little later, some two hundred yards east of the school on the lakeside, Maurice Crillon poled the motor-boat gently off the strand and when it was a hundred yards out shipped the oar he was using and sat facing Trudi. Until now they had spoken only a few brief and — on Trudi's side — guarded words together.

Crillon said, 'Because of the men outside the school we drift up the lake some way before I start the motor. Happily the wind is in the right direction. Maybe that it is so is a good sign. It is also a good sign for us both that you have decided to join me.'

'Have I?'

'Oh, yes. One day you will fully understand your own character. I think you begin to now. Underneath that Trudi you show the world is the other Trudi — the one I first knew and then loved in Zürich. Since I have treated you so badly, you could long ago have cut yourself free from me. But you did not — because deep in your heart there was something in you of the same nature as myself.'

'This talk tells me nothing. If you now want something from me — then tell me what it is. Then you shall have my answer. Yes or No. And yes — you go away and leave me, and I hate you and then you come back and at the first touch I forget my hate. I despise myself for it. For being like that.'

'And I despise myself for being what I am. But God made us both this way. Perhaps one day we shall understand why. In a little while when we have drifted far enough up the lake — *le bon Dieu* has favoured us with the wind — I shall start the motor and we shall cross over to Spiez. You remember how sometimes in the old days we would take the steamer across for the weekend and stay in the Eden-Kurhaus and then make excursions to the Kandertal and Simmental?'

'I remember. But you do not talk to me

281

now, Maurice, out of the memory of good but past days. You talk because you are, you think, gentling me, beginning to woo me again, because you have something to ask me — something which will save your own skin. Underneath everything I think you are — maybe for the first time in your life — frightened for yourself. You have followed some fantasy, tried to live this life like a dream life — everything for Maurice — and now it has all gone sour for you. Maybe, even, made you for the first time frightened.'

'Maybe.'

'So what do you want from me?'

Crillon smiled, his face clear in the starlight to her, and somewhere in her heart a rising sadness for him. He could have been good and done so much with the great gifts God had given him. But he had treated all these gifts like a small and over-pampered boy — tired of a new toy presented in the morning long before the morning had worn away.

It was some time before he answered, and then he said, 'Just to bear witness to something which is going to happen. To do as I say and ask no questions. To play a true part and know that you will be rewarded for it.'

'You ask me to do something for money?'

'There would be that, of course, among

other things. But I am asking you for far more than that. My freedom from certain things in my past.'

Trudi shook her head. 'I make no promise until I hear what it is you wish from me — it could be that you will ask too much.'

'Very well, I will be frank. I will tell you after we have reached Spiez.'

He leaned forward from the stern thwart, bending to start the little marine engine, and smiled at her in the bows. Seeing the starlight on his face Trudi sighed, knowing in her heart that she could never find a way to a final rejection of this man who took life so lightly and love so waywardly.

The engine came to life and Crillon, knowing that everything would be as he wanted it, had to be as he wanted it, pushed the tiller round and headed the boat southwards across the lake to Spiez where his car waited.

It was some time after midnight before they arrived at the Merligen hotel. Trudi went up to their room and to bed, but Crillon stayed in the hotel lounge and called for a bottle of whisky. He sat with it for an hour, exasperating the night waiter with chatter which became more and more wayward and inconsistent as he drank. Finally he stumbled away and up to their room where Trudi lay in bed. He was drunker than she had ever seen him. For an odd moment or two her heart found genuine sympathy for him, and admiration. Maurice in all he did — good and bad — was no believer in half measures. When he finally tumbled into the adjoining single bed she put out the light and lay in the darkness, and as the first heavy snoring broke from him, memory took her back to that first day when he had walked into her father's yard and — so typically — had charmed his way into a job and into her heart.

The next morning Crillon woke late and with a heavy hangover. Trudi had already gone to breakfast. When he came down, looking as she had never seen him before — hung-over and genuinely jittery — she wondered why, even for the simplest deception, he would always insist on doing his utmost (even to the point of exaggeration) not just to play the part he had designated for himself, but actually to abandon the normal Crillon to become the one which fitted his needs. But this time it was different for her because she understood his danger and was now far from lost to any sympathy for him.

He quarrelled and complained over a breakfast which he hardly touched, and insisted on having two large brandies. He was short with her to the point of rudeness.

During breakfast he asked for a picnic lunch for the two of them and arranged for the hire of a rowing boat.

When they finally left the hotel to walk through its garden to the small jetty and their boat, the dining room waiter, watching them go, said to the waitress, 'There is a pig of a man. With such a fine-looking woman, too. I never tell you this, *liebe* Lotte, but so was my father with my mother. Terrible . . . so terrible that my brother and I decide it must finish and we must do the finishing. But the good Lord spares us the trouble. He is staggering home one night in Berne when he staggers too far into the road and under a lorry. You know something, too? Ah, women . . . my mother weeps for him and is in mourning for over a year. What is it about some women that a man can treat them like dirt and abuse them and yet they take their martyrdom with patience and remember only the few good things that marriage gave them?'

* * *

Five days later Warboys, a rose in the lapel of his light grey suit, the memory of the girl in the Shepherd Market flower shop warm and promising, as, indeed, he hoped the day would be, fingered briefly his old Etonian tie and looked up with a bright and almost youthful smile as Kerslake came in.

He waved him to a chair and said, 'Splendid morning. Pippa passes and all that, what? And so, we must presume, has our elusive Maurice Crillon. Such sadness. Cut off, if not exactly in the springtime of life, at least in full manhood. Death as it must . . . and all that. And no body yet found. Possibly never to be found.' He tapped the report in front of him. 'You've seen this, of course?'

'Yes, but I'm not inclined to believe it.'

'Why not? Dead drunk. Had been most of the weekend. Strips to his bathing trunks and goes into the lake for a cool-off. Then — *Hey presto!* — goes down like a lead plummet. Had an uncle, you know — Regius Professor of Theology or something at Oxford. Not sure which now. Salmon fishing on the Wye one June . . . no fish, low water, bloody bored, too much port at lunch, so strips and goes in and never comes up again. And Crillon — let's face it — was sooner or later for the high jump with Andretti after him.'

'He'd hardly have tucked the documents in his bathing trunks. There was nothing with his clothes and luggage.'

'True. But they could be in some safety deposit box. After all, it was Switzerland.

What secrets and what fortunes do the little gnomes there protect?'

'If the drowning were faked then Trudi Keller must have been in the know.'

'Finger to the side of the nose? Arranged?'

'Could be, sir.'

'How?'

'Her statement to the Swiss authorities says that they rowed the boat up the lakeside some way towards Interlaken and then went ashore to sunbathe and have lunch. His, according to her, was chiefly an alcoholic one.'

'Drunk — and then insists on going for a swim. My father was a martinet about that — no bathing until two hours after a meal. And then?'

'He gets into difficulties. Goes down, comes up and shouts for help — and then goes down again.'

'At which, like Grace Darling in different circumstances, she mans the boat and rows to his help.'

'Quite so — and goes in after him. But she can't find him and there's nothing she can do.'

Warboys smiled. 'I can see the scene. Dreadful.'

'If it ever occurred.'

'You're doubting the word of a lady?'

'And an actress of sorts. Member of long

standing with a Zürich Amateur Dramatic Society, and produces the children's school plays at Gunten — according to our man out there.'

'Who must still have a very red face at being hoodwinked by Crillon. But go on — the main point has still to rise above the dawn-flushed Eastern horizon.'

'She goes back to the hotel and carries on the act. She's playing a part and giving it everything.'

'If I don't ask why yet it is because first I'd like to know what really happened, do you imagine, to Crillon?'

'He'd got it all arranged. He never went into the water at all, I think he simply walked off, leaving her — with her agreement — and caught a bus on the lakeside road. There's a Thun — Interlaken service.'

'Dark glasses? False moustache? Don't tell me he was a Dramatic Society buff?'

'He didn't have to be. He was, or is, a born natural. For him — 'All the world's a stage . . .''

'Ah — *Hanc personam induisti: agenda est?*'

'You escape me, sir.'

'Seneca — 'You have assumed this part: it must be acted.''

'Hopefully I'll come to that level one day, sir. But, to revert to Crillon. He had it all arranged before he even co-opted her help.'

'I don't quarrel with that. But — why on earth did she agree to help him, lie for him, act the distraught woman in the hotel, and the grief-stricken girl friend at the official enquiry? She had no reason to do him any favour.'

'There must have been a *quid pro quo*. And a very substantial or compelling one, too.'

'I wonder what?'

'I've no idea, sir.'

'Full marks for frankness. But perhaps time will show. Your time, not mine. Only a little while to go, Kerslake. So, there we are. Freedom lies only a few bow shots ahead of me. Sir Julian is never going to get what he wants. Nor are the archive blokes here. And for that I shall weep no more nor sigh nor groan. Our late enemies, now staunch Nato companions, will have a permanent gap in their archives, too. And Sir Andrew — with whom I have lunch at Lord's today before enjoying the slow delights of cricket — my father, as a stripling of sixteen, once bowled out the great W. G. Grace but irascibly he not only refused to leave the wicket, but also to give chapter and verse for his reasons — and to come back, belatedly, to Sir Andrew . . . well, in his coarse English-before-Agincourt manner he will no doubt utter some jolly profanity. Quite frankly, I'm sick and tired of this whole business.'

Kerslake said gently, 'Are you asking me to close the file?'

Feigning horror, Warboys raised his hands. 'Good God, man — that is the blasphemy of all blasphemies. The archive boys still have hundreds of ancient files open. They still hope that one day something will turn up to prove conclusively who murdered the Princes in the Tower.'

'I think, sir, that we should keep an eye on the girl, Trudi.'

'Poor heart-broken lass. But yes — why not. Also, I think a call to Signor Andretti would be a politeness. There is no more he can do. But tell him that we will honour our side of the bargain appertaining to his gambling relation. We may, who knows, need him for some other quite different help in the future. Allies, no matter how reprehensible, must be treated with outward courtesy.'

Later, after lunch at Lord's, and sitting in the Long Room while an unexpected gentle summer drizzle fell outside and the covers were on the wickets, looking like the canopy of a sunken canal barge, Warboys — undeterred by the other people close around them, knowing that the best security for secrets was to pass them in a crowd, particularly this crowd, well-fed and wined, and still wining

— said to Sir Andrew, 'Bit of news for you, my old dear.'

'Good, I hope. Why does it always bloody rain when I come here? Perhaps I've offended the rain gods. Touchy buggers. Have been ever since Noah cocked a snook at them.'

'Well, not so good — since you took quite a fancy to him. Your artist laddie — Crillon.'

'What about him, the dear chap?'

'Well, he was week-ending with some girl friend on Lake Thun. Boating excursion. Lap, lap of wavelets as they loitered in paradise. Sip, sip, too, of *vino*. Girl said he was well away. Decides to go for a swim. Wades in — strikes out — and then suddenly goes under never to come up.'

'Good God! I always thought that bit about never bathing right after a meal was apocryphal. Poor chap. What an end! What a waste! Still, there you are . . . in the midst of life. You're absolutely certain about all this?'

'Certain. Girl went in after him. Couldn't find him.'

'Plucky. Got guts some girls. I say, old chap — this has really upset me. Won't mind, will you, if I give this caper up? Rain's in for the day, anyway. Dear, dear — such talent. Christine will be quite cut up. She took a fancy to him. She'll be home soon from France, you know. Oh, dear — slog all the way up here to be rained off, and now you tell me this.'

'Sorry, Andrew. But I felt you would want to know.'

When Sir Andrew had gone Warboys lit a cigar and watched the rain fall on the covers. He sat, puzzled. Sir Andrew had he wished could have simulated grief . . . in his time he had played many parts. But the odd thing was that he had no doubt that his friend had been reacting quite genuinely.

★ ★ ★

Signor Andretti — at a table in the great window bay which held as though framed in a picture a view over the garden and distant Florence — gently lifted one of the pieces of a vast jig-saw puzzle based on the Hieronymus Bosch painting *The Garden of Earthly Delights* thus completing the flowing tresses of a naked woman in the act — though this he had not completed yet but knew from memory of the original — of being embraced or raped by a naked youth — looked up at Berini and said, 'The one thing about the English is that you can trust their given word. It is, perhaps, the most endearing of their many stupidities. Your cousin in London will come to no harm.'

'And do you believe that Crillon is dead?'

'The girl, Trudi, says so. Drowned.'

'There's only her word. Why should she do him any favour — even a last one?'

'Perhaps he gave her something in return.'

'The document?'

'Idiot. No — something which she couldn't refuse.'

'But what?'

'Something. But don't ask me what because I have no idea.'

'And Crillon? Do we still go after him? He has insulted and humiliated me.'

'Just write it off to experience.'

Berini sighed. 'Very well. But he is a man I can't understand. To insult and defy you so.'

Signor Andretti dropped another piece into place and found it was the gleaming eye in the head, now revealed, of a bird like a goldfinch. His mind went to the shooting of little birds in the foothills far up the Arno. Spitted and roasted in the open and eaten with rough Chianti . . . delightful. In old age one went back to simple pleasures.

He looked up, shook his head, and said, 'Then you are very stupid. The world is full of such men. They are born out of their time. And the world needs them. Good or bad. Garibaldi. Mussolini. Dante. Cortez . . . Maestro Bosch here — ' He fitted another piece and part of the naked rump of the lover with the girl in the water took shape.

'If he lives, he has insulted us. We should go after him!'

'Idiot. This is no vendetta. Has he raped your sister? Or cheated like some night-club owner over his protection money?'

'He has broken the heart of a woman. Maybe many women.'

Signor Andretti looked up and laughed. 'Now you are a double idiot. No man can break the heart of a woman. While she weeps her eyes rove looking for the next lover. Women are incurable optimists. Your aunt, my dear departed wife, may her soul rest in peace . . . ' He crossed himself. 'She was a woman. But also — when she wished — she was a man. I married her knowing nothing. She taught me much, and when she had made a man of me she went back to being a woman. You understand that?'

'No.'

'Perhaps not. It has to be experienced. You should go find such a woman for yourself. One who will love you and deceive you and educate you. If you need a suggestion — then I give you one. Go marry Aldo Pandolfi's sister. Carla I think her name is. No?'

'Yes. But why her?'

'Because she saw — though not absolutely

clearly — what there was in this Crillon for her to make. She might make something of you. And this you certainly need. What man watches the front of a school and has not the wit to remember that there is a back entrance to it?'

'But, I understand she is . . . *gravidanza*.'

Signor Andretti shook his head. 'No. Aldo tells me not. She makes up this story for Crillon's benefit — hoping to keep him with her. It is time you married. And it would be good to have Aldo in the family for do not think he is nothing, all puffing and blowing. He has the eye for truth in paintings and will find someone else to take Crillon's place. You think there is only one Crillon in the world? It is full of them. All most of them need is a little encouragement. Now go down to the good Pandolfi *casa* and tell them that Crillon is dead. Carla will weep for your benefit and Aldo will weep more truly for the loss of an almost irreplaceable partner. But neither will weep long. You will not find written above their doorway — *Lasciate ogni speranza, voi ch'entrate*.'

'You mean go now — this moment?'

'Idiot. If you delay you may find — to be coarse, which mostly I do not approve of — that another man's trousers are already hanging over the rail at the bottom of the bed. *Mamma mia* — for an intelligent man you can be extraordinarily stupid at times. *Va via* — you are spoiling my pleasure in this puzzle.'

★   ★   ★

Kerslake — now behind Warboys' desk — was enjoying Sir Julian's discomfiture. The dark eyes shone angrily. But even so — with no gleam of hope in them.

Sir Julian said, 'I don't believe a word of any of this story. Why can't you at least be frank with me and tell me that no power on God's earth was ever going to let you give the documents back to me?'

'What does it matter? They are now rotting somewhere on the bed of Lake Thun. The story has been a long one. But now comes the final chapter. Either the body, from buoyant accumulation of decomposition gases, will surface and something will be salvaged — unless, of course, some passing steamer or speedboat rips into it unknowingly and it is Hail briefly and Farewell finally. But your last point is true — as you have long known — that we could not let you have the documents back. You've known that. That's why you went to Andretti. So why do you come here, Sir Julian? There is nothing we can do.'

'You really think he's dead? You believe all that story?'

'What do your German friends believe?'

'God knows. That he is dead, I suppose, and that he will never surface.'

'Sensible of them. All State archives have *lacunae*.' He stressed the plural ending purely for his own pleasure and then took more pleasure silently in the faint oral conjunction with *lacustrine*. Here, indeed was truly a lake secret — about which he had his own reservations. He added, 'No records are ever complete. History is an iceberg. There's more below than ever shows above.' He was — though not showing it — pleased with himself — a council school, then grammar school, moon-faced yokel from the leafy lanes of Devon . . . *Where I have been and still am sad in this dull Devonshire.* He could have said it aloud to Warboys and got a pat on the back for remembering his Herrick.

Sir Julian rose, and then — to Kerslake's concealed surprise — smiled, the change of features suddenly revealing something maybe of the long ago, uncorrupted, ambitious Julian Markover. He said almost cheerfully, 'Well, one thing I'm glad about and that is that probably nobody is ever going to see them again.'

Kerslake nodded, but not entirely in

agreement. Though there was no logic in him to make him think otherwise. Life, however, was full of surprises. Part of the fun was trying to anticipate their advent. He said, 'I'll let Mr Warboys know you called. He'll be very sorry to have missed you.'

Sir Julian said, 'I doubt it. But it is polite of you to say so. And if I may say so again — if you ever get tired of this place I could find you something very worthwhile in my organization. Think it over.'

With Sir Julian gone Kerslake did think it over briefly but not seriously. He saw vividly one of his father's sleek Scandaroon pigeons perched on the stump of his mutilated hand.

9

Monsieur Bonivard pulled his car up outside the cottage and sat for a moment or two admiring the neat strip of garden which fronted the road. Albertine roses flourished in profusion over the front wall of the cottage. The little roadside strip was planted with yellow and red hollyhocks and multi-coloured petunias and a bordering of pansies. House martins nested under the eaves, busily hawking the surrounding country for food to bring to their second broods. The window frames he noticed had recently been freshly painted. Gaston kept the place well, always had, and always for the sake of Madame Crillon.

He got out of the car and walked into the side garden where the part open cottage door told him that Gaston was around somewhere working. He turned towards the large vegetable garden in search of him. From up the river came the sound of children shouting and playing, the thuds of a football being kicked bruising the air. Any ball that came over into the garden was held by Gaston for a week before it was restored to its owner.

Transiently for a moment or two as he walked down the path to the river he wondered at the state of a mind which could hold so tenaciously to agnosticism as Gaston's did. *L'homme moderne* . . . without belief and so without prayer. Such souls were waterless wastes . . . however God in His mercy understood all and was of infinite wisdom and forgiveness right up to the last moment. Miss that chance of supplication and Hell awaited. He had prayed that in his last moment Maurice had found such grace. Gaston, he knew, would never seek it. But the man had goodness in him.

He found him taking a rest by the river, watching the swifts hawk low over it and the little rings of water where fish rose to take the insects that fell from the overhanging riverside foliage.

Sitting by him, briefly greeted, he said, 'I hear, Gaston, that your son is to be married?'

'That is so, monsieur.'

'Did you know that long ago Madame Crillon made her will such that on her death the cottage was to go to her son for his lifetime, and then at his death it was to come to the Church?'

'No, monsieur.'

'Well, it is so. And now poor Maurice has gone. The cottage is ours. Will it be against your principles to look after the place for us?'

'Yes, monsieur.'

'Ah, at least you are consistent in your beliefs. One day, though, you will understand them to be wrong. In the meantime I have a proposal to make to you. Madame Crillon was of the Faith, but you had no objection to working for her.'

'Why should I have? She was a good woman. I did not look further than that.'

'And is your son a good man?'

'Who says he is not?'

'No one that I know. He is a good son of the Church, too.'

'Every man decides his own beliefs. I do not interfere with his or others', monsieur.'

'There is virtue in that. I was thinking that since you love this garden, and your son will need somewhere to live when he is married, I could let him have it at a small rent and you could carry on here. Does that appeal to you?'

'I shall have to think about it, monsieur.'

'Do that, Gaston.'

'I will, monsieur . . . and, monsieur, thank you. I am grateful . . . on my son's behalf.'

'I understand.'

The priest stood up, felt his arm begin to move automatically to bless the man and stopped the movement. All in good time, he thought. God is ever patient and so must his servants be . . . aye, even to the last second of an unbeliever's life.

As he went back to his car he was thinking of the lady who had visited him some days ago, surprising him on his hands and knees as he clipped the grass around his church's old yew, and the talk they had had before she made confession . . . small sins of greed and envy . . . of the bottle and the table . . . and one small peculation in a tourist shop at Domme where she had stolen two china mugs on the spur of the moment — 'Father, I really don't know what came over me. But you see one had the name Maurice on it and the other the name Andrew . . . father and son . . . it was irresistible. But I sent the money anonymously two days later, though I do know that does not wash away the sin.' Yes, a very pleasant lady whose husband's distant ancestors had carried the Cross against the infidels and during their far from incontinent absence ensured the virtue of their own women with chastity belts.

At that moment, sitting out on the balcony of their first-floor drawing room were Sir Andrew and Lady Starr. Sir Andrew, his eyes on the setting sun, waiting for its lower rim to be nibbled by the pinnation of a group of firs on the crest of the western slope of the hills across the river so that he could ring for Hanson and drinks, said, 'It's damned refreshin' to have you back again, my dear. 'Fraid I've got into a lot of sloppy habits while you've been away. Hanson's been chivvying me — but he lacks your charming authority. Tell you one thing I can't find. Used to have rather fancy dress shirt . . . ruffles down the front, you know. Damn thing's gone.'

'I know my love. I sent it to the Women's Institute jumble sale. Made you look like some pouting old fan-tail dove. My love . . . it is nice to be back. Do we have to go through all the sun and tree ritual. This is special . . . I'm back, and I need a drink.'

Sir Andrew smiled. 'For you — anything.' He reached back and pressed the bell push on the wall behind him, saying, 'Tough titty about our dear Maurice Crillon, what? I mean one can't feel as one would if it were all as it should have been and he had actually been with us bed and board, private school and Eton and all that from nappy days. But nevertheless . . . For whom the bell tolls, and you never know what day it's going to. That's why it makes good sense to start each day with a prayer. Rise every morning with the sun your daily course of whatever it is to run. Or something. Memory going a touch these days.'

'You sound as though you've had one or two already, dear.'

'Swear not. Delayed emotion, now released — you're home and my heart leaps up. So you looked up this Trudi Keller gal?'

'I tried to. I drove back by Thun and went out to Gunten. She'd left her lodgings and the school and gone back to Zürich. I really couldn't be bothered then to go all the way up there.'

'Of course not.'

'You're not too upset are you, Andrew . . . about his being dead?'

'Well, a little of course. You know, although it was a question of son and no son, I did really take to the chap.'

'Yes, of course. Well, I brought you something. When I unpack I'll give it to you. It's a little framed photograph of him as a boy. When I called on monsieur *le curé* we went round to the cottage and there it was hanging on the wall. He was charming about letting me have it.'

'Good chap, was he?'

'Splendid. We did the right thing, you know, dear. It would never have worked. You do agree?'

'Yes. I agree. But the thought of that poncing, priest-loving great-nephew of mine taking over here . . . Well, that's the way the world wags.' He leaned back again and thumbed the bell push.

When Hanson arrived, Sir Andrew said, 'Where the devil have you been, Hanson? We've been sitting up here with our tongues hanging out and the sun already well below the yard arm.'

'I'm sorry, Sir Andrew, there's been a little trouble below stairs.'

'I don't care if there's been an earthquake. Get us some drinks.'

'Yes, sir.'

Hanson gone, Lady Starr said, 'You do bully the poor fellow, Andrew.'

'Bully my foot. He thrives on it. And anyway it's part of his job. Told him twenty years ago when he first came — remember him then? A ham-fisted, foot-shuffling young feller, unemployed miner from Kent, wanting to go into service. Why not? Better than breaking your back at the coal face. Can't think why I took him on and trained him. Told him then it was a dog's life being in service.'

'Your memory is going, dear. It was his father who was the miner. Hanson was a barman at the Hotel Metropole in Brighton.'

'Was he? Well, damme, whatever he was I told him that there would be nothing cushy about working here. Up with the lark and no bed some nights until cock-crow.' He turned as Hanson, coming up behind him, laid the drinks tray on their table. 'That right, Hanson?'

'More or less, sir. Yes.' Hanson deftly made and served their drinks; a large gin-Campari soda for Lady Starr, and a large Glenfiddich pure malt whisky, neat, for Sir Andrew who asked, 'Why Glenfiddich, Hanson?'

'Ignore him, Hanson,' said Lady Starr.

Sir Andrew grinned. 'Oh, yes, I see . . . Special occasion. Madam has returned from her Continental summer caperings.' He raised his glass and sipped her health, then continued, 'And now what's all this about trouble below stairs?'

'Not exactly below stairs. In the main hallway. A young foreign person who wishes to speak to you.'

'Is that so? What sort of a young foreign person? Black, red, yellow, white — and, of course, sex. And anyway — the garden shut fifteen minutes ago and I'm off duty. Tell it to go away.'

'I don't think she will, sir. If I may say so, sir — she's a very determined sort of young . . . well, not so young lady. She asked me to tell you that her name was Fräulein Trudi Keller.'

'Would you mind repeating that name?'

Lady Starr said, 'I got it very clearly, Andrew. Fräulein Trudi Keller.'

Sir Andrew leaned back in his chair, drank some more of his whisky and then put the glass down on the table, his hand shaking a little, and said, 'Well, I'm damned.'

'Yes, sir.'

'What do you mean — Yes, *sir* — Hanson?'

'That you're damned, dear — we all know it.' Lady Starr gave the butler a smile and went on, 'Show her up, Hanson.'

'Yes, my lady.'

When Hanson had gone Sir Andrew said, 'Pretty rum turnup for the book, eh? But what's she doing here?'

'I think she'll tell us that — and probably more.'

'You having one of your good-as-a-witch spells?'

'Maybe.'

'Well, I can't think what about.'

'I shouldn't try to anticipate. And do be nice, Andrew. You know . . . your really nice and sincere nice bit.'

'How could I be anything else to a woman — no matter what kind? My dear father tanned my arse for being rude to an under house-maid when I was seven. You know what he said as he whacked me? 'Courtesy to all is fundamental for the maintenance of good society. Hence, I impress this on you through your fundament. Never forget it.' I never have. I couldn't sit comfortably for three days.'

Trudi Keller was ushered through the french windows on to the balcony by Hanson who announced, 'Fräulein Keller, madame.'

Lady Starr rose and took the hand which Trudi held out a little hesitantly, saying, 'Fräulein — how nice to see you. Oh, forgive me. My husband, Sir Andrew.'

Sir Andrew, already on his feet, gave her a big smile and said, 'Surprise, surprise — but very welcome. Do sit down. Would you like a drink?'

As Trudi sat, she said, 'You are both very kind. Could I have, perhaps, a glass of milk? I am not very alcoholic, except now and then a little wine at meals.'

'Bully for you, my dear. Hanson — a glass of milk for Fräulein Keller.'

Lady Starr said, 'This is your first visit to England?'

'No, Madame. I am once here with a school party when I was sixteen. It is a country which I very much admire. You must have guessed, of course, that my being here now is to do with Monsieur Crillon. He talked often about you when we last met.'

'Ah, yes. And how sad, too . . . we have

308

heard about his death,' said Lady Starr. 'In fact on my way back home from France I tried to find you in Thun — but you had gone. We both wanted to know so much about . . . well — '

'I understand, Madame.' Trudi crossed her legs under her pleated white skirt, settled her handbag on her knees, and went on, 'It is difficult to begin at the beginning of all things with Maurice . . . so you will excuse if I do it as it comes to me.'

'You do it any way you like, my dear. Never did believe in begin at the beginning and end at the end. You know . . . *Crack! A pistol shot shattered the silence of the night.* Well that's a hell of a way from the beginning. Though, of course, a sure sign that it ain't going to be great literature so — '

'Andrew!'

'Sorry, my love.'

'I understand, please. Sir Starr is being kind.'

'Sir *Andrew* you must call him.'

'That is correct?'

'Yes, dear.'

'Ah, so. Well, I will tell you about Maurice. But first I must do other things. When he came to see me last, he said that he was worried that something bad might happen to him. Very worried. It is that which makes him drink so much. To forget. With Maurice, you understand, it is no good asking for reasons. You do as he says or you don't. With me I could never say no and mean it for long.' As she spoke she opened her large white summer handbag and pulled from it a half-folded long brown foolscap envelope. She handed it to Sir Andrew, saying, 'He did not tell me what was in it, but he said if anything happened to him I should come to you and say, 'Find a safer place for them this time.' Does that make sense to you, Sir Andrew?'

Sir Andrew, fingering the envelope, made no attempt to open it. It could only hold one thing and this time he would put them away safely . . . double-bolted and double-locked and forever part of the family records, snug and warm within the family archives . . . Crusaders' letters, the diary of the Starr who went down with his ship on the day Nelson died aboard *H.M.S. Victory* . . . his father's account of the last ever cavalry charge in the 1914–1918 war . . . dear girl, what a gift, and dear boy, chip off the old block. And more to come, he sensed, good as a witch, something in the air tonight . . . Prospero and Merlin. Magic still lived and worked, and a two-fingered gesture of contempt for all the Sir Julians of this world . . . Aye, and the same for Birdcage. Pity though he could never tell dear

Warboys about it. Trust no one.

At this point Lady Starr said gently, 'Perhaps you will tell us about . . . the boating and what happened on the lake?'

'Oh, that . . . well, he comes and finds me at the school one evening late. It is a Friday when I am on duty there for that is the evening that the *Frau Direktorin* goes out to play bridge with friends. He is in a bad state . . . already drinking, you know. Which is not like Maurice. So I see that he is really upset and very worried.'

They listened, the light beginning to fade a little as the sun dropped from sight behind the hills. They heard about his heavy drinking all that week-end and then his insisting on bathing from the boat on the Saturday afternoon.

' . . . he dives in and does not come up soon, but I think at first he plays a joke with me . . . staying under as long as he can. But in the end . . . he does not come up at all . . . Ah, such a moment I shall never forget.' She took a small handkerchief from her bag and touched her eyes with it.

Sir Andrew reached out and gently patted her arm and said, 'Nothing you could have done, my dear. Nothing . . . '

'I try to find him, but I cannot. So there is nothing I can do. Nothing. Still they do not find his body.'

'Happens sometimes, dear girl.'

'He was not a good husband to me, but I loved him. The heart, you know, refuses to listen to the head. So, when all the business about his death is done, I leave the school and go back to my parents in Zürich. That is where we first met and got married. He worked for my father. His hands, you know, were as good with a mallet and chisel as they were with paint brushes.'

Lady Starr said, 'You were married to him?'

'Oh, yes. My parents were against it so we went off together. In the end he leaves me — only coming back when he wants something or is in trouble. At Gunten I used my maiden name because I do not want people always asking questions about where is my husband. So, too, I leave Johan with my parents in Zürich. You say to yourself 'How could anyone fall in love with a man like that?' I say it to myself still. But it happens. After a time though, the pain goes. And now he has gone for good. I shall learn to live with that. I am a woman, and can be very sensible. When some men are what they are there is nothing else but to be . . . what you say? . . . *philosophisch*?'

'Philosophical. Quite right,' said Lady Starr.

'Yes, so. But it is hard for others. The ones who are small and ask the questions that tear at one's heart. Poor little Johan . . . he still does not understand. Still he says at times now, as he always used to say when Maurice was alive, 'When comes pappa to play with me again and to take me on the carousel?'' She dabbed her eyes with her handkerchief.

There was silence for a while as she sat there with her head slightly bowed, her face hidden from them. Sir Andrew looked across at his wife. She nodded gently to him.

Sir Andrew said, 'And how old is your little boy, Frau Crillon?'

Trudi looked up. 'It is right of you to call me that. He is seven the fifteenth of last month.'

'And where is he now?'

'Oh, he is a good, obedient boy. He waits for me in the car still.'

Lady Starr asked, 'And where are you staying?'

'Oh, we go back to a hotel in Salisbury.'

Sir Andrew stood up and touched her shoulder, and said, 'No. Not tonight. Not any night. You stay here. I will go down and bring the boy up. In the meantime my wife will take care of you.'

'Oh, no — that is not necessary. You are being too kind.'

'Nonsense. You go and I will bring the boy

up. And Hanson will see to your luggage. No argument now, my dear girl. We do this because we too were very fond of Maurice. Very, very fond as you will understand a little later.'

★ ★ ★

The car — a dusty Volkswagen — was parked close to the edge of the sunken garden. When he got to it there was no one inside. But that did not worry him. No seven-year old was going to sit patiently on his arse in a car while grown-ups gabbed away. At least, no seven-year-old with his blood carrying its full and legal proportion of the ancient Starr ancestry. He took a handkerchief from his pocket and blew his nose in it with a foghorn blast, feeling the tears prick close behind his eyes. My God, he thought, what a day for a miracle to happen. All homecoming and happiness. Dear Christine back, dear Trudi — and who would ever know whether on that last day Maurice had unbuttoned himself and told her that he was the heir to a baronetcy, and at his death his son would inherit? Probably he had — but it made no difference. Didn't signify a sparrow's fart. He had a grandson. Maurice now dead, his heir. And now that priest-loving great-nephew of his could go seek sympathy with his bishops and rectors and deacons and the whole gang of them who had had the almighty gall to muck about with the language of Latimer and Ridley and Cranmer or whoever it was — and bad cess to the lot of them. Watertight — he couldn't fight it.

Johan — damned soon to be turned into plain John, legal or not legal, for the boy's sake. Though come to think of it there was one of the old Templars sleeping in the chapel who had been a Johannus. Might keep Johan, then. What's in a name?

He found Johan leaning perilously over the edge of the fountain basin, watching the fish. He wore tight shorts, white socks, one wrinkled down to his shoe, light-weight red windbreaker, big Micky Mouse emblem on the back, and turned to face him as he heard his footsteps on the gravel.

He spoke in German, 'You're Johan Crillon, aren't you?'

'Yes, sir.'

'I've come to take you into the house to your mother.'

'Why?'

'Good question. Answer it later. Like fishes?'

'Yes, sir.'

'And fishing?'

'Yes, sir.'

315

'Good, we'll do some together soon.'

'Who are you, sir . . . please.'

'I'm your grandfather.'

The boy laughed. Nice teeth. Nice grin. And by God, yes — and not kidding himself, something of Maurice there and something of himself, too . . . well, wouldn't swear to the last . . . too young yet for the genes to get busy and make their mark.

'My grandfather is in Zürich, sir.'

'I'm the other one. Your father was my son.'

'Really, sir?'

'Yes, really.'

'I never knew that. I wonder why he never told me? He's dead now you know. Mummy told me — he was drowned. She cried a bit. We didn't often see him, you know. Did you know him?'

'That's a silly question, isn't it? He was my son.'

'Yes, of course.' He laughed. 'I'm a bit stupid sometimes. Don't stop to think, my mother says.'

'Doesn't do any harm sometimes. Act first, think later, live longer. Come on — we'll have plently more time to talk soon.'

He took Johan's hand and led him away. As they passed the car, Johan said, 'Should we lock the car?'

'Good question. But no need for it now. We

let the bloodhounds out when the place is shut up. Any strangers come along and, by God, they're mincemeat before they know what's hit them.'

Johan laughed. 'You talk like my father used to — but I suppose that's why. Because you were his father . . . ' He paused for a moment, frowning, and then went on, 'But how could you have been? My father was French.'

'Bright as a button, aren't you? I'll explain that to you sometime.'

⋆ ⋆ ⋆

The stable clock striking twelve, one window of Lady Starr's bedroom open to let the cool night air in after the heat of the day, Sir Andrew came through in his dressing gown, holding a balloon brandy glass in his hand, and sat on the side of her bed. She reached out and took the glass from him, sipped at it, and retained the glass, saying, 'You've had enough of that for one day.'

'No question of enough on a day like this, my dear.' He flicked his hand at a moth that blundered past his head, and went on, 'Can't understand why you have a window open. Place full of moths.'

'They go when I put the light out. I like moths.'

'Well, what do you think of them?'

'Charming. Give it a few months and they'll fit in. She's no fool.'

'You think she understands all that is involved . . . her son heir to a baronetcy?'

'Don't be an ass. Of course she does. Maurice must have told her. But she isn't going to bring it up first. You'll have to do that.'

'And the boy? What did you make of him?'

She laughed gently. 'My dear Andrew — if you could see your face.'

'Cheshire cat?'

'More than.' She handed him back the glass. 'Here, I'll be generous. A big day for you — and for me. Finish it. He'll fight it, you know, your prissy-mouthed great-nephew.'

'Let him. He'll get nowhere. Hasn't got a hassock to stand on. And if he does I can always go to Birdcage and play a trump card that would produce him a crack over the head by the Archbishop of Canterbury with his crozier. It is crozier, isn't it?'

'I think so. You're sure you've got a trump card?'

'Oh, yes. Abso-bloody-lutely.'

'The lease on the dower house runs out in two months. She could take over. You'd have the boy to hand.' She sighed. 'I suppose sometime we'll have to have the Zürich

318

stonemason and his wife over? Oh, Gawd!'

'Takes all sorts. After all, trade is now the breeding ground of the new nobility.'

'*Tant pis* — why do I always make that sound rude?'

'Because at heart you're a common slut.'

'If only — then I could have some fun.' She paused and then said seriously, 'Do you believe all that story about Crillon's drowning?'

'Absolutely. Don't you?'

'Oh, yes — absolutely, my love. Now off you pop and get a good night's sleep. I want the light out and the moths. Oh, yes — I meant to tell you. She rides, you know.'

'My dear, who doesn't these days? The world is full of people bumping around on sorry old nags with their legs semaphoring and their elbows wagging as though they wanted to take off and fly. Pleasant dreams . . . '

Sir Andrew went back to his bedroom and switching on the lights stood for a while, his spirits roseate, the smile on his face probably — he told himself — to stay fixed there even while he slept. What a good day. A day of true grace. After all the storms and shipwrecks, the peace of harbour.

★ ★ ★

Warboys, coming in late, the summer night near lipping into the beginning of a summer morning, found Kerslake sitting at his desk, jacket off and shirt sleeves neatly folded back, the electric fan purring softly and making little impression on the stifling night air. Before him was a great pile of folders and one open from which he had been making notes.

'Midnight zeal and midnight oil. Dear, dear, shall I miss it after tomorrow? Big Ben has already signalled the beginning of the last day. I've just come back from dining with one of the Pursuivants of the College of Heralds.'

'Which one, may I ask?' Kerslake, tired, wiped his hot brow with his handkerchief.

'Timmy Anderson — Portcullis. Just filled a long vacancy. Now sits in style with Bluemantle, Rouge Croix — '

' — and Rouge Dragon. Lot of old medieval nonsense!'

'Never underrate continuity. Kind hearts and coronets and never mind the colour of the blood. He was interesting on Sir Andrew's little turn-up for the book.'

'You told him about it?'

'Broad outline. He said that it was a matter for the Standing Council of the Baronetage. But as far as he could see the grandchild is O.K.'

'Even if Crillon is alive somewhere?'

'Time will solve that. Seven years to be exact. After that he's dead. Declared so — and not a dry eye in the house. I was down at Avoncourt a few days ago. If Sir Andrew were a dog he would have two tails. Nice little boy, too. And a fair share of the Starr look and temperament. He's learning English fast — the polite above stairs from doting grandfather and grandmother, and the plebeian from the stable and garden staff.'

'So now we know why the fair Trudi put on all that act about Crillon drowning. She couldn't resist what he had to offer her and the boy.'

'Quite. Any other woman in her position would have done the same. I've always found that given the right incentive there's no man living can compare with a woman when it comes to — *Mentiri splendide.*'

'To lie magnificently?'

'Splendid — you've been burning the midnight oil.'

'And the German papers?'

'If he's got them they're certainly not in the back of any picture. All very interesting, ain't it? Curiouser and curiouser — as Alice said.'

Kerslake smiled. 'We could shoot a bow at a venture for Crillon . . . yes?'

'No point. Not our job. He'd done nothing wrong. Nice to know now, though, the reason he took the risk of thumbing his nose at Andretti. For us he's still at the bottom of the lake. Not all drowned bodies finally surface. Some float up, maybe for a last fleeting glimpse of the world they hated or made their oyster. Others stay put. Either way there is no impediment to — *Est quaedam flere voluptas; Expletur lacrimis egeriturque dolor.*'

'I'm afraid that's well beyond me.'

'Persevere. You have the years ahead for it. 'There is a certain pleasure in weeping; grief is appeased and expelled by tears . . . ' though, of course, I think it should always be done in private. You seem to have an extraordinary number of files there.'

Kerslake smiled. 'I am reading through some old cases. To see how things were done in the past.'

'Much as they are in the present. Make and mend. Guess and gamble. Treat your triumphs modestly and your failures with a bland smile. Leave emotion to the poets — who will make money, if they're lucky, out of it — and to the peasants who regard it as a form of grace before the funeral meats and wine. Well, I must be off. A nice walk home. Pray God, no muggers, and then to bed.'

Kerslake smiled. 'Would you like a subject for thought or conjecture on your way back? Since you walk — we could call it a footnote.'

'Tease me.'

'I learned today from the Wiltshire police who have kindly been keeping an eye on some things for us that a certain Margery Littleton, solicitor's confidential clerk or whatever, has started a month's holiday, brought forward somewhat since she wanted to spend it in Scotland with an ailing aunt.'

'Good girl. How often the young lack such devotion.'

'She hired a car to Heathrow — boarded a plane to Madrid.'

Warboys smiled. 'Well, well — that does seem a long way round to get to Edinburgh.'

'Dundee exactly.'

'*C'est la même chose.* When lovely woman stoops to folly . . . So?'

'I just thought you'd like to know. Not that it's of any great interest.'

'No. But pleasing. Good night, my dear Kerslake.'

We do hope that you have enjoyed reading this large print book.

Did you know that all of our titles are available for purchase?

We publish a wide range of high quality large print books including:
Romances, Mysteries, Classics
General Fiction
Non Fiction and Westerns

Special interest titles available in large print are:
The Little Oxford Dictionary
Music Book
Song Book
Hymn Book
Service Book

Also available from us courtesy of Oxford University Press:
Young Readers' Dictionary
(large print edition)
Young Readers' Thesaurus
(large print edition)

For further information or a free brochure, please contact us at:
Ulverscroft Large Print Books Ltd.,
The Green, Bradgate Road, Anstey,
Leicester, LE7 7FU, England.
Tel: (00 44) **0116 236 4325**
Fax: (00 44) **0116 234 0205**

Other titles published by
The House of Ulverscroft:

THE CRIMSON CHALICE

Victor Canning

When a party of marauding Saxons destroy her father's villa, young Roman girl Gratia, 'Tia' escapes. She comes upon the body of the heir to the chieftanship of a British tribe in the west. Baradoc, a prisoner of Phoenician traders, was sold as a slave and is also escaping the Saxons. However, after being attacked he was left for dead by his cousin, the next heir. Tia nurses him back to health, and they continue together to the safety of her uncle's villa in Aquae Sulis . . . Their son, Arturo, inherits his father's desire for uniting Britain against the Saxons.

THE CIRCLE OF THE GODS

Victor Canning

Arturo's dream, like that of his father, Baradoc, is to unite Britain against the marauding Saxons. Always a wild and arrogant youth, he grows up and leads a rebellion against Count Ambrosius. He raises a small force of men which attacks Saxon settlements. Then, with Durstan and Lancelo to lead the troops, Arturo's great campaign begins . . .

THE IMMORTAL WOUND

Victor Canning

The Saxons face increasing opposition as Arturo secures his garrisons and his army strengthens. But Count Ambrosius poisons Arturo's wife, Daria, who was pregnant with the warrior's child. However, he subsequently meets and marries Gwennifer. Arturo faces many bloody battles against the Saxons — culminating in the most ferocious clash of armies yet, the Battle of Badon Hill . . .

THE DOOMSDAY CARRIER

Victor Canning

Jean Blackwell works at Fadledean, a Ministry of Defence research station. Involved in a new project, her work with a chimpanzee named Charlie involves research into biological warfare. But security there is severely compromised when, alone on duty, Jean falls down in a faint. And despite Fadledean's strict safety regime, Charlie is able to make his escape from the station. The chimpanzee, having been injected with plague bacilli, will become highly infectious after a three-week incubation period. Now, the hunt is on for Charlie . . .